REDLINE

by Terry Green

With best wishes
Terry Green

Copyright

First published in Great Britain in 2024
Copyright © 2024 Terry Green
The moral right of Terry Green to be identified as the author of this work has been asserted in accordance with the Copyright, Designs and Patents Act, 1988.
All rights reserved. No part of this publication may be reproduced or transmitted in any form or by any means, electronic or mechanical, including photocopy, recording, or any information storage and retrieval system, without permission in writing from the author.

This book is a work of fiction. Names, characters, businesses, organisations, places and events are either the product of the author's imagination or used fictitiously. Any resemblance to actual persons, living or dead, events or locales is entirely coincidental.

To my wonderful teachers of History and English Literature, who, many years ago, inspired me with their stories of great lives and deeds and unravelled the mystery of how to tell a really gripping story.

Mr Trevor England and Ms L. Anderson – I salute you

Contents

1: Monday: Start Your Engines 1
2: Warming Up 7
3: Appealing to the Crowd 22
4: Tuesday: Select First Gear 41
5: Women Drivers 87
6: Wednesday: Drop the Clutch 102
7: Up through the Gears 112
8: Thursday: Change Down 149
9: Diversion 186
10: Friday: Double De-Clutch 196
11: Flat Out and Down the Straight 240
12: Passing on the inside 270
13: From the Commentary Box 280
14: The Last Lap 296
15: Saturday: The Chequered Flag 316
16: Spray the Champagne 335
A Free Gift for My Readers! 338
Afterword 339
About the Author 345

1: Monday: Start Your Engines

5th May 1997.

There's a phrase that's supposed to keep the noses of us have-nots pressed firmly to the grindstone. You know the one, it's often attributed to smug, successful bastards as they grin at you from the pages of the latest business magazine. It goes something like this – "People say I've been lucky but, you know, the harder I work, the luckier I get."

Well, here's the truth. Luck needs hard work like a rabbit needs a space-hopper. Seems to me some fortunate types have everything good land in their lap whilst the rest of us poor fools get to put up with the dross life throws at us.

Do I sound bitter? Bloody right, I do. Accused of a crime I didn't commit, out of a job and, the real kick in the aspidistras, broken-hearted after the love of my life deserted me without so much as a bye, I'm leaving.

A phone call at half seven in the morning wasn't going to improve matters. Which is why I let my ancient Panasonic answer machine pick it up. Anthony Browne's nasal, upper-class bray filled the room.

'Morning Jake. Listen chap, don't bother coming in today. Seems our vacancy's been filled. Sorry and all that. Ciao.'

The tape whirred in rewind and the answerphone reset. Bastard. The Panasonic's winking red eye mocked me from the top of the oak-effect sideboard until I reached across and hit the button, erasing the mendacious Browne from its memory and my Christmas card list.

Now what?

I left the scatter of unpaid bills lying across the heavy set, dark wood dining table and took all of three steps across my "compact kitchen stroke diner" - rental agents have such a way with words, don't they? – to the sink. I peered through the kitchen window despondently, at the small, tousled square of unkempt lawn with its neglected borders.

Filling the kettle, I flicked the radio on in time to hear the eight am news. Blair again, sounding smug and earnest now he'd become Prime Minister. Lucky bugger, he'd be earning. A robin caught my attention as he landed on a gnarled rose bush, staring back at me belligerently. Clever though, the way our Tony had snatched the centre ground from the Tories whilst keeping a lid on the unions.

Still, as long as there's coffee there's hope. I spooned instant into a mug, squeezed out the last drops of milk, chucked the carton in the bin and placed the dirty spoon in the sink. Back to my makeshift workspace to mastermind my next move.

What the hell was I going to do? All my usual contacts had stopped answering the phone since the court case. Accusations, even false ones, have a way of putting people off. Even Anthony Bloody Browne's book-keeping job, hardly a role for a fully-qualified accountant, had disappeared as soon as they'd realised it was me. I'd lost everything; my home, a promising career in a well-respected firm, and the biggest blow, Ella, the girl of my dreams, barely giving me the chance to explain before she left.

The letterbox rattled, signalling the arrival of another wodge of envelopes. More bills? Replies to my latest job applications? I perched my coffee on the table and made the dozen strides through the small, under-furnished sitting room to the front door of my terraced Victorian cottage. I scooped the mail from the mat and took a quick flick through. Strictly bin fodder.

A familiar, if unexpected, shadow loomed through the opaque door glass. Too curious for my own good, I snatched the door open to confront my ex-boss, his clenched fist raised to a knocker no longer within his reach.

'Morning, David. What can I do for you?' Best to be civil, at least until I knew what he wanted.

David Lansdowne always made me feel underdressed. He stood, straight-backed and immaculate as ever in sports jacket and twill trousers. His regimental tie precisely squared against his carefully pressed, pale blue shirt. Brown brogues held a mirror finish. He slowly lowered his arm as if completing a salute. Clear blue eyes, under bushy salt and pepper brows, studied my face. His professional smile hinted at his purpose; a man who was here to do business. Interesting.

'Morning Jake. Thought I'd see how you're doing.'

'You'll be wanting coffee,' I said, standing back and ushering him towards the kitchen. He joined me at the sink as we waited for the kettle to boil. The rose bush quivered as the robin launched himself into a fly past in David's honour. Time to make polite conversation.

'Are you a gardener, David?'

He looked at me quizzically, then comprehension dawned and a broad smile graced his lips and softened his eyes, 'I leave such things to Mrs Lansdowne. Tilda.'

'Perhaps you could send her round here?'

David guffawed. In all the time I'd known him, I'd never heard him make such a sound before. We really were in new territory. I poured steaming water onto coffee granules in a second mug.

'There's no milk.'

'No matter. Black will do the job.' He added a touch of cold water from the kitchen tap and followed me to the dining table.

Taking a seat opposite me, his eyes strayed to the notepad where I'd been working out the grand scale of my debts. I gathered up bills and jottings and dropped them into a single pile on the floor. My business, David.

'What can I do for you?'

'You didn't have to leave, you know,' he said sympathetically.

'Any hint of suspicion sticks like gum to a schoolboy's desk. Your words not mine.'

He had the grace to look uncomfortable. The silence between us was broken by the familiar sound of next door's toddler colliding with the furniture and landing with a thump. Over-cheery maternal tones gradually overcame the sound of wailing.

David cleared his throat, 'I've come with a proposition. One, which I believe can take you past your recent difficulties. It concerns Race Engineering.' He took a mouthful of coffee and swallowed reluctantly.

'The sports car people,' I said, 'Flashy toys for well-off boys.'

Laughing at David's expression, I relaxed a little, 'I worked on a couple of their audits when I was first with you.'

'Indeed. And now they're in trouble. On the verge of bankruptcy.' He lifted his coffee mug, hesitated, then put it down again, untouched. 'I want you in there. Find out what's gone wrong, then show them how to get out of the hole they're in. You'd be their consultant.'

'With my reputation? Why the hell would they hire me?'

David leaned in, smiling, 'I know you. You'll do your research and come up with a convincing plan to get them out of trouble. My influence will get you through the door. All you've got to do is use your charm.'

I sipped my instant and made a show of enjoying it. 'You don't think landscape gardening's for me then?'

'Not if you want to eat. So, how about it?' Why would David put me up for this when he'd got a plethora of talent to choose from. Did he think he owed me?

He pursed his lips impatiently, then looked at his watch, the prized rose gold Jaeger-LeCoultre Reverso presented to him last year, marking twenty-five years of loyal, lucrative service. 'I won't lie to you. They're difficult people and it's a messy situation. Most of my colleagues would run a mile rather than get involved. But I know you. You're tenacious and now you've something to prove.'

This was my chance to get back in the game; to put the disasters of the past months behind me, prove my honesty and get on with my life. What had I got to lose? Absolutely nothing. 'I'll need a day rate, first week up front.'

'I'd expect nothing less.' Standing, he placed his nearly full mug in the kitchen sink. 'I have to go.' He paused by my front door, frowning, 'They'll take some saving. Especially from themselves.'

2: Warming Up

David had lingered just long enough to be convinced I would turn up for a meeting with the directors that evening before striding off to his waiting Jaguar. He needn't have worried, what with the legal bills I was facing for my defence and no salary coming in, if he'd suggested popping up to the moon to fetch some green cheese, I'd have offered to get my rocket out. And besides, after my career had stalled so dramatically, who was I to refuse a bump start?

Within the hour a courier arrived at my door with a couple of large boxes. I had my orders, report to reception at Race Engineering, six p.m. sharp, ready to be grilled.

The files drew me an eloquent picture of a company on its last legs but I wanted the narrative that went with the numbers. I knew just the man.

It was lunchtime when I left the early May sunshine behind on Union Street and sauntered down shady steps into the dimly-lit subterranean bar known as The Glovemaker's Arms. A handful of earnest drinkers were already in occupation, if you included the barman and two blokes playing pool.

I didn't see him at first, his slim form half-hidden in the gloom. Ned Drake, editor, reporter, advertising salesman and - for all I knew- head of toilet cleaning for the Stratford Courier, sitting alone in his usual booth, poring over an advance copy of this week's edition, checking for any howlers before his readership's critical eye got the chance. I'd known him for years and we'd helped each other out from time-to-time, swapping snippets of information as we'd progressed through our respective careers. I never thought I would be the subject of one of his columns. Last time I'd seen him was three months ago, across a crowded courtroom.

His expression didn't change as I approached but he flicked his head up quickly in a kind of nervous tick, acknowledging my arrival. A gasp of ambient light caught the sheen in his short, black, slicked-down hair. I walked up to the bar, ordered a pint and put down a handful of change. I took the seat opposite Ned, placing the beer on the table in front of him. They call it reciprocity. Offer something up before you go for the gimme. Of course, a little threatening behaviour always helps seal the deal.

'All right, Jake?' he asked, a smug look behind his watchful eyes.

I smiled, 'Oh, I'm fine Ned, couldn't be better. But you have a small problem.'

He drew smoke from his slim panatela, carefully blowing it sideways, away from my face, as he balanced the cigar back on the ashtray.

He returned my smile, 'What's that, then?'

'Me,' I said.

I picked up his cigar and stabbed the hot end down towards the back of his hand, stopping a hairsbreadth above it.

'Jesus,' he muttered under his breath, examining his heated flesh carefully. 'What d'you wanna go and do that for?' Stress brought out his Black Country accent.

'That's the difference between us, Ned. I could have burnt you but chose not to. You, on the other hand, lost me my job without a second thought.'

'I heard you resigned,' he whined.

'No choice after the way you covered the story.'

'You was the one in the dock.'

'I was innocent,' I responded.

'Like I haven't heard that before,' he smirked. 'The public had a right to know.'

I'd made my point. Time to get on with the job, 'I want a favour.'

Ned watched me balefully and started in on his pint, 'I'm listening.'

'I'm after everything you have and everything you've guessed about Race Engineering.'

Ned took a long pull at his beer, his dark eyes unblinking over the rim of his glass. He tapped the side of his nose. 'You're on to something, aren't you? OK, but let's get one thing straight. If you pick up even a hint of a story, it's mine. Do we understand each other?'

'We do,' I said.

He held up his half-empty glass and waggled it towards the bar, followed by a polite two finger salute.

The barman made a house call, placing a beer in front of each of us. I took a mouthful from my glass as Ned spilled out his story.

I already knew Race Engineering had been started a couple of decades ago by Roderick Race, an ex-racing driver. I hadn't known he'd got his nickname, "Hot Rod," in honour of his supposed conquests in the bedroom. Ned reminded me Race had been joined in the business by James Bishop, the ex-chief engineer of his racing team. Together they'd launched a sports car called the Vixen. They'd done well. A race series across Europe and lots of private sales. But, as always happens, after a while, the market started to look around for the latest shiny thing and, in consequence, sales started to decline.

Before it became critical, a well-placed rumour led the affluent anoraks who follow the brand to fall over each other showering the company with speculative deposits for Race's next car, the Siren.

Ned continued, 'Race's finished last year with a full order book and Hot Rod was having a whale of a time, jetting all over the world, doing deals with his cronies.' He finished his first beer and an made impressive inroad into the second. 'And then, back in February, whilst you were otherwise engaged…'

'Fighting off trumped-up charges, you mean.'

'They found him lying in the car park out at their test track.'

'Heart attack?'

Ned leaned in and took a final pull at his pint. 'Bloody hell. Don't you ever read my paper?'

'I wasn't much in the mood for comics back then.'

'He'd been hit by a car.'

'What happened?'

Ned shrugged. 'No witnesses, no tyre tracks. The ground was as dry as old Mother Shakespeare's bones and the car park surfaced with loose gravel. Left the forensics people scratching their heads.'

'Accident?'

'If that were an accident my Aunt Nell's a badger.' He stopped talking long enough to look at his mobile phone, jot a note on the edge of his paper, tear the strip off and pass it to me. 'This copper's on the investigation team. You can mention my name if it helps.'

I examined his barely-legible scribble, "DS Guy Cooper" and a phone number.

'The test track's out at Long Marston, you know, the old airfield?' he said. 'Inquest was adjourned for further evidence. Buggered if I know where they're going to find that.'

'What happened then?' I asked.

He chuckled, 'That daughter's a feisty one. Hard as nails. Took charge of the business and got the new car launched. It started well but there were more bad news to come. I should know, I broke the story.'

'You're like a vulture sitting in a tree and waiting for something to die, aren't you?

Ned chuckled thickly. 'It's not me, it's the dear old paper-buying public. Nothing sells like a wealthy local family going tits up.'

'And then there's the valuable public service you perform, I suppose?'

'Do you want to hear this or not?'

I gestured for him to continue.

'Couple of Sirens were out on the test track. One of 'em went sideways and took the other one out. Wonder no one was killed.' He started laughing and shook his head.

'What's funny about that?'

'Not a lot. But what happened to me was. It was last Monday. I'd just got the paper ready and were in here having a quiet pint when I got a call from the office. An urgent special delivery. Prints, negatives and the bare bones of the story. Anonymous, like. I rang Race's and got hold of the daughter, Carina, to check it out. She rubbished it and gave me an earful so I sent copies of the pictures across. Ten minutes later I got some garbled nonsense on a fax from her lawyers admitting it was true but offering no explanation. I ran the story in last week's paper. It's been a good earner, been syndicated round the nationals.'

'How come you're not more pleased then?'

He frowned. 'It was a tuck up. Like finding a rat's bum floating in yer pint. I mightn't have a clue as to who did for old man Race but it was me as finished off the Siren.'

Back at home, I dialled the number Ned had given me and left a message. I'd stopped to buy milk, putting coffee on the menu once more, much needed after that lunchtime beer.

The thought of Race's body lying in a car park put my own troubles in context. Why hadn't David mentioned it? And now, three months later, the new car had disgraced itself at the same circuit. Coincidence? I hoped so. I pushed the thought to the back of my mind. Time to get ready for the grilling.

It had been a while since I'd worn the Hugo Boss. Donning my charcoal pin-striped business armour increased my confidence a little. My sharp-suited persona formed a protective veneer over the bundle of nerves within me. What if these people wouldn't listen to David? What if I fluffed the pitch?

My image stared soberly back at me from the full-length mirror of the wardrobe door. I could just about see the top of my head without bending at the knee. I pondered, reflectively, pulling in my belt a notch. It would have been nice if the suit had shrunk a little to match my new, leaner profile. In some ways, being away at "college" had been good for me. Twelve weeks of disciplined routine and regular exercise had curbed bad habits and eliminated my recreational consumption of alcohol, forging a sharper, fitter me. And my always galloping ambition had been honed into a steely determination to prove myself.

I finger-combed my dark locks into some sort of order, straightening the tie and shoulders, discovering that if I tweaked my shirt sleeves up a little, no-one would notice the slightly frayed left cuff. I tried a rakish grin. Not bad.

Back at the dining table, I dropped my papers into a battered leather document case, adding my slim Filofax before zipping up. I stepped into the street, closing the door behind me.

I'd quickly settled into Old Town on my return to Stratford. The rows of terraced Victorian houses in their modest streets were somehow comforting. Originally built for the workers who'd brought the railway to the town, the area had matured into a fashionable, bohemian district peopled by the middle classes. One or two darlings of the stage living quietly amongst the teachers and retired professionals, with an occasional radio producer thrown in. It was handy for the theatre and the shops. Back in the 1860's this would have been a tight-knit community, self-reliant and hostile to outsiders. Round the corner from me, in Bull Street there had been four pubs in one relatively short road. My cottage was in Narrow Lane, then called Love Lane; an excellent address if you happened to be in the bliss business.

I'd lived quietly these last weeks, nursing my wounded pride, screened by the self-absorbed bustle of life around me. But here I was stepping back into the everyday stream of events. A semi-colon in my life; not the end of the sentence but definitely a new beginning.

Late afternoon sunshine anointed the buildings, warming the red brick and reflecting off the densely parked cars lining the street. At the top of the road, casually abandoned Volvo estates and people carriers signalled the imminent escape of squadrons of small people from the prep school. I felt a sense of camaraderie with them, after all, I knew what involuntary incarceration felt like.

My thoughts turned to the task ahead of me. Directors of failing companies aren't generally noted for their calm manner and positive outlook. At one end of the scale would be the garrulous confessions of a profligate board. At the other, inarticulate misery. I hoped for something in the middle. Either way, as father confessor, I had a duty of care which meant giving them enough stick to test their resolve. Well, you have to get your kicks where you can, don't you?

I crossed the street and turned north, walking past the end of Maidenhead Road, where my old life used to be.

My lips moved in a calming mantra, 'when the going gets tough'. I caught a glimpse of myself in a nearby shop window. I gave myself a confident grin, catching the attention of a passing "yumai mumai," as Ned would say. I noticed her straighten her shoulders and push out her chest, tossing her red hair.

All of the tourists who come to view "Will Spokeshave's" birthplace, to catch one of his plays, or simply to stroll by the river and feed the swans, probably never notice the small but thriving manufacturing base tucked away, to the north of the town. That's where I was heading, walking briskly towards my fate. Prospero Road Industrial Estate, our modest local engine of commerce, stays largely out of the limelight of Stratford's international reputation. Race Engineering had been, until recently, the one notable exception, its image underpinned by the fast, stylish sports cars it builds for rich, glamorous customers, lending it something to shout about. Till it lost its voice.

The building I was heading for was something out of the ordinary. Built in the 1930's, the two symmetrical, white-painted wings of offices, each with a double row of steel-framed Crittal windows, met in the middle, joining a rectangular tower which reached above the roof line. A clock at its apex proudly bore Race's logo. At the base of the tower was a short flight of white marble steps leading up to a pair of polished aluminium and glass doors, over which projected a flat canopy porch. The whole looked rather as if two white cruise liners had collided simultaneously into an art deco lighthouse. The clock showed five minutes to six.

High gates at the entrance to the car park were firmly closed. A uniformed security guard stood behind them with arms folded and a "not on your nelly" expression of firm defiance on his face. A huddle of people gathered on the pavement outside. The guard moved forward to unlock the gates as a car came up behind. The driver edged forward gently, not looking left or right. A man in his mid-forties, accompanied by a colleague sporting a fancy camera, gestured a "winding down the window" motion. When the driver didn't comply, the reporter banged on the roof and shouted his question at the impervious glass.

I approached the back of the group and gently but firmly pushed my way through. At first, they ignored me but as I reached the gate and explained to the security guard I had an appointment, they turned on me, firing off a myriad of questions. I kept my expression in neutral and walked through. The gate closed behind me and I found myself standing in the car park.

A wide expanse of tarmac stretched in front of me. In normal times, it would have easily provided enough parking space for the workforce, visitors and any attention-seeking celebrity who insisted on picking up their latest acquisition under the glare of the waiting paparazzi's cameras. Today was a different story.

Every parking space and grass verge between the fence and offices was occupied by a low-slung sinuous shape. But it was as if an artist with a bad hangover had captured the scene. Each car's paintwork was embalmed with a thick layer of dull, dreary wax. Every roof, windscreen and set of side windows was obscured by a fitted cover of drab, oatmeal coloured canvas. Each wheel was shrouded in thick layers of translucent plastic. Unregistered, unsold Sirens. Lots of them.

Only one car in the place had plates and shiny paint and it was right in front of the steps to reception. I edged my way carefully around the gleaming metallic blue bodywork and black soft top, noting the registration number S11REN. The interior was, of course, trimmed in tan leather and walnut, the perfect executive plaything for the man or woman who didn't need to care about the cost.

Once inside the building I approached the front desk. Unanswered telephones rang out intermittently in the background. The receptionist looked like he'd had a hard day.

I smiled pleasantly. 'Hi. I'm Jake Elderfield. I'm here to meet David Lansdowne.'

He pulled his careworn face into a pale imitation of a greeting, 'Certainly Mr Elderfield, I'll let him know you're here. Please take a seat,' he said.

I walked across the light-filled, double-height lobby, admiring the severe, clinical décor and the way it set off the building's simple aesthetic. I settled into a wine-red leather sofa and channelled positive thoughts.

A door at the back of the lobby opened, admitting the faintest smell of engine oil and I recognised the familiar strains of D: Ream's "Things can only get better" playing through the factory's public address system, over the low mechanised hum of machinery. How appropriate. A man in smartly pressed motor racing overalls walked through. He looked tired and thoughtful as he left the building.

An array of two-week old motoring journals lay on the coffee table in front of me. I picked up a magazine which was full of macho praise for Race's new car, billed as "the seductive Siren, a stylish masterpiece with plenty of grunt."

The slap of leather soles descending the marble stairs alerted me to Lansdowne's arrival. David glided down with the simple grace of an accomplished ballroom dancer. Still attired in this morning's ensemble, he looked fresh and eager for the coming confrontation.

'Jake. Glad you could join us this evening.'

I stood and we shook hands. 'Well, here I am, David. How are things?'

'Challenging, but there are grounds for optimism, not least because you're here.'

I grinned as he ushered me towards the grand staircase, leading up to the first floor.

'I've borrowed an office. We can talk there.'

We climbed higher in the airy central atrium. Early evening sunshine pooled across the floor below us, projected from the four elongated, vertical windows in the building's front elevation, like the claw marks of a very large cat.

At the head of the stairs, we turned right into a parquet-floored corridor. Windows to our left looked down across the factory floor. To our right lay individual offices. The clear glass in the top half of each door allowed a glimpse of oak-panelled interiors and the opportunity to spy the rural view, beyond the edge of the industrial estate, that each occupant could enjoy from their desks. We came to an office with "Chairman" written in gold lettering across the door glass. David ushered me inside. A collection of wall-mounted photographs caught my eye; a shrine to the ego of one man. Blond, blue-eyed Roderick Race shaking hands with a minor royal during a factory visit. Another showed Race on the podium, his face grubby and hair dishevelled, spraying champagne over adoring onlookers. A third had him in black tie at a film premiere, accompanied by an attractive blonde, glass in hand, chatting companionably with several familiar Hollywood faces of twenty years ago. A glass-fronted cabinet displaying racing trophies and memorabilia sat against the far wall. An oak battleship of a desk occupied the central area of the office, with an ancient executive chair parked behind it. A scale model of the Siren, crafted from solid aluminium and perfect in its detail, sat in the centre of the otherwise empty desk.

It felt like trespassing, being amongst so many of the dead man's personal effects.

'Take a seat,' said David, gesturing to the two guest chairs and perching on the edge of the desk facing me. 'You've looked through the papers I sent across?'

'In detail.'

David moved behind the desk and settled himself into the comfortable-looking, faded leather seat. He reached for the model of the Siren, turning it slowly in his hands as he spoke.

'And what do you make of the situation?'

I frowned, 'They started well enough and had some good years but relied on the one model for too long. Still, credit where it's due; it was impressive, the way Carina and her team knuckled down to get the new car launched after Race's death. But this crash at the test track has left them teetering on a cliff edge. Have I missed anything?'

'I should say not. A good summary. I should tell you that they're minded to call in receivers but I'll make them listen to what you have to say first. There's a lot of emotion flying around in there and you'll need to dial down the heat and shine a light on the facts.' He placed the model car back on the desk.

And then he said something more prophetic than I could possibly have realised.

'You know, we had a saying in the army,' he said.

'If it moves salute it?'

'Not the one I'm thinking of. When your thirsty, everything looks like an oasis.'

I smiled, 'No, you've lost me.'

'Beware the simplest solutions that appear to fit the facts.' He checked his watch, 'Shall we go through?'

3: Appealing to the Crowd

A head-and-shoulders portrait of the late Roderick Race posing in his racing overalls dominated the period-panelled, plush-carpeted boardroom. His middle-distance stare was on you wherever you stood. Proudly posed, he was a caricature of a nineteenth century industrial magnate in twentieth century overalls.

I wasn't sure the artist had taken his commission entirely seriously. It made the flamboyantly-tiled, art deco fireplace below seem positively staid. The full-width window at the far end of the room provided an excellent view of the ranks of slumbering Sirens awaiting the outcome of our deliberations. A long, highly-polished table occupied the centre ground. Five chairs were clustered around the near end with more lined up against the wall, should anyone feel the need to host a banquet. The seat at the head of the table was empty, reserved for David, no doubt. The other four were already occupied. A side table held a collection of thermos jugs, milk, sugar, mugs, a carafe of water and glasses. No biscuits. Things must be bad.

David placed his briefcase on the floor and rested his hands lightly on the back of the chair. I stood next to him, studying the four impassive faces turned towards us.

'I'd like you all to meet an old friend of mine, Jake Elderfield,' said David. 'Jake, may I first introduce Carina Race, managing director?'

She was a year or four older than me, maybe late thirties. Attractive certainly. A generous mouth and long nose dominated her features. High cheek bones, large expressive eyes, full red lips and a determined chin. Her lightly-tanned skin radiated health. When she spoke, her voice was surprisingly deep and inviting. Shame her greeting wasn't.

'I thought this was to be a private meeting, David? No place for hangers-on, surely?'

'Please think of Jake as a specialist to whom I've referred you.'

Nice touch, David. Carina didn't respond straight away. My eyes followed her as she went to refill her coffee mug. Graceful yet precise. Well-dressed, business-like but elegant in her smart, double-breasted, navy-blue suit. A silver slide in the shape of a Celtic knot positioned at the nape of her neck kept her shoulder-length mane of auburn hair under control. She was gripping her coffee in her right hand as she came back towards me, her long, slim fingers, wrapped around the mug, displaying red, talon-like nails. The large diamond solitaire on her ring finger refracted a distracting beam of multi-coloured light towards my eyes. She'd have been tall even without her heels but with them, we were almost the same height. As she came in close, I was hemmed in by her heady, intoxicating perfume. Her expression was amused, confident.

'Here to see what you can grab at our expense, no doubt. I suppose I could get a couple of my burliest chargehands to throw you out?' She seemed to consider the idea as she sipped her coffee. 'On reflection, it might be more amusing to hear what you have to say, first.'

Returning to her seat she directed her words across the table to the chap with the look of a young plant in desperate need of sunlight and a kind word. Arching an expensively shaped eyebrow, she commented, 'It all seems so obvious to me, I don't know why we're even discussing it.'

The plant looked angry. 'It's not your decision to make, Carina, I …'

'Oh, save it,' she snapped, 'When I want your opinion, I'll tell you what it is.'

Her victim lowered his eyes and said nothing.

The well-groomed, fifty-something man sitting next to Carina was striving to appear younger in his fashionably-cut suit with a white, open-necked shirt. The "stress highlights" in his collar-length, dark, wavy hair somehow enhanced his sophisticated bohemian look. The faint pink pinstripes in the charcoal fabric of his suit added a touch of colour to his otherwise monochrome appearance. He remained seated and waved a languorous left-handed greeting in my direction. He beamed an engaging smile around the table, softening his mouth and crinkling his eyes.

'I've always had a fond regard for a happy ending, however unrealistic. You know, unlikely hero rescues the leading lady from the burning building just as the roof collapses. Welcome, Jake. I'm James, engineering director of this humble manufactory and owner of Berrington Pressings, supplier of parts to car makers large and small. Glad you made it before our closing down sale.'

I generously awarded him a half smile. 'You're not beaten yet.'

'The fat lady may not have burst into song but she's certainly taken a deep breath.'

Opposite James was a familiar looking blonde woman of about the same age as him. Her pale blue dress and cream cardigan were understated elegance itself. She wore an expensive watch but no rings. I recognised her from the iconic film premiere photo on Race's office wall.

'Helen Race, Mr Elderfield. Please excuse my daughter's hostility and James's flippancy. This is a very trying time for us all. I, for one, am very keen to hear what you have to say.' She spoke like a BBC radio announcer from a different era, precisely articulating vowels and clipping sentences. Her handshake was cool and dry. I noticed her clear-varnished, closely-cut finger nails as she reached for an expensive-looking eyewear case. The steel-framed glasses she put on lent her an air of calm authority. I felt like a shy five-year-old, facing a scary doctor for the first time.

The slim young man with the close-cropped blond hair, who'd already been admonished by Carina, unfolded his long lean body and stood, seemingly genuinely pleased to see me. 'Allen Race, Mr Elderfield. Finance director.' He reached out a pale hand and gripped mine, pumping it enthusiastically, his blue eyes conveying sincerity.

James smirked. 'And I thought you just made the coffee round here, Boy Wonder.'

Ignoring him, Allen took up a chair from the side of the room and placed it between David's and his own.

'Call me Jake,' I said, taking the proffered seat.

He smiled and placed a glass of water in front of me.

David brought the meeting to order in a calm, confident voice. 'Thank you all for making yourselves available at short notice. We're here to consider Race Engineering's current difficulties and decide our course of action. If everyone agrees, I will act as your chair this evening. Any dissenters? No? Good. Allen, may I ask you to record the minutes?'

Allen nodded quickly, unscrewed the cap of his fountain pen and sat ready with his notepad.

David continued. 'Jake, perhaps you would lead us off.'

I opened my Filofax and leafed through the notes I'd made earlier. I'd already piled my other papers on the table in front of me; their purpose to intimidate my audience.

Carina sat back, arms folded, lips pressed tightly together. James doodled myopically on his pad. Allen waited with pen poised whilst Helen emanated calm discipline.

In my world, the call for help usually comes in so late the only option is to pay the workers off and put a for-sale sign on everything that doesn't move. Making this a novel experience; the chance to fix the business before it hit the wall.

'How does our charge, ladies and gentlemen, do we have a pulse?' I asked.

Allen opened his mouth to speak but Carina beat him to it.

'Shouldn't you be telling us?'

'I've only just arrived but you people have been on the scene all the time.'

James jumped in. 'Sales have tanked since the Courier's article and there's nothing left in the bank account. I'd say we're done, wouldn't you?' He shrugged and went back to his illustrative works.

Allen looked up from his papers, his brows furrowed into a frown. 'You're the reason we've no money James, you've spent every last cent.'

'Perhaps if we'd had this conversation, before we committed the expenditure?' said James.

'We did, if you remember. Repeatedly.'

'I'm afraid the miserable bleating noise you made didn't register. Perhaps you should have tried harder.'

'Enough,' I said, directing my gaze at Helen.

'I have nothing to say at present,' she said.

'How very Helen,' said James. 'When she finally shows up for a meeting, she has nothing to say.'

'Nevertheless, as a director you have a voice,' I said.

'And when I have something to add you shall hear it.'

'Ok. Let's try a different tack.' I smiled pleasantly. 'Anyone been through an insolvency before?'

Blank faces, dismissive shakes of the head.

'Thought not. The law says if you're unable to meet your obligations, you should call in an administrator who will take control of the business. Their job will be to recover as much money as they can for your creditors. They'll be all sympathy at first but it's just a ruse to extract information; which they'll use against you if they think it'll lead them to more funds.' I leaned forward for emphasis. 'You'll be under the microscope. Any mistakes or signs of fraud and they'll be at your throats.'

Carina was dismissive. 'Nothing to find here. The quicker this is over, the sooner we can get on with our lives.'

I smiled, 'It'll be thorough and unpleasant. It'll take weeks but will feel like months. If I was appointed, the first thing I'd look at would be your handling of the Siren.'

'What specifically?' asked Helen, her icy blue eyes lasering in on me.

'Let's start with the crash. What was the cause, James?'

James smiled, 'It's my turn in the tyre bath, is it? Well, bring it on. I say driver error.'

'Why would two professional drivers make such a dramatic mistake?'

'They're used to hacking around the circuit in Vixens. The new car is a completely different proposition, with a larger engine and different handling characteristics. Any powerful car requires one's full concentration to get the best from it.'

'If an experienced driver could lose control, it must call your design into question.'

'Should a knife manufacturer be held responsible when one cuts oneself preparing dinner? I don't think so.'

'So, what then? The driver just took his eye off the ball?'

James smiled, 'Or, in this case, the road.'

'Where's your evidence?'

'You asked me what I thought and I've told you.'

'Where's your analysis? Interviews with the drivers? Have you even examined the wreckage?'

James stared back impassively.

Carina shrugged dismissively. 'Let's move on. We saw no point in a detailed investigation after the Courier's article. Everyone had their money back and none of the cars got into the open market.'

'So, no investigation. And without any actual evidence James decided it was the driver's fault. I don't suppose you bothered to discuss this with the other board members?'

'James and I made the decision together,' said Carina reasonably.

'Three black marks so far,' I said. 'Firstly, when your finance director suggested you were overspending, you ignored him. Secondly, you failed to investigate the crash, bringing about the current crisis. And finally, the two of you took a key decision without consulting your fellow directors.'

Carina shrugged. 'Why are we even bothering to talk about this? The outcome wouldn't have changed.'

'Not the point. You didn't follow due process.'

'Anyone can be clever after the event. You're supposed to be advising us. Why don't you get on with it?' she retorted angrily.

'And I'm not done yet. Let's move on to this fateful press release, shall we? I took the single sheet from the top of the pile in front of me and waved it under their noses for emphasis. 'This says the crash happened but with no attempt to explain it. And now we know why, don't we? You don't actually know.'

James grinned and shook his head, whilst Carina stayed silent, her eyes flashing at me.

I waved the paper. 'What could you possibly believe this would achieve?'

'It's called damage limitation. Our lawyers advised us to keep the release to a minimum,' said Carina sharply. 'The offer to refund customer deposits demonstrated our confidence in the car,' she added.

'Incredible. All you accomplished was to empty your bank account for no benefit. Did you all sign up to this?'

Helen spoke. 'It was Carina's decision.'

'I was told afterwards,' said Allen.

I shook my head.

'There wasn't time to drink tea and debate the mysteries of the universe,' said James.

Carina was emphatic in her agreement, 'Someone has to face up to the difficult decisions around here and I don't see any other volunteers.'

'But you didn't go about it the right way. You're vulnerable. Let me tell you what's going to happen if you make that call. A team of expensively suited vandals will come calling. They'll be nice as pie to begin with. They'll sit you down individually and the questions will start. They'll demand an office for their exclusive use from which you'll be banned.'

Helen sipped water from her glass.

'They'll exclude you from their conversations. They'll bury you and your team with requests for information, wearing you down and keeping you guessing. And then the threats will start; disqualification as a director, fines, losing your house, maybe even a prison term. Signing up as a company director is far too easy; people don't realise what's at stake if they don't do the job properly. And guess what? Ignorance is no defence.'

Allen had been watching me intensely. I paused, but he looked down at his papers.

'They won't spare your blushes when they start looking for a buyer. Your friends, neighbours and everyone in the trade will know that you've crashed your company.' I plucked a set of their accounts from my pile and flung the papers into the middle of the table. 'There won't be any obvious takers with these liabilities so it'll mean a break up. Your workforce will be paid off at statutory minimums – that's poverty wages. They'll auction off your fixtures and fittings – anything that doesn't sell will go on the scrap heap. Some of your people may be lucky enough to get a job stacking shelves in the supermarket which will almost certainly get built on this site. By then Race Engineering will be just a fond twinkle in the eye of a few enthusiasts and you'll be pariahs.'

'Jake's right,' said David. 'You should listen to him. I've known these situations become quite difficult. Smashed windows, unpleasant scenes when you're out for a quiet dinner. One managing director was beaten up by an aggrieved supplier.'

An awkward silence ensued. I let them sweat.

'There's plenty of ammunition here to give you a hard time,' I directed my words at James and Carina, 'Especially for you two.'

'Yes, yes. We understand it's not an attractive option but what choice do we have?' Helen's steely gaze caught my eye.

'None,' said Carina.

David smiled, watching me.

'What if I can show you a better way?' I leaned forward,' Tell me, why do you think this company has been around for so long?'

James looked up from his pad, 'Oh, I know this. Some of us were stupid enough to be taken in by Roderick and we made quite a success of it despite him.'

'Must you always reduce everything to a joke, James?' said Helen acidly.

James shrugged, 'I've always believed it's better to see the humour in life than dwell on its tragedies.'

'Anyone else? What about you, Allen?' I asked.

'Because the Vixen's a good, dependable sports car.'

'This is a waste of time,' muttered Carina.

I shrugged and made to close my Filofax. 'We don't have to do this. The powers of darkness are just a phone call away.'

'Please continue, Mr Elderfield,' said Helen.

'Jake, please. Answer's simple.' I waved an arm towards the leery portrait over the fireplace. 'Your founder's reputation became the essence of your brand. It made a promise which the Vixen fulfilled, allowing you to profit from selling cars your customers love.'

'Oh, so that's what marketing's all about, it is?' asked James.

'Why don't you just shut up and listen? You might learn something,' said Helen sharply.

I ignored the interruption. 'You've as much chance of reaching Mars on an armadillo as selling a Siren right now. But there's an alternative, if you're willing to consider it.'

James had even stopped sketching. Was he the artist who'd produced masterpiece over the fireplace? Unlikely. I'd say he was a man of taste. 'You've a hardcore of loyal fans who've bought Vixens from you. They can help.'

'Preposterous,' said James. 'They're hardly going to rush out and buy another one, are they?'

'James's hit the nail right between the eyes. Those cars are up to twenty years old. How many of them could do with a little TLC or maybe even a complete rebuild? And who better to reinvigorate your beloved motor than the people who made it? Upgrades, you know, tuning, suspension, retrims, hi-fi, you name it.' Was I getting through to them? At least I had their attention. I continued the pitch. 'You'd make money whilst restoring your reputation. Every Vixen you've ever sold would be a sales opportunity. The owners would thank you for increasing the value of their investment whilst they enjoy a better driving experience. Everyone wins.'

No smiles. I really must work on my delivery.

'You'll need to cut your costs to make it work; suspend directors' salaries, send home all non-essential staff and make it harder to spend money round here than finding a unicorn's tooth.'

'You expect us to work for nothing?' snapped Carina.

I shrugged, 'It's your call but unless you reduce your outgoings now you may never see another penny out of this business.'

'Shouldn't we make redundancies?' asked Allen.

'Common mistake. Redundancies burn cash. Better to agree lay-offs. Besides, when this plan works, we'll need them back pronto.'

He nodded, adding to his notes.

I continued. 'Once we've stabilised things, we'll see if we can't reduce your working capital by selling off anything you don't need and reducing your stock-holding. So, there's the plan. Four steps to solvency, ladies and gentlemen, cut costs, generate more sales, repay short term debt and then restructure the finances.'

Rock solid principles, detail to come later. James sat back in his chair, legs stretched in front of him, hands behind his head and a smug expression on his face.

I continued, 'If we're going to make this work, we'll need to stay so close even our sworn enemies couldn't slip a stiletto between us. I suggest we meet daily until we're through the worst of it, making all our key decisions together.'

And the punchline. 'And let's see if we can't get your shipwrecked Siren off the rocks whilst we're at it.'

David took over.

'It would be helpful to hear everyone's thoughts.'

It wasn't going to take an Einstein to work out Allen was up for it but James and Carina would rather swim the channel pursued by killer whales. Helen was a puzzle.

Which side was she on? And did it matter? If she was for the plan, the best I could hope for was stalemate. Unless I was wrong about Carina, who was now staring at me with a half-smile on her lips.

'We build cars, we don't service them.' she said, grinning sarcastically. 'That's what dealers are for. Think again or go away. I don't care which.'

Even-stevens then. I couldn't see this working.

Helen removed her glasses and appraised me carefully. 'What reassurances can you give?'

I made ready to pack away my papers. There seemed barely any point in answering.

'I can offer you only one certainty; unless you sign up for this, the company will fail,' I said.

'Think of our people and their families, Mum. Don't we have a responsibility to them?' asked Allen. 'Jake's proposal would allow us to protect some of their jobs at least.'

James laughed and shook his head.

Ignoring him, Helen nodded thoughtfully. 'Yes, I see.'

'What about you, James?' asked David.

'I'd say the fun's over, ladies and gentlemen. High time for a dose of reality.'

Carina came back into the discussion. 'I agree with James. Let's make the phone call.'

David gave an almost imperceptible shake of his head, forestalling my cutting response.

'Thank you, Carina. I propose a motion for the board's consideration. Race Engineering should hire Jake to report to me, working closely with the directors to create a survival plan. I would ask each of you now to vote on the motion. All those in favour?'

Allen raised his hand.

'Thank you. All those against?'

James and Carina raised their hands.

Two to one against. Tied vote at best. Back to the situations vacant for me.

Helen still hadn't spoken. David looked at her expectantly. She smiled at Carina. 'I've supported Carina in every decision she's made here.'

Carina smiled triumphantly. 'Thank you, Mother…'

Helen held up her hand, 'Let me finish. But this time I can't. I have to agree with Allen. We must take every opportunity to save Race Engineering, however slim its chances of success.'

'Which means the four directors are deadlocked, with two votes for the proposal and two against,' said David. 'Let's examine the situation with respect to shareholdings.'

David leafed through his papers, displaying a confidence I didn't feel. Was I still in with a chance? A shareholder's majority would outrank a director's vote every time. The one document I hadn't seen was a list of who owned what.

'For the proposal, Helen has twenty per cent and Allen ten.'

Helen's face was unreadable. Allen looked nervous, refusing to meet anyone's gaze.

37

'That makes thirty percent for. Agin... Carina has thirty-five per cent.'

She was trying hard not to smile. Like a snake trying not to hiss. Elegant but deadly.

'James has ten. Forty-five percent in total.'

James snorted. There was a chunk of shares floating in the ether. David held up a piece of paper.

'This is a proxy form from the trustees of the Race Engineering Pension Fund authorising me to vote their shares. The fund holds twenty-five thousand shares or twenty-five per cent of the equity. 'I vote in favour of the motion. The proposal is carried fifty-five per cent to forty-five. Congratulations Jake, consider yourself hired. You and I can sort out the details.'

Carina's smile was more of a grimace. She clapped her hands sarcastically half a dozen times.

'Apparently, we've had a boardroom coup. I suppose under the circumstances, I should offer the board my resignation.'

'Don't minute that, Allen,' said David. 'Perhaps Carina should reflect before such a move.'

Gathering up her belongings, she stood, 'I'll say good night, for now.' Carina banged the door closed behind her, the staccato clicks of her stiletto heels receding through the office.

With the meeting breaking up, David and Helen stood together as James sauntered casually over to me. He seemed sanguine about losing the vote, offering me his hand to shake.

'Congratulations, dear boy. Welcome to the sinking ship.'

I shook the proffered hand but didn't reply.

'I'll go after Carina,' he added with a smile. 'Once she calms down, I'm sure she'll see the logic of working closely with you, even if it's only to keep an eye on what you are up to.' He chuckled, shaking his head as he walked away.

Helen chatted quietly with David before returning her glasses, notebook and pen to her handbag, offering me a brief smile of acknowledgement. I went over to them.

'I'm so sorry, Jake. What must you think of us?' she said.

'No issue. I'm just here to do a job.' I smiled.

Helen left, as Allen joined David and me.

'I'd like a copy of those minutes to sign first thing in the morning and then, Jake, you and I need to go and have a chat with the bank and outline our intentions,' said David.

'Of course,' said Allen.

'I hope you didn't have any plans for this evening?'

Allen looked puzzled, 'No, why?'

'I want to go through all of your costs, line by line and build a new cash flow model.'

'No problem. And you'll need somewhere to work. There's Dad's office. It's hardly been used since he died. All his things are still in there. I'm only next door so I'll be on hand for anything you need.'

'Great.'

David looked grim-faced as Allen left the room. 'Well, we carried the day, my lad, but you're going to need to work on Carina and James. You must take these people with you, even if you have to chase them along with fixed bayonet. I want to see a real grip on the detail by the time we meet the bank tomorrow.' He smiled, 'And they won't be fooled by those superficial headlines you presented tonight and neither will I.'

He began to move away and then did an about turn to my side.

'Here's an idea, why don't I bring in breakfast tomorrow at seven am and you can demonstrate to me precisely how you are going to keep these people out of the brown stuff.'

4: Tuesday: Select First Gear

Allen's mobile phone rang at six-fifty-nine the next morning and he went downstairs to let David in at the front door. I sat back in the large leather chair behind the desk and reflected. It had been a pretty intense night, paused only for a Chinese takeaway at midnight. We'd made really good progress in bringing together the first stage of a viable survival plan.

I stood, stretched and turned off the lights. The windows behind me faced out over the car park. I opened all of them, exchanging fusty air, heavy with calculation and egg fried rice, for the fresh smell of a new day in Bard's town.

I took a couple of lungs full of the clean, sweet morning, looking beyond the industrial estate towards the lush green of the Welcombe Hills. It was going to be another warm day. The pale, early sunlight illuminated the mothballed legion of Sirens below me.

Between working on the numbers, I'd used the opportunity to get to know Allen better. Last night's board had shown the way things had been run around here. Allen had spent most of the meeting passively taking notes or staring at his papers. But, judging by what I'd seen of his work, he had strong technical skills. Ok, he was young for the job. I'd put him at no more than twenty-five or twenty-six. But even so, Carina and James should have given him more credit.

Helen was a puzzle. She'd given very little away. Allen's comment about employees and their families seemed to be the pivotal moment last night and yet she didn't seem like the emotional type. Did I detect a social conscience?

Allen and I had met up in my borrowed office last night. Eager to please, he'd faced me across the desk, practically quivering on the edge of his seat, pen and pad at the ready.

I was down to shirt sleeves, the jacket and tie draped over the back of my chair. 'I could do with a drink. What about you?'

'Of course, I'll warm up The Beast.' He smiled, 'My coffee machine.' He glanced lovingly towards the glass separating our two offices, behind which stood the chrome and stainless-steel monster perched on top of his two filing cabinets.

I sat back in my chair. 'Nice idea, but I was dreaming of a cold beer right now.'

'Then you're in luck.' Allen pulled the lower door of the display cabinet open, revealing the interior of a fridge. He took out two cans of lager and handed one to me before slipping off his jacket, folding it fastidiously and placing it carefully on the seat next to his.

'Cheers,' I said, pulling the tab and taking a long drink. Just what I needed. As Allen sipped from his own can, I asked him about his background.

'I studied Economics at Liverpool Uni. What about you?'

'Warwick. Economics too. Did you have a good time?'

Allen looked uncomfortable. 'I hated it at first, the others on my corridor thought I was stuck-up but I was just shy.'

The only time I'd seen him smile was when I first met him. He looked care-worn and beaten. I noticed that his hair was thinning on the crown. Judging by his figure, he must enjoy the diet of an under-nourished supermodel.

I'd taken every opportunity to turn my time at Warwick into a three-year-long hooley. I'd grown up as an only child and the inner-city school I'd attended had been scant preparation for what followed. University had been a revelation. Most of the kids I met were from far better-off families than mine and whilst no one had needed to show me which knife and fork to use there had been times when I'd felt out of my depth. But the upper crust Nelly (Neville) Bosworth and I had clicked like the snap of a provocatively-worn suspender. In no time at all we'd rented a small house in the back streets of Coventry and settled down to a hectic social life leaving barely enough time for our studies. If it hadn't been for the Blessed Liz, Nellie's girlfriend, I would never have learned to cook a decent meal or iron a shirt.

'And after Uni?' I asked.

'I did my exams at a practice in Birmingham.'

It felt like I was interviewing him. In a way I was. I'd be depending on his judgement and knowledge over the coming days. 'And then back to the family business?'

'I'd just qualified when Dad came home from one of his trips with a bottle of Champagne and took me into his study. He, James and Mum were the directors and Carina was marketing for the racing team. Dad had me join finance as its most junior member.' He took a pull from his can. 'For practically the first time in my life I felt like one of the boys. I'd just settled in nicely when Dad surprised everyone by elevating me to the board.'

'Nice. Daddy gave you a leg up.'

'No one spoke to me. Dad brushed it off, said I'd have to deal with it.'

'What did you do?'

'I threw myself into the job. Most weekends would find me at one motorsport event or another. Everyone could see how hard I was trying and it gradually made a difference. And then Dad put Carina in charge of the whole business.'

'How did that work?' I asked.

He grimaced. 'Not well. She insisted everything, however trivial, go across her desk. I suggested it would be more efficient if we each looked after our own area and reported around the board table. She refused. I called Dad and set up a conference call. He was in China and it was the middle of the night there. He was furious when he realised what it was about, said he hadn't got time for such trivia and told Carina to sort it out. From then on, she ran it like she owned the place.'

'Sounds pretty hellish.'

'Dad was always overseas, or if he was here, he'd be locked away with James. I hardly ever saw him.'

'Carina and James ran the show between them, then?'

He shrugged, 'Everything I said was shouted down or ignored.'

'Making it impossible for you.'

He sighed, his honest, open face, a picture of distress, 'David lent a sympathetic ear when he could and tried to mediate. But it's been really difficult. It was only when the bank started bouncing our cheques that everyone agreed to David's request for a meeting.' He looked hunted, on edge.

'May I offer some advice?'

'I'm open to any suggestions,' he said.

'Carina favours intimidation over analysis. Ignore her insults and focus on the facts. Stay calm and resist the temptation to fill the silences. Best of all, credit your instincts with the respect they deserve.'

Allen seemed pleasantly surprised by my words. He kept grinning to himself when he thought I wasn't looking. A bit of coaching and some positive strokes could go a long way.

I ran my fingers over the stubble on my chin as I looked down across the car park. The gates were open, yesterday's throng of journalists was nowhere to be seen, no doubt covering someone else's crisis. Workers were streaming in, ready to start their day in the factory. I turned back into the room as the office door opened behind me.

'Morning, Jake. You boys made a night of it, then.' David came in, bearing a carrier bag in each hand.

'Morning, David,' I responded.

I picked up the waste paper basket and swept screwed-up papers and a number of empty beer cans into it. David placed one of his bags in the centre of the desk. The other he parked on the floor.

Allen appeared behind him, 'The Beast is warming up.'

Over bacon rolls and strong black coffee, Allen presented the fruit of our night's labours, the new cashflow model. We'd been able to detail our cost reductions and forecast a new sales line. One of Allen's first tasks today would be to check our maths with his team. David was content with the outline plan and we quickly moved into mapping out priorities for the day. By the time we'd boosted our caffeine levels with a second mug, Allen's to do list was as long as a wet Sunday afternoon with nothing on TV. He left David and me talking, eager to crack on with his day.

David took a last appreciative swig of coffee and put his mug down decisively on the desk. He looked at his watch, 'Nine o'clock. I'm going to head over to my office. I'll ring the bank and book us a meeting for this morning.'

'Will they fit us in so easily?'

'Oh, I was in the Welsh Cavalry with their manager, Trevor Woods, we'll be ok.'

'Welsh Cavalry?'

'Surely you know this about me, Jake?'

'I knew you'd been in the army.'

David smiled, 'I was a Lieutenant Colonel in the 1st The Queens Dragoon Guards, an armoured regiment, known as the "Welsh Cavalry" because we recruited from the Borders. Trevor and I served together in the Aden emergency in sixty-six.'

I pictured David in uniform, standing stiffly to attention, squinting through bright sunlight into the middle distance, calm and resolute.

'And what's your plan now, Jake?'

'Assuming Carina's come in, I want to see if she's prepared to work with me to sort this mess out. Then it's James' turn. Can I break through his negativity and get him on side?'

'He's been less than candid about the Siren incident. We need to know what really happened.'

'Agreed. I can't believe he's so relaxed about it. Think of the damage to his reputation.'

'Before you do any of those things, you might want to use these.'

David reached down and put the other carrier bag he'd brought with him onto the table. I looked inside. A clean white shirt in my size, aftershave, a toothbrush and paste, a comb and a razor.

I grinned. 'Thanks David. You really do think of everything, don't you?'

He opened the door. 'I'll see you later – I'll leave a message once I have a time for the bank.'

I found the "Executive Washroom" a few doors down from my adopted office. It was a faithfully restored icon of its era, complete with octagonal, gilt-framed mirrors, marble shelving, large white porcelain sinks and heavy chrome taps. I quickly stripped to the waist, filled the sink with hot water and set about tidying myself up.

Splashing water over my face and head felt really good, washing away the blur of fatigue behind my eyes. I fumbled for the towel which I remembered would be somewhere on the wall over to my left.

My fingers connected with soft, silky material smoothly contoured over warm flesh.

'This might work better for you.'

I opened my eyes, grabbed the proffered towel and buried my face to hide my embarrassment, before looking towards the voice. Carina was standing there, looking immaculate, apart from the wet finger marks on the right breast of her red silk dress.

'I'm so sorry. I didn't hear you come in.'
'I can be quiet. Sometimes.'
'Sorry about your dress.'
'It's ok. It'll dry.'

'But won't it stain?'

She examined herself quizzically in the mirror, plumping up her hair, styled more loosely today and pouting her lips before examining the front of her dress. 'Well, if it does, I'll just tell everyone you did it.'

'I was on my way to see you.'

'Really?' She continued to tease her hair and examine her face in the mirror.

'I wanted to apologise. I feel I've been thrust upon you like an unwelcome gift.' I flexed the winning smile. 'But, you know, if you and I can work together, I really think we can save your company.'

She scowled at me.

I covered my naked nipples with the tips of my forefingers and kept the grin going.

She laughed. A full-on, dirty laugh. Mouth wide open, showing those perfect teeth between full red lips, head thrown back. I could almost see what she'd had for breakfast. 'How can I stay mad at you?' She shook her head. 'You really pissed me off last night. I've had to battle twice as hard as any man to prove a strong woman can succeed in this industry. And where has it got me? Managing director of a bankrupt company. I knew he'd conned me as soon as I got this job, the bastard.'

'Who do you mean?'

'Our late, glorious leader, of course, Rod bloody Race. It was never about me, his blue-eyed girl, winning his trust. He just wanted to spend his time with his cronies, fancying himself doing incredible deals up and down the motor racing circuits of the world, whilst Cinderella did his chores.'

'He stitched you up?'

Carina frowned, 'I expected to make some real money once I took over.'

'Perhaps a few under-the-table cash deals?' I offered.

Carina grinned and wagged her finger. 'By the time I got into the seat, the old man had all the wrinkles sewn up. Ever since he died, it's been hand to mouth. I've spent my whole time scrimping and scraping, whilst barely earning enough to keep body and soul together.'

'Your eyes are green.'

'I'm touched you noticed, Brown Eyes,' she said, drily.

I shook out the clean shirt, shrugged into it and started buttoning up. 'Truce?' I asked.

She appraised me critically.

'In my experience, men are either pirates or wimps. My question, Mr Elderfield, is, which are you?'

I studied the comb in my hand before flicking it though my hair and examining my reflection. Interesting choice. 'Maybe you've missed a third option?'

'Which is?'

'The hero, who rides into town, minding his own business, gets dragged reluctantly into the fight and saves the day before disappearing into the sunset.'

She studied my face in the mirror as I tucked in my shirt. 'I'll allow you the benefit of the doubt, for now.'

She looked me directly in the eye, her decision made. 'Why don't you come for dinner this evening?'

Worth a try. I knotted my tie into place and put my jacket back on, 'A great idea, thank you.'

She smiled. 'Good. Well, if we are going to be on the same side, what do you need from me?'

'A communications meeting with the whole team. As soon as we can – what about lunchtime today?'

'Why not? We'll use the canteen. What's the form?'

'We need to hit just the right note, serious but reassuring. You should kick it off and explain the situation and then hand over to me and I'll do the rest.'

'Ok, I'll get the message around. We'll get everyone together at noon. And I'll see you tonight at my place? Say seven-thirty?'

I smiled, 'Sounds like a plan.'

'Ok. I'll have Kat make something special for us. See you at High Noon, pardner.'

'Who's Ka...?' I started to say but she was already leaving, her heels tapping across the tiled floor, the door closing behind her.

I put my head into Allen's office on the way back through.

'David's been on the phone,' he said. 'He has an appointment for you both with our bankers at ten-thirty. He'll pick you up from here at ten-fifteen.'

'Great. Then I just have time for a chat with James before I go. How are you getting on?'

'All in order. I'm working my way down the list,' he beamed.

I left him at the centre of the maelstrom of activity he'd created. His team were scurrying like ants in a wrecked nest. I stood aside as a junior member of his team arrived with a pile of printouts.

At reception I was directed into the factory and up to a large office perched on a mezzanine floor. I could hear the muffled strains of opera, Madame Butterfly, I think, as I approached.

Opening the door, my ears were assailed by a wall of sound.

'Mr Elderfield,' James shouted, looking up from the papers on his desk. 'Come in and take a seat. Welcome to the final remains of Race Engineering, maker of sports cars. Here we are, limping into the pits with smoke pouring from our engine.'

I looked around his office at the eclectic mix of engineering gizmos on shelves, framed drawings and photographs on the walls. Every surface crammed with bits of technology. In the corner, a life-size stone statue acted as a coat rack, the lady in question sporting a black Fedora on her head and a long dark coat draped around her shoulders. She held a hunting bow in her hands at half stretch whilst a pair of stone dogs stood loyally at her feet. James noticed my look of surprise and reached behind him to turn off the cassette player.

Lowering his voice to a normal speaking volume, he smiled and waved an arm at the statue, 'The Greeks called her Artemis and the Romans, Diana. Not only was she a huntress but she was also the guardian of roadways and in particular, the one which leads to the underworld. Rather appropriate don't you think? She is my inspiration when I am confronted by the latest engineering challenge thrown at me by the Race family.'

'Not something I expected to see in a car factory. Thank you for speaking to Carina last night. I don't know how you did it but she seems willing to work with me now.'

'All part of the service. My powers of persuasion are not resistible.'

So smug. How could I unsettle him? 'Well, you certainly seem to enjoy the sound of your own voice.'

James laughed heartily, 'But it is such a good voice, isn't it? I flirted briefly with the idea of a career on the stage.' James twitched an anticipatory smile into place, warning me his distinctive sense of humour was about to strike. 'At school they said my Coriolanus was legendary. But one still has to make a living, you know.'

I smiled politely. 'I'd like to hear your story. What brought you to Race Engineering?'

He paused, resting his elbows on his desk and steepling his fingers in front of his face. His gaze rested just above my head, as if he were addressing the gallery. I surveyed the office, realising what I'd taken for haphazard clutter, was, in fact, meticulously curated.

Similar components, groups of photographs and framed sketches clustered together in orderly groups. And someone was thorough with a duster around here.

'I was with Roderick right from the start. He drove, while I kept the cars running.'

'A partnership, then?'

James smiled reflectively. 'Perhaps, but not of equals. He was the one in the public eye, winning the prizes and the ladies' attention. I simply wielded my spanners.'

'But then you started your own business?'

'Inherited, dear boy. From my uncle. At just about the same time Roderick got an offer to drive for one of the big teams.'

'Quite a change, I should think?'

He smiled, like a tiger who'd spotted a lonesome sheep. 'It was and I loved it. At first, anyway. Money in the bank and the freedom to make my own decisions. Along with the factory, I inherited my uncle's dream machine, a Bristol 403. Designed by aero engineers. Mine was built at the pinnacle of their might, in nineteen-fifty-three. In my humble opinion it's the closest thing to automotive perfection, ever.'

It was hard to keep a straight face. There was nothing humble about James.

He turned the photo frame on his desk around to face me, 'Quite a rarity. It's still my daily drive. We should go for a spin some time.' A shadow flitted across his face, 'But what am I thinking? Off the road at the moment… for an engine rebuild. Another time.'

The picture showed a younger James standing next to a classic sports saloon in a deep burgundy colour. He looked at the picture fondly.

'Taken just after the repaint. I even inherited the registration plate, JB101, from my uncle. His name was Jack Berrington.'

'How did you come to be involved with Race Engineering?'

'I was seduced. Like a blushing virgin.' He paused and grinned wickedly, 'Roderick had been driving for class teams for about ten years by then. He wasn't as quick as he used to be and the wins were becoming fewer and further between. It was time to leave before he was pushed out. And he'd spent all his money on beautiful cars and fast women. Hitched in holy deadlock by then, of course, but playing through.'

I was mystified and it showed on my face.

'Oh please,' said James in exasperation. 'I despair of the youth of today. Is English really your first language, dear boy? That is to say, he was married but still having the odd dalliance. He approached me with what he described as the opportunity of a lifetime. "Let's use your talent and my name to make sports cars. We'll have lots of fun and make fistfuls of cash." Bloody liar, he turned out to be. He knew I was struggling by then. The big manufacturers were forcing price reductions on the small fry. He suggested Berrington could be a key supplier. It only dawned on me later that, without his own capital, Roderick needed my line of credit. The cheeky bugger even got me to use my pension fund to buy shares. Nuts, bolts and bloody wheel-brace. I fell for it all. And what do I have to show for it? A minority holding in a worthless business.'

'How can you say that? The accounts look pretty good until the last two years.'

'I've hardly seen a penny from it,' James glowered.

'Tell me about the new car?'

'What's to tell? The Siren was to be a class leader. The magnanimous Mr Race let me get on with it until funds became tight and then he instructed me to, in his words, stop buggering about and the get the car finished.'

'What did you have in mind?'

'Ancient history, dear boy. It matters not.'

'Humour me.'

He smiled wistfully. 'Very well. Updated styling, build quality to match the mainstream makers, superior performance and handling, with lower fuel consumption.'

'Faster *and* less thirsty? Don't those work against each other?'

'Not necessarily. A larger engine needn't work so hard and of course we improved the aerodynamics over the old car.'

'I thought you said the handling wasn't as good as the Vixen's?'

'It just needed more work. It can be our little secret.' He held his finger to his lips and grinned conspiratorially. His smile turned wolfish.

'But you went along with it?'

'What else could I do? Berrington was owed a small fortune. Still is, actually. I had to comply.'

'Surely then, it's very much in your interests for Race to survive and prosper?'

Although James' mouth still smiled, his eyes had grown wary. 'It's time for a dose of realism, dear boy. I really don't believe your ideas will ever generate enough income to pay off all the debts, save the Siren and restore Race's fortunes.'

I persisted, 'Our new forecast says otherwise, which means I'm the best chance you have of seeing your money.'

He leaned back in his chair and put both hands behind his head, smiling with the certainty of a man who knew he was right. 'It's very kind of you to take an interest in my affairs but you mustn't worry on my account.'

One last attempt to engage him. 'What would it take for you to resurrect your original vision for the Siren?'

James looked at his watch. 'Are we nearly finished with this nonsense? I have a lot to get through today.'

I smiled, 'I'd appreciate an answer.'

He shrugged his indifference. 'Things move fast in this business. One of the majors will have surpassed my thinking by now. Besides, who knows what happened to my papers and prototypes? We'd be starting all over again, virtually from scratch.'

'And the crash? Wouldn't you like to silence the critics? What about your personal reputation in all this?'

As the engineering director of a failing company, responsible for a new car which had been in a high-speed accident, I was convinced James should have looked a lot more concerned. Or at least, a little perturbed. But no, he was as relaxed as the man who'd just won the Nobel prize for being laid back.

'Let them think what they want. As far as I'm concerned, the Siren's dead and buried and Race Engineering won't be far behind it.'

'If this company fails, your creditors will want answers. Without evidence to the contrary, they'll blame you and the other directors for this wreck.'

James was implacable. 'They can make up their own answers, I have nothing more to say on this subject.'

I got up to leave. 'Thank you for being so candid. It allows me to do what I think best.' There was just time to add to Allen's task list before I dashed out to the car park.

I opened the passenger door of the waiting Jaguar and seated myself next to David. 'When are you going to spoil yourself and dump this old heap?'

David roared with laughter, 'I'll have you know this car is a classic.'

The immaculate red leather interior of the cherished ten-year-old XJ12 smelt exactly as I imagined an Edwardian gentlemen's club would, of cigars and aftershave. The gleaming black bonnet stretched down to the leaping cat riding on the prow. We nosed gently away from the entrance.

'How did you get on with Carina this morning?'

'I have an invitation to dinner.'

David's Jag pulled slowly up to the front gates, giving the guard time to open them, before cruising out into the street.

'Are you the starter or main course?'

'Very funny. Actually, she seems to be welcoming me into the team. James did a good job on her last night.'

'And how was he this morning?'

'Camp and uncooperative. Dug his heels in over the crash investigation.'

'He's always been somewhat theatrical but his lack of cooperation is very disappointing, particularly after he persuaded Carina to work with you, don't you think? What will you do?'

'It's in hand.'

David's Jag purred gently through the town centre traffic and we arrived outside the bank branch just in time to take possession of an on-street parking space being vacated by a camper van with Italian plates.

'Lucky,' I said.

'Fortune favours those who keep their eyes peeled,' said David.

Our local branch of the National Alliance Bank was in a beautiful building erected in eighteen-seventy-six. Originally a cornerstone branch of the Warwickshire and Worcestershire Savings Bank, through a long series of amalgamations, it found itself today representing one of the "Big Four". In contrast to the everyday red brick

Victoriana around it, the finely chiselled stonework and leaded windows looked positively religious. Its Victorian architects were clearly reaching for a high moral tone, inspiring thoughts of trust and integrity alongside threats of fire and brimstone for defaulters.

David announced us at reception. After a few moments, the security door at the side of the counter opened and Trevor Woods stepped sideways through the door, like a lean, fit bullfighter entering the arena. His hair had surrendered to gravity, no longer growing across the shiny dome of his head. He kept what little was left on the sides short and neat. He greeted David warmly, a conspiratorial smile confirming their long association as they clasped hands. After introductions, we were ushered through to his office, where an unwelcome surprise awaited me. A crisply pinstriped suit jacket hung possessively over the back of a visitor's chair. The occupant's richly-striped, blue-and-white shirt, teamed with his red braces, jarred against the office's restrained décor.

'Anglo Mercantile thrown you out at last, Keating?' Adrian Keating and I had crossed swords before. And the weaselly toad had dropped me right in it. And now here he was, with his gelled hair and shiny, smirking visage; a face I could never tire of punching.

He stayed seated, glancing casually in our direction. 'Jake, David,' he said. 'Of course. I'd forgotten, you weren't around when I moved, were you? Here at NAB, I'm with the BRU.'

'Bastards R Us?' I asked.

Keating smiled thinly. 'Business Recovery Unit, actually. It's where all our doubtful debts go to die.'

'Anglo fired you then?'

'I took the opportunity to review my career and decided it would be better served elsewhere.'

'I take it they didn't approve of your ways of doing business?'

Woods intervened, 'Gentlemen, please. We're here to talk about Race Engineering.'

David took over the conversation. 'I want Jake to brief you both on a rescue plan. He was tasked by Race's board last night with refocussing the business and getting it back into the black.'

Keating raised an eyebrow, 'I would have thought with your history you would be the last person they would want advising them about their future.'

'I'll thank you to keep a civil tongue in your head *Mr* Keating,' barked David in his parade ground voice. 'Our focus is to save the business. It just so happens Jake's experience and abilities equip him uniquely for this task.'

'That's a matter of opinion,' retorted Keating.

Woods interjected, 'Let's just hear the facts.'

Taking my cue from Woods, I summarised the current situation at Race and the shape of our plan to correct it.

Keating was dismissive. 'It sounds to me like the bank should pull its loans before things get any worse.'

I returned his hostile glare. 'Do that and you'll crystallize your losses and kill the business. Of course, if you're happy to live with the adverse publicity, then go ahead. But, just so you're clear, before you leap off the bridge and take us all down with you, I'm not looking for any additional borrowings, simply for you to honour the existing facility until the start of next week, by which time I will have a fully fleshed-out rescue plan and can offer the bank a repayment schedule which will bring your risk down progressively.'

Keating offered a hyena's smile, 'Well, you've certainly got balls.'

Woods directed his gaze at Keating as he spoke, 'Race Engineering is still a customer of this branch. And I hold the directors and David Lansdowne in the highest regard. We've benefitted considerably as their business has prospered and as long as I am manager here, we'll not shirk from our responsibilities and abandon these good people.'

Keating stood, scooped up his jacket and put it on, pulling the shoulders carefully into line and adjusting his cuffs to show a pedantic centimetre below the sleeves of his jacket, 'Then there's no more to be said, for the moment, at least. But I'll want to see daily figures. At the first sign things are going off the rails, I'll have the Race account in my portfolio and then we'll see what's what.' He opened the door and looked back at me, a smirk on his face, 'I would wish you luck, Elderfield but we both know I wouldn't mean it. I'll see you again, very soon.'

Woods was quiet as he escorted us back to the lobby. He and David stood close, shook hands and exchanged a meaningful look.

David spoke, 'Thanks, Trevor. We are most grateful for your support. We'll keep you posted on any and all developments.'

Back in the car I tackled David with my suspicions, 'You knew Keating would be there, didn't you?'

David completed his manoeuvre out of the parking space and back into the traffic before he answered. 'Bankers like Keating either end up at the top of their game or in jail. You were going to have to meet him sooner or later, best to get it over with.'

I took a deep breath and stared through the windscreen. 'Thanks for the warning.'

'You handled it well. Didn't give any ground.' David was conciliatory but he wouldn't be drawn further.

'Anything else you want to spring on me?'

'I believe you'll find more than enough at Race to keep you entertained for a while.'

We finished our journey in silence. David dropped me back at the office where I found my second surprise of the day.

Walking through the lobby, the receptionist drew my attention to a visitor who was waiting for me. A man of about my age, wearing pristine leathers, sat on the sofa, where I had been sitting the evening before, reading a motoring magazine. There was an expensive-looking motor cycle helmet on the table in front of him. He put his journal down and stood up as I approached. Like many tall men he was a little round-shouldered. Six-four maybe? His unruly mop of tightly curled brown hair hung over the back of his jacket collar. Widely-set, startlingly blue eyes looked out at me from his smooth-skinned, innocent face.

'Jake Elderfield?'

I nodded my acknowledgement.

'I'm Detective Sergeant Cooper.' He fished in the innermost reaches of his jacket for his warrant card, letting me study it briefly, before returning it to his pocket.

'I would never have taken you for police,' I said.

He smiled. 'That can have its advantages. Forgive the get-up but I'm officially on a day off, on my way to a bike race at Donnington this afternoon. I made the mistake of popping into the station this morning and the boss collared me for this errand.'

He paused and looked around him. 'Is there somewhere we can chat?'

I took him up to my office. The pixies had done a good job of restoring order after last night and this morning. All was clean and tidy. There was just one item on the desk I didn't recognise. Carina's business card. I picked it up and turned it over. On the back was scrawled a message "12 Greville Terrace, Leamington Spa, 7.30 don't be late."

Cooper placed his helmet on the corner of the desk and gravitated across to the display cabinet to examine the trophies and memorabilia.

'So how can I help you, Sergeant?'

I yawned, my all-nighter catching up with me.

'It's something of nothing, Mr Elderfield. I have a new boss who's just taken over the investigation into Roderick Race's death and, as I said, I'd just dropped into the station this morning to go over the case notes with him.'

Sergeant Cooper's eyes traversed across the contents of the cabinet, reaching the photographs. The picture taken at the film premiere stopped him in his tracks.

'Who's that with Mr Race?' he said. 'Is that…?'

'Yes, I believe it is,' I said.

Cooper turned towards me. 'Fascinating. Apparently, he was known as "Hot Rod" because of his success with the ladies.'

'I wouldn't know,' I said, looking at my watch meaningfully. What the hell was this about?

Cooper gave me his full attention. 'You left a message for me and then, out of the blue, the boss received a call to say you're working here.' He smiled apologetically, 'Obviously, we know Mr Race died before your time but when your name went into the computer, we saw your recent history with our colleagues in London.'

'You'll know, of course, the charges against me were dropped?'

He smiled. 'Lack of evidence as I understand it.'

'Because I didn't do it.'

Cooper's disarming smile barely left his face. 'I'm pleased to hear it,' he said. He unzipped the breast pocket of his jacket and took out a notebook, flipping open the cover. 'The case is still open.'

'Well, it's nothing to do with me.'

Cooper studied my face for a moment and put his notebook away, leaning back against the wall.

'May I ask what your role is here?'

'We're trying to save the business from bankruptcy. My job is to get it back into profit as quickly as possible.'

'You'll be digging around and asking lots of questions then?'

'Absolutely right, Sergeant.'

He gave me his wide, guileless smile again and held out his hand. 'Guy.'

I reciprocated. 'Jake.'

'Good to meet you.'

'It's been three months since Mr Race died and we are no further forward in finding out how it happened. The boss can see this one going nowhere and he has other cases piling up. Someone must be responsible for what happened and I'd like to find them.' He hesitated, frowning. 'I thought maybe we could help each other? I can understand how your previous difficulties could still be causing problems for you and meanwhile I have an unsolved death on my hands, without the resources to investigate properly.'

'What are you suggesting?'

'If you come across anything you think might be relevant to Mr Race's death you let me know and I'll look over your file in my spare time. If either of us finds something useful to the other, we share it.'

'What's in it for you?'

He grinned and stood away from the wall decisively, preparing to leave.

'I'm not going to make Inspector by just sitting-around, am I?'

'Do we have a deal?' he said.

'Ok, why not?' I said as I saw him to the door.

It was five to twelve. I went downstairs and joined the stream of employees as they made their way to the canteen for the staff briefing.

The room had been laid out theatre style with a central aisle and a block of seating on either side. Canteen tables had been lined up at the back. Two urns, one containing tea, the other coffee, sat next to a stack of mugs. Knots of two and three workers were standing, talking and waiting.

I picked up a yellow mug with "Race Engineering" stencilled across it in bold blue type. I needed more caffeine to stave off sleep.

I was still under the radar as far as most people here were concerned. I stood quietly sipping my coffee and listening to snatches of conversation around me. Nothing I heard was unexpected. The rumour mill had been in full grind. And you'd have to be blind and daft to miss the unsold cars out front.

There was a stir as Carina entered the room. She moved down the middle like a fashion designer at the end of an haute couture show. People took their seats and silence descended. Carina was cool and composed; an accomplished performer. A matching jacket had now been added to the dress I'd seen earlier. Her freshly applied make-up and brushed out hair completed her immaculate appearance. She waited patiently until everyone was settled. I found a seat at the back, next to Helen, who'd come in especially.

'Good afternoon, everyone.'

There was a murmur of response.

'I'm sure you're all aware of the difficulties we're in. Sales have collapsed and there's no doubt we're in serious trouble.' Carina prowled restlessly in front of her audience, walking to her left for a few paces, stopping to face her audience and deliver her next line and then walking to her right and repeating the manoeuvre. It was a compelling delivery. She came across as sincere and passionate, caring deeply about the business and each and every employee. I was convinced most of the predominantly male audience was more than a little in lust with her. 'Last night, your directors had a very difficult meeting. Carina stood still and looked slowly around the room, making eye contact with as many people as possible. 'We decided to bring in an adviser to work with us, to try to improve our prospects for the future. I won't lie to you. I was dead against this but I have been persuaded to give it a try.'

Someone shouted, 'Will there be redundancies?'

She ignored the question and slipped off her jacket, placing it over the back of a nearby chair. The move seemed natural, not staged, but the impact on the audience was measurable. Her tanned arms, together with the tailored, close-fitting silk dress, made her look more glamorous than ever. The water mark I'd left on her dress had disappeared. She was looking directly at me.

'Let me hand over to Jake Elderfield. What happens next is down to him.'

Talk about being put on the spot. The pantomime villain ready to be booed off stage at any minute.

'Thanks Carina,' I said, as I stood, trying to articulate more enthusiasm than I felt. I walked slowly to the front of the room, turned and faced the expectant audience. Carina took a seat in the front row. A host of pale, anxious faces looked back at me. Some were close to retirement, others just setting out on their careers. I'd lived this moment of truth many times before but it always had the same effect on me. This was in-your-face, real. These people's lives would change as a result of my actions.

Allen sat in the second row, leaning forward in his seat, all rapt attention. Helen was still at the back, next to my vacant seat and James had come to watch, leaning against the side wall, arms folded.

For a whole minute I stood silently, looking down at my feet, mirroring the quietness of the audience.

'First things, first. No redundancies. For now, at least. But the next chapter of Race Engineering's history is going to be tough. We must act quickly and decisively if we are going to save this company and everyone's jobs. I can make no promises to you other than we will use every means possible to try to turn this situation around. We'll clamp down on all unnecessary costs and do everything possible to boost sales. There will be lay-offs and your managers will talk to those of you who are affected, as soon as possible. But please be assured we plan to keep these to a minimum. It's essential we demonstrate to our lenders we are in control of the situation.'

I handed back to Carina.

'Thanks Jake. Does anyone have any questions?'

A troubled silence settled over the room. Everyone was preoccupied with their own thoughts.

'Then let's get back to work.' Carina said after a moment. 'Thanks everyone.'

As they filed out, Carina turned to me, 'I thought that went surprisingly well, all things considered.'

'Nobody likes to look stupid or self-serving in front of an audience. The questions will come later.'

'I suppose. I'll see you this evening,' she said.

I caught up with Helen on her way out. 'I wonder if I might have a word?' I asked.

'What about?' she asked.

'Let's go up to the office.'

We settled ourselves into the two guest chairs and Allen insisted on making us a coffee from his shiny machine before I banished him. I had to admit it tasted a lot better than the stuff in the canteen. Helen's cool blue eyes appraised my expression carefully.

'How can I help you, Jake?'

'It's like this. Unless I make the right decisions in the next few days all the bad things we talked about last night are going to happen. There's no room for mistakes; I need absolute confidence in the abilities of our senior team and an understanding of how they'll react in every situation.'

Helen looked thoughtful. 'Go on.'

'Here's where I've got to – Allen is talented but no one has been listening to him. I plan to build his confidence and take him along with me. Carina is a bright, sassy handful. She has a lot of useful knowledge in her head but she'll make me pay to get it. James is an enigma. He seems like he knows what he's talking about but he's stepped out of the tent and is throwing hand grenades under the flap at every opportunity. I don't understand why. That leaves you.'

'I'm not sure I like being analysed in this way,' Helen said.

'Nevertheless, you are part of the team. Apart from David, you were the most rational person in the room last night. You challenged James and Carina and seemed genuinely motivated to do the right thing by all stakeholders. In my experience, that's rare. And yet, checking Allen's records, that was the first board meeting you've attended for some time.'

I let silence float around us whilst I drank my coffee.

'I really don't see how any of this is relevant. These matters are private and must remain so,' said Helen.

'There were more undercurrents in last night's conversation than you'd find at the beach when the red flag's flying.' I got up and made to pull my papers together.

'Where are you going?' she asked.

'I can't do this job blindfold. There's no point in me staying unless you're prepared to be completely open with me.'

'Wait, please wait,' she said. 'You are asking a lot of me but I want this to work. Not just for Allen and Carina's sakes; everyone that works here is practically family, I've been to funerals, weddings, even christenings. Please help us Jake, please.'

'I promise you, whatever you are able to tell me will be in the strictest confidence.'

She hesitated, blinking back tears and pursing her lips. 'This is difficult for me but I will help where I can.' She took a deep breath and brushed at her eyes with the back of her hand. 'You need to know my husband was a very selfish man, much more so than I realised.' She smiled 'Perhaps, after thirty odd years of marriage, most women would say the same.' She took a sip of her coffee, 'But I wouldn't expect them to say they'd married a liar and a cheat.'

I maintained a sympathetic expression whilst wondering where this was going to take us.

She spoke quietly, reflectively. 'What made it worse was only finding out just how unprincipled he really was on the night he died. I was robbed of the chance to have it out with him.'

I wondered if I'd need the clean handkerchief that wasn't in my pocket but her tears stayed firmly in check. Back in control. More steel about her than any of the cars outside.

'He'd been away on one of his many trips to France and was due back that evening. Whilst I was waiting for him, I'd been going through his wardrobe picking out items for dry cleaning. I took out a couple of his suits and as usual, I checked the pockets to make sure there was nothing of value in them. I found this.' She took a cream envelope with a ripped-open flap from her handbag. 'I keep it close to remind me of how angry I should be.'

She passed it across to me and I turned it over to see the foreign postmark and the flowing blue-black ink, addressing the letter to M. Roderick Race at this office.

'Paris,' she added, unnecessarily. 'From her.'

I handed the envelope back.

She shrugged. 'How stupid can one be?' She smiled bitterly, 'Oh, there were always rumours, of course, but I never believed them.' She looked up at the framed pictures on the wall, showing her husband in his prime.

I kept quiet. Knowing this wasn't going to save the business. I sat in polite, uncomfortable silence.

Helen continued with her story. 'I was in a trance. I left the suits lying across our bed, went downstairs and poured myself a very large Scotch. I still had the letter in my hand so I read it again. I couldn't believe my eyes. He'd been seeing her all of the time we were married. I felt as if my whole world was deflating around me. Before I realised it, an hour had passed and I was sitting in the dark. As I got up to close the curtains, I saw headlights in the drive and I braced myself for the argument we were going to have. But when I threw the front door open... it was James, not Rod, standing there.'

'I can only imagine how you must have felt-'

'Oh, there's more. You need to hear me out.'

I offered her a watery smile.

'Rod had always bullied James appallingly. James used to laugh it off, saying public school had prepared him for much worse. But beneath the bravado I could see it hurt him deeply. I confronted Rod about his behaviour but he was dismissive, saying he intended to wring every good idea out of James and make our fortune. It was an awful situation and my sympathy was entirely with James. We became quite close. When Rod was out of the country, James and I would spend time together. The children saw more of him when they were growing up than they did of their own father.'

She stopped for a moment and smiled apologetically. 'Rather than face up to the tension between them, I'm afraid that I withdrew. I became a trustee of the Mary Arden Hospice and that has occupied much of my free time.'

She finished the last of her coffee and replaced the cup on its saucer. 'Well, anyway,' she said, 'When I opened the door that night, James could see something was very wrong. He led me back into the sitting room and sat me down. He poured drinks and I poured out my heart. He listened patiently without comment, until I'd finished.'

'How did he respond?'

'This is the worst part. Very embarrassing, actually. His words came as a complete surprise. He took my hand, looked deep into my eyes and told me I was the reason for his putting up with Rod's behaviour for all of those years. I'd never thought of him as being interested in women, let alone in me. We were friends, nothing more. I tried to make a joke of it, asking why he'd never thought to mention it. He said he'd been waiting for his chance; that the truth about Rod's affair would come out sooner or later. He tried to kiss me. It was disgusting. I was shocked and didn't believe a word of it. I pushed him away and told him to get out. He became angry, asking why we shouldn't be together when we had both been treated so badly by the same man. I told him to go.'

'What happened then?'

She offered me a humourless smile. 'It was very sudden. One moment he was ardent, passionate even. The next he was the James I had always known, humorous, suave and seemingly without feelings.' She shrugged her shoulders, dismissively. 'He put down his glass, straightened his tie, made some quip about the time and left.'

Helen's face crumpled and she looked down into her lap.

I leaned forward, touching her arm gently.

Her smile was sad, distant, her thoughts elsewhere. 'I'm fine,' she said. 'Yesterday's meeting was the first time I have been able to face him since it happened.'

It was my turn to say something, anything, to cover our mutual embarrassment. I could only admire Helen's candour in the face of my relentless questioning. It was a tribute to her commitment to saving this business that she was prepared to bare her soul like this.

'Thank you, Helen, for being so honest with me. It really helps if I understand how these relationships fit together.'

We sat in silence for several minutes until her spirits rallied. We walked down to her car together. On the way back up to the office I reflected on what I'd just heard. Piecing it together with what I'd learned so far, I could see why this board was so deeply dysfunctional. Carina's bitter feelings towards Rod Race; James, with every reason to feel aggrieved by Rod and now Helen, barely on speaking terms with James and deeply hurt by Rod. As for Allen; whilst his mother might love him, James and his sister alternately ignored or made fun of him.

Back in the boardroom, I found a lively and enthusiastic Allen waiting for me with the sales manager. Surprising, after the hours we'd put in last night. We three spread our papers over the table to review the forecasts together. Within a couple of hours, we'd refreshed the marketing plan to focus on Vixen owners and briefed the sales team to make an immediate start. Where the Siren had been designed as a luxury sports car, the Vixen was a no-nonsense coupe. A stripped-down speed machine, leaving plenty of scope for performance and trim upgrades, alongside servicing and renovation work.

'Great work, Allen. We'll review this with the directors first thing in the morning before pushing it across to the bank. It should keep them in our rear-view mirror for a while.' I changed the subject, 'How did you get on with finding us an engineer?'

Allen smiled enthusiastically, 'Hired and already on site at the test track. He understands the urgency and has committed to turn the task around quickly.'

I forgot how tired I'd been feeling. 'Excellent. Can't wait to meet him.'

Allen smiled. 'Why don't I drive you over there now? We can see how they're getting on and you can meet the head of the racing team?'

'Why not? I think we deserve a break.'

During the fifteen-minute journey to Long Marston, Allen explained that the facility had been an airfield in the Second World War but his father had leased it and built a circuit where there used to be a runway. With its perimeter fence and useful array of lock-up workshops and office buildings, it was perfect for testing cars away from prying eyes. Security had been increased significantly since Race's death, which had only made it doubly surprising someone had been able to smuggle in a camera on the very night of the accident. How could our snapper know what was going to happen?

We were met at the gates by a security guard with a clipboard and a ferocious-looking dog. He exchanged a few words with Allen and carefully checked his identity card and car registration. We were waved through to make the short drive to the global headquarters of Race Engineering's racing team, pulling up in the car park. I watched Allen's face. This was where his father died. How would he react?

'This must be difficult' I said.

'I can't visit this place without wondering what Dad was thinking at the end.' He shook his head, 'What the hell happened?'

I put my hand on his upper arm and squeezed gently. I thought a hug might be too much.

He looked around him, as if seeking an answer. 'He was a difficult man to love.'

I was saved the need to find a reply by the arrival of a compact man in racing overalls, as we climbed out of the car. Allen introduced him as Mike Rowe, head of the team. He looked like the action figure I'd had as a kid but without the scar down the side of his face. And he was quite a bit taller. There was an obvious affection between him and Allen.

'How're you, laddie?' and turning to me, 'and you must be Jake.' We shook hands.

'Yes, I must be,' I said.

Allen grinned, 'Mike's a clever man, Jake. He has hundreds of inventions to his name. Haven't you ever heard of the Mike Rowe Chip?'

Mike let out a wheezy chuckle at what was obviously a well-worn joke between them, 'Hawd yer wheesht young Race, enough of yer nonsense.' Mike hammed up his gentle Scottish burr for our benefit.

'I wanted Jake to see what you get up to here, Mike,' said Allen, 'and we thought it would be good to meet the chap looking at the Sirens.'

Mike stroked his neat designer stubble, which somehow seemed to be the same short wiry texture and thickness as the hair on his head. 'Aye, no problem. The guided tour will take all of ten minutes. We'll finish up in the sheds where he's working. They've been here a couple of hours already and have made a good start.'

'That's what we're paying him for,' I chipped in.

'I'll meet you inside,' said Allen.

Mike frowned at me as we moved away from Allen. He waited until we were out of earshot before he spoke. 'Now listen,' he said. 'I've a lot o' time for Allen and I won't have any rubbish from you about firing him.'

'What makes you say that?' I responded.

'I keep ma ear to the ground. I know what goes on in the boardroom. He's a good lad. Sharp and trustworthy.'

'It's early days but I agree. I'll be relying on him heavily so it's good to have your endorsement.'

His point made; Mike became business-like as we walked around the buildings. He introduced his small team to me.

'We work closely with James. Mostly, it's about proving endurance and trying to find a good compromise between road-going and track performance. And o' course, we've also been heavily involved in winning type approval for the new car.'

'What's type approval?'

'A regulation that keeps all the cars we buy roadworthy. We're allowed to go through a simplified process because we're not a volume producer. Type approval has been suspended until the accident has been investigated.'

'You're saying we couldn't sell another Siren even if we had a buyer?'

'Aye. I canna understand why James wasna looking at this before now. It makes no sense.'

'What do you make of the guy Allen found?'

'He comes highly recommended.' His face split into a broad grin. 'By me. He's an old contact o' mine. He's just finished an assignment in Birmingham so I knew he was in the country. Come on, I'll introduce you.'

A large workshop stood across the yard, at the end of the pit lane. Mike opened a side door and we joined

Allen, who was propped against a wall watching the floor show. The building was spacious and well lit. The far wall was covered in component drawings showing the make-up of the car. A Siren was parked near it, a deep wound scarring its side. Bright metal showed the point where the second car had first impacted before scraping along its full length. The partly-dismantled rogue Siren stood in the middle of the space as two men in white laboratory coats, latex gloves on their hands and plastic covers on their shoes, meticulously dissected it. Components and battered panels were being laid out systematically onto large white sheets stretched across the floor.

One of the two, a tall, thin, studious-looking man in his late fifties came towards us, leaving his colleague elbow-deep in surgery. As I watched, the younger man picked up an angle grinder and set about the car's mangled front wing. Bright sparks arced up towards the ceiling and the metal parted, revealing the twisted remains of the engine bay.

Mike introduced us to the distinguished-looking man who had joined us. 'This is Dr Jan Phillips. His work at the Technical University in Delft makes him one o' the foremost automotive engineers of our day.'

Phillips smiled and gave a formal half bow in acknowledgement of Mike's introduction. His half-moon glasses, short grey hair and lab coat lent him a medical air.

He issued us with shoe protectors and took us over to the wreck.

'How are you getting on?' asked Allen.

'Well, we've almost completed the disassembly of the key parts of the vehicle and we will be starting to examine the componentry and look for failures in the next hour or so.'

He spoke excellent, slightly accented English, his "v's" sounding more like "f's".

I surveyed the myriad pieces making up the three-dimensional jigsaw puzzle. 'It looks like you have plenty to keep you busy.'

'I am confident by tomorrow morning we will have answers,' he said, peering over his glasses at me.

'Any first thoughts?' I asked.

'I am a scientist, not a soothsayer. You will have my report first thing in the morning, once we have all the facts.'

As we left the workshop, Mike turned to me, 'D'you fancy a spin around the circuit wi' me?'

Allen laughed.

'Depends,' I said.

'On what?'

'We've just left the good doctor slicing up a car which nearly killed its driver out there. Just how stupid do you think I am?'

'Away with you, man. All the Sirens are grounded but I can take you around in a Vixen.'

'Well, why didn't you say so? Let's go.'

Mike walked me to a garage half way along the pit lane. He passed me a crash helmet. Whilst I was putting it on, he called up one of the drivers and summoned a car in from the track. The dark red, metallic sports coupe snarled into the pit lane and stopped just in front of us. The driver climbed out, leaving his door open for Mike. The idling engine emitted a throaty burble and I could feel the heat coming off the machine as we stood by it. As if reading my thoughts, Mike turned to me with an explanation, 'This car has now been out on the track for almost twenty hours continuously. A team of three drivers work together to keep it running around the clock until the test is complete or something breaks. Bill, here, is about to take an unscheduled tea break whilst I show you how it's done.' The driver took off his helmet, grinned at Mike and strolled into the garage to put the kettle on.

'Aye, it's all glamour, this job,' said Mike, grinning.

The car's paintwork was dull with dirt from the track and there were smears across the windscreen where the wash wipes had sluiced the driver's field of vision. The alloy wheels were black with brake dust and the chrome tail pipes on the twin exhausts grey with sooty deposits.

'This Vixen is very like the one Allen drove you over in today, almost identical in fact. The cockpit on the road-going version is nicely trimmed in leather and such. Mind you, there are a few concessions for you Sassenach fairies, you know, a radio and the like. But it was originally designed as a track day car for enthusiasts.' He grinned, 'You'll see what I mean when we get inside. Watch your head on the roll cage.'

Once I was in my seat, Mike checked my helmet and my racing harness, before walking around the car and climbing in behind the wheel. Looking around the cockpit, I noted the large red fire extinguishers at the side of each footwell and the fuel cut off switch on the dash.

We accelerated smoothly out of the pit lane and onto the circuit. By the first bend we had reached one hundred and thirty miles per hour before Mike applied the brakes firmly and we cornered right on the apex, with a slight squeal of protest from the tyres. He was relaxed. This was just a normal day at the office for him. One hand on the wheel, he made polite small talk, whilst I hung on to the roll cage with my left hand, knuckles going white with the strain. Looking across at the dials, I could tell Mike was using gear changes to keep the revs high. He saw me looking.

Shouting over the engine, he explained. 'It's tuned to deliver more power at higher revs. Above six thousand.'

'You're closer to nine thousand most of the time,' I yelled back.

'Aye, I'm giving it some stick. Our job is to break these cars and to see what gives out first. We can then decide if they're good enough or if they need beefing up. We can run it safely up to nine thousand revs all day long – it's tough as old boots.'

The black dial showed a red segment starting at nine thousand revs.

'And what happens if you go over the redline?'

'Do it once or twice and it's not a problem. But the more you do it, the more you risk. Sooner or later, it'll blow up in your face.'

I laughed. 'Sounds like my life.'

We completed the lap and pulled back into the pit lane where the test driver was waiting to continue. Mike grinned as we got out of the car, 'That gives you some idea of what these cars can do, even on a soft lap.'

Allen joined us. 'Not bad eh, Jake?'

'Well, let's just say next time I aim to rob a bank, I know where to find a decent get-away driver!'

'Och, away with you!'

'To more serious matters, Allen, Mike, what about the team finances? We are looking closely at how we can keep the factory viable but what about the situation here?'

Allen responded, 'Mike and I reviewed things whilst you were at the bank. Racing is currently holding its own. There are quite a few Vixens in use on European circuits and the parts and racing accessories sales are the bread and butter to this operation. The bank account is very much in the black since the team hooked a new sponsor, Nalco, for the planned race series in the States featuring the Siren.'

'Nalco?' I asked.

'The North American Lubricant Company,' added Mike.

'Will they still go ahead after the crash?' I asked.

'I have to say I'm more confident now you've hired Dr Phillips.'

'Let's hope he comes up with the goods then,' I grinned, 'Thanks for the lap, Mike. I could get into these cars.'

'What do you drive at the moment?'

'You could say I'm between cars right now but I hope to be in the market soon.'

'You need to get yer hands on a Siren whilst they're goin' cheap.'

With a cheery wave Mike walked back to his office and Allen drove us both back to Stratford and Race Engineering. I called a cab to take me over to Carina's for dinner.

5: Women Drivers

My taxi pulled up outside an elegant, double-fronted Regency town house in Leamington Spa. Its crisp, white-rendered walls reminded me of a carefully iced cake. I paid the driver and crunched up the gravel drive towards the front door, passing a gleaming white Vixen with mirror finish chrome alloy wheels on the way. Evidence of serious spend on this house was everywhere. New sash windows with a star pattern etched into the lower panes of glass ensured privacy whilst adding glamour. Tasteful, minimalist planting occupied neat flower beds at each side of the driveway. These large, expensive properties, in their quiet streets, offered sanctuary to commuters who made their daily pilgrimage to Birmingham.

At the front door, an old-fashioned porcelain bell-pull set into the wall produced an answering chime somewhere inside.

I stood back to look up at the front of the handsome house, just in time to catch the twitch of a curtain as it fell back into place. Moments later, the door opened and a petite young woman in a short, close-fitting black dress and white apron stood in front of me.

Black eyeliner emphasised blue/grey eyes and her cheekbones were carefully accentuated by the skilful application of blusher to her pale skin. Her jet-black hair was cut in a severe urchin style and she had one of those doily things in her hair that maids wear. She performed a neat curtsy.

'You are Mr Elderfield,' she announced in heavily accented English, 'Madam is expecting you. I take you to garden room. Please, to come in.'

I was admitted to the hallway and she closed the door behind me. Her scarlet nail varnish exactly matched the bright shade of her lipstick. Her generously applied make-up seemed at odds with the formality of her uniform. Strange.

'Please, to follow me,' she said. She turned and walked slowly, further into the house.

The hallway was expensively decorated in a contemporary style whilst acknowledging the building's heritage. The lower part of the walls was panelled, in a pale cream finish. Dark green paper with the lustre of silk sat above this. A large, contemporary chandelier, with about fifty candle bulbs, hung from the high ceiling and a grand oak staircase disappeared up towards the next floor.

But I confess that having spent too much time living like a monk recently, the rear view of my companion, with her shapely legs sheathed in glossy black nylon, commanded much of my attention. I caught up with her.

The half-glazed door at the end of the hall, with its twin panels of Arts and Crafts-style, stained glass, opened onto a classical garden room which overlooked the carefully manicured outside space.

'Madam will be here shortly. Would you like wine?'
'Lovely, thank you.'
'Is Chablis, Sir. Is chilled.'
'Thank you.'

I took a seat and studied the garden in the fading light. Formal beds were laid around a water feature; a life-size nymph, kneeling towards me, in a large open clam shell, her head bowed, her hands raised and cupped in front of her face, water trickling through her fingers. Four lights, at ground level, transfixed her within their convergent beams. A hi-fi was playing quietly in the corner of the room and twin wall lights softly illuminated the space. It was relaxing and I felt myself drifting towards sleep. I snapped back into consciousness as the door opened and Carina came in. I stood quickly. Partly from politeness but mainly to jog my mind into wakefulness. Her hair was piled up on her head in a way that looked casual but must have taken many pins and infinite patience. Glamorous yet informal. Dark swirls of hair framed her cheek bones. She'd been poured into her close-fitting, strapless, full-length, black silk dress. The long split in her skirt served two purposes; as well as providing an alluring "now you see it, now you don't" view of her physique, it also enabled her to walk. I felt grubby and under-dressed in the business suit I'd been wearing since yesterday. Our serious-faced servant girl followed her into the room, bearing a silver tray with two thoroughly chilled glasses of white wine, beads of condensation forming on the outside of each vessel.

'Good evening, Jake. Kat, you are very slow with our guest's wine tonight,' said Carina as she sat demurely in the chair facing me.

The girl curtsied formally, bowing her head and offering the tray towards Carina.

'I apologise, Madam.'

Carina took a glass and the girl presented the tray to me. The crystal was deliciously cold.

'Inform us when you are ready to serve dinner. You may go until then. We will ring if we require anything else.'

'Thank you, Madam.' Facing away from me, the girl bent at the waist and leaned forward to where Carina was sitting. They kissed slowly and deeply, the girl clasping the empty tray in both hands behind her back.

She straightened, tucking the empty tray under one arm. She turned, smirked at me and left the room, closing the door behind her. I took a sip of wine. It was very good.

'Are you always so familiar with your staff?'

Carina laughed, 'It's just a little fun between grown-up girls.' She raised her glass. 'To secrets. Now you've seen mine and I know something of yours.'

'What do you mean?'

She smiled, baring her perfect white teeth.

'Only the privileged few get to meet Kat, you know.'

She gave me a quizzical look. 'And it seems you are something of a dark horse, Mr Elderfield.' Relaxing back in her chair, she crossed her legs.

My eyes were drawn to the split in her long skirt as it parted, revealing tanned flesh from ankle to thigh. I brought my gaze back to her face. She was studying me, with a provocative half smile playing around her lips, whilst her eyes signalled, 'I dare you.'

'I've been asking around. David was less than candid when he introduced you last night.'

I put my glass down on a side table and tried to stay calm.

'What have you heard?'

'You were considered to be a rising star before you suddenly resigned from Lansdowne & Partners three months ago.'

She paused to sip her wine.

'Moreish, isn't it? But, you know, what's really intriguing is the visit you had from the boys in blue just before you quit.'

I shrugged. 'Old news. I'm surprised you didn't hear about it at the time. But then you had your own issues to deal with.'

'There was something of a scandal, wasn't there? Accused of raiding the coffee money, perhaps?'

'Like I say, old news. All dealt with now.'

'I hope so. If we're going to rely on you to help us, the last thing we need is another visit from the police.'

Did she know Guy Cooper had been to see me today? I paused. How best to respond?

'Nothing you need worry about. Let's get on with saving the business, shall we?'

'Fine. But I'm curious. Why resign from David's? You were on your way to becoming a partner. Did you develop a conscience about the fees you were charging?'

Good. She was moving away from the point. Time for a cliché.

'The role was making me feel claustrophobic. Time to become my own boss; to choose my own challenges.'

'How ironic. Wasn't it David who secured this job for you? I am right, aren't I? After leaving Lansdowne's, you've not worked until this,' she laughed. 'I suppose trouble with the police must have affected your employability.'

Ok. Enough. 'I thought we were here to talk about Race?'

She smiled, in control. Or so she thought. 'Not good at being teased, are you?' She shook her head, 'Time to relax. Let me take charge.' She got up from her chair, turned up the stereo and walked towards me. Tony Hadley was belting out "Only when you leave" as she put down her glass.

'Dance with me,' she said. She reached out her hand and as I took it, she pulled me up to her, in close, wrapping her arms around me, moving her body in time to the music, slowly, sensuously.

'C'mon, Jake. Relax.'

I'd been expecting a business-like chat over a quiet dinner, not a full-blown assault on my senses. What the hell was she up to? And what was the thing with the servant-girl she'd just snogged? I could feel Carina's body pressed against mine, her hands stroking slowly up and down my back. Her perfume was heady and strong. Her left hand reached down my back, below my waist. I stiffened, ready to pull away, when the door opened and light from the hall broke into the moment.

The girl stood at the door, a neutral expression on her face. 'Dinner is served, Madam,' she said. I wondered how long she'd been there.

Carina beamed a slow smile at me and then at her. 'Thank you, my angel,' she said as she stood back, keeping hold of my hand, 'Let's go through.'

The table in the dining room was set formally, for two, with elegant wine glasses, lavish cutlery and a candelabra, candles burning bright, casting shadows on the dark red walls. The traditional crystal chandelier, hanging above the table, gave off a dim, background level of light. The girl pulled a chair back for Carina and then hurried around the table to do the same for me.

'The table looks lovely, Kat. You may serve us.'

'Thank you, Madam.' The girl busied herself with dishes.

'I haven't introduced you two properly, have I? Jake this is Katerina Dominova, Kat for short. She's from Prague. You might say we are very, very good friends.'

Kat curtsied for a second time and grinned at Carina.

'Kat likes to cook, don't you darling? What are we having this evening?'

'Tonight, Madam, I make Polish dishes. Zupa Buraczkowa, red beetroot soup, Baranina, lamb with roast vegetables and to finish Blueberry Mazurka and coffee.'

She poured more wine into fresh glasses.

Carina was effusive. 'Sounds wonderful, doesn't it, Jake?'

I nodded and smiled.

'Your good health. Are your plans for Race taking shape?'

I took a deep breath and, as Kat served the beetroot soup from a shining silver tureen, began to answer.

Carina interrupted. 'I heard Mike took you around the circuit today. Surely you didn't go all the way out there for a cheap thrill, did you?'

'I wanted to meet the man we've hired to examine the Siren.'

Carina's polite smile switched off abruptly.

'Who gave you permission to do that?'

'I don't need anyone's say-so. I have a job to do.'

'James won't be happy.'

Well bully for James. Time to tell it like it is. 'If we're going to save this business, you people need to get your act together.'

I gulped my wine. Tired and irritated. This whole evening seemed designed to wrong foot me. I smiled and made an effort to sound more reasonable than I felt.

'Ask yourself why you're in this mess. Maybe if you'd communicated better- shown each other a little love even - it would have helped.'

'Love? You can't be serious? I've never heard anything so ridiculous.'

'C'mon Carina - every relationship – business or pleasure – needs trust and commitment to stand any chance of working. You don't want to call it love? Fine. How would you describe it?'

'Weakness. Some of us are born to lead where the rest follow. One sets the rules, the others do as they're told.'

'That's cack and you know it. Every pair of hands that does a job, comes with a free brain. Which is why just handing out orders is such a bad idea. You're missing all of that valuable, direct experience – some of which might save you a stack of time and money. Craziness.'

'Someone has to take charge, otherwise there'd be chaos.'

'Sure, someone has to own the big picture but it's not about being a dictator. Carry people with you, share your vision of the future and they'll support you with their energy, enthusiasm and brilliant insights.' I sipped wine, feeling calmer after my rant. 'Hasn't anyone ever told you they love you?'

She smiled, 'Just words. You, on the other hand, have some strange ideas for a business consultant. I'm beginning to wonder what you're going to come out with next.'

I shook my head. 'Beyond reason and beyond doubt. An act of faith. Love is more than just a word.'

'You've really thought about this haven't you?'

I watched Kat as I replied. 'Dishing out orders and not listening to feedback is just arrogant. That's a red line to steer clear of, in my book. But with the right approach, you can unlock people's inventiveness, fire up their imagination and bind them to you. Think for a moment. Just imagine the power you'd create if you could harness the creativity of everyone who works for Race Engineering. You'd be unstoppable.'

'I didn't realise you could be so passionate.'

Carina saluted me with her glass. 'Impressive. What do you say, Kat?'

When I'd started speaking the girl had been looking at her feet, the very picture of characterised servitude. Now she was looking at me. With a spark of life in her eyes which disappeared as she turned to answer Carina.

'Certainly, Madam,' she said, now standing decorously to attention by the sideboard.

What was the relationship between these two? Had Carina hired an actress for this charade? Did I care? I was here to learn about Carina and save the business. 'Long Marston was useful in another way, too. It got me thinking about how we can reenergise enthusiasm for Race.'

Carina's smile didn't touch her inquisitive green eyes. 'Full of good ideas, aren't you?'

'If we could put a handful of influential motoring journalists where I sat today it would get them believing in the brand again.'

'How's your starter?'

'Delicious.' I turned to the girl. 'Thank you, Kat, this is wonderful.'

'Thank you, Mr Elderfield,' she simpered.

'Please call me Jake.'

'Certainly, if it pleases you, Mr Jake.'

'Just Jake is fine. Aren't you taking this whole mistress, servant game a little too far?' I asked.

Carina smiled, 'You get your kicks saving companies. We need a little more spice. So, tell me, do you enjoy playing with people's lives and fortunes?'

'It's what I know and I'm good at it.'

Her expression became thoughtful. 'I suppose, in a way, you've just as much at stake as we do.' She took up her wine glass. 'If you save us, your reputation is made but if it goes wrong...'

'I win a trip to the job centre.'

'Exactly. Let's not squabble.' Green eyes softened, 'James was very persuasive last night. But if we're going to work together, you do need to keep me fully in the picture.'

I raised my glass, 'To our unholy alliance then.'

Carina laughed and had Kat join our toast.

I finished my soup, leaned back in my chair and enjoyed the wine, after all I wasn't driving anywhere. I relaxed and half closed my eyes. Two beautiful women, entertaining and distracting me. A warm, elegant dining room burnished by soft light. Fantastic food and wine. Whatever Carina was up to, I could enjoy it and stay focused on the job.

Kat curtsied to Carina before turning to face me. As she collected our soup plates her glance drifted up until she met my gaze. She grinned. The first natural thing she'd done all night. She took her tray out to the kitchen, closing the door softly behind her.

'Tell me about this house, Carina. How long have you lived here?'

'It was a wreck. It's taken two years of hard work to make it what you see today. My architect, builder and interior designer brought it back to life. My principal contribution was the enormous cheques I had to write and then, of course, there were my own glamorous touches. Chic with a hint of drama.'

'Quite a project.'

'It's my palace of pleasure: a perfect place to worship beauty.' Carina's gaze followed Kat as she came back into the room bearing a bottle of red wine. 'I believe money's only purpose is to enable us to have and do whatever we want.'

Kat served the main course as she joined the conversation, 'Madam likes to collect beautiful things.'

Carina held her gaze as Kat filled our glasses. 'I do. And when I collect something, it stays mine forever.'

Kat's fingers trembled a little as she poured.

'Clumsy girl, you've spilled the wine,' Carina lifted the offending hand to her mouth and looked deep into the girl's eyes as she licked hungrily at the red droplets anointing the pale skin. Kat shuddered and a low moan escaped her lips.

I levered my thoughts away from what I was witnessing. 'How did you come to join the business, Carina?'

'It was Rod's idea. I was a headstrong, lippy teenager and I believed I could change the world. At first, I worked in the racing team, helping to manage the sponsors. Anything from ferrying them around to helping to make the most of their spend. It was a short jump from there into the main business when Rod decided he wanted to play chairman.'

'You never call him Dad, do you? You weren't close?'

She shook her head and twizzled her wine glass thoughtfully.

'I saw him as others did - a legend in his own mind.'

'And you, Jake, did you grow up in a loving family?'

'My parents were always very supportive.'

'And is there no one special in your life?'

'She left. A while ago now. Not heard from her since.'

'Silly girl. Well at least Kat and I won't have to compete with anyone for your attention.'

I smiled, covering my true feelings about my recent past. 'Will you ever stop teasing me?'

She laughed, 'How else am I going to find you out?'

'Well, it's been an interesting evening and I'm pleased we've found a way to work together. But I should make a move. Another busy day ahead of us tomorrow.'

Kat came back in with dessert. She looked me in the eye, her face close to mine, and licked her lips, 'Cream?' she said.

'I'm sorry?'

'On dessert. You want cream, Mr Jake?'

Carina interrupted. 'You may serve our coffee now. As I don't believe we've tempted Mr Jake to stay for breakfast, once you've called him a taxi, you may clear and get ready to retire for the night.'

'Thank you, Madam.' Kat provided brandy and coffee in the garden room. With service completed, she sat provocatively close to me on the wicker two-seater. Her eyes stared into mine as she reached down with both hands and slowly removed the red-soled high heel from her right foot. Letting the shoe drop gently to the floor, she rubbed both of her hands slowly and sensuously across the sheer black nylon encasing her shapely foot. I couldn't help but notice her carefully manicured toenails were painted to match the red gloss of her fingernails. She arched her foot and placed her toes on the ground, repeating the exercise with her left foot. I couldn't decide which she was enjoying more; the languorous self-massage or the effect she was having on me. She half closed her eyes, pouting her lips and arching an eyebrow as she watched me watching her.

'I'll say goodnight, Mr Jake. It was a great pleasure to meet you.'

Her accent had softened considerably. She picked up her shoes and stood facing me. Putting her hand to her mouth, she blew me a slow kiss, winked and grinned widely before turning a solemn face to Carina and curtseying. She left the room, closing the door softly behind her.

Older but probably none the wiser, I finished my coffee, said goodnight and left, looking forward to my bed.

6: Wednesday: Drop the Clutch

The shareholders gathered in the boardroom at the civilized hour of nine-thirty to receive an update. Carina wore a stylish, figure-hugging, dark grey trouser suit, with her hair carefully tousled around her face, softening her features. Allen had moved The Beast into the boardroom in order to preside over refreshments. David and Helen were chatting and James stood moodily by the window.

'Good morning, Jake,' said Carina in a soft voice, enjoying her coffee and smiling, 'Pleasant dreams last night?'

'I had a great evening, thank you. And I enjoyed meeting Kat.'

'Should I be jealous?' she asked, a wicked smile playing on her lips.

'I think it's time we started the meeting, don't you?' I asked.

She grinned, 'I'm not embarrassing you, am I?'

I ushered everyone to their seats whilst Allen made more coffee. David called on us both to report progress.

'What's this I hear about you hiring in some engineer, Elderfield?' James interrupted.

'Maybe I didn't make myself clear, James. Without a thorough investigation I can't save the Siren.'

'So, a second-rater gets to fabricate a fairy tale?'

'He happens to be extremely well qualified for the job and he's waiting to speak to us now. Shall we ask him for his opinion?'

My visitor was sitting patiently in my office, knees pressed primly together with his battered, satchel-style, leather briefcase on his lap. His brightly checked three-piece suit, white shirt and a blue bow tie seemed eccentric; more suited to a day at the races than a discussion about the future of Race Engineering. Despite his late night he looked as fresh as a newly-picked peach. I was jealous.

Back in the boardroom, Allen drew up an extra chair. Dr Phillips stood to attention and bowed his head formally as I introduced him. He rejected Allen's offer of coffee in favour of camomile tea. Phillips slowly unbuckled the straps of his briefcase, removing a small black case with the flourish of a conjuror. He took out a cloth and a pair of glasses, using one to carefully polish the other. Placing the half-moons on his nose, he peered at each of us, like a short-sighted mongoose.

James looked at his watch and gave a loud sigh, 'For God's sake. I thought we were going to get a lecture on saving the business, not watch this old fart juggling his eyewear.'

David interjected, 'Patience, James, let's hear what Dr Phillips has to say.'

Phillips removed a slim folder from his briefcase and studied the contents. He began to speak in his strong, mildly-accented voice. 'Good morning, ladies and gentlemen. I am here to offer you my preliminary report on the Siren.'

There was a shuffling noise at the far end of the table.

'Stay where you are, James,' growled David in a low voice.

Ignoring the interruption, Phillips carried on. 'After examining the two vehicles and interviewing the drivers, we were able to obtain copies of the crash photographs from the local newspaper and these proved extremely helpful. I can say, for certain, the driver lost control of the vehicle when a pressed steel component in the offside front suspension failed due to metal fatigue.'

'And in simple terms?' I chipped in.

Dr Phillips pursed his lips and examined me carefully, making me feel like the dimmest pupil in his class. 'Bad metal causes crash.'

James looked bored and irritated, giving the impression of a recalcitrant sixth former waiting to see the headmaster.

Helen was first to comment. 'The Siren's design is not at fault then?'

Phillips pursed his lips and glanced over his glasses at her. 'I can say the car's aerodynamics are good. It has crisp, contemporary styling, although the centre of gravity is a little too far forward for my taste.' Phillips saw the expression on my face and sighed. 'For the nontechnical amongst us I am suggesting the Siren's dynamics could be improved by counterbalancing the weight of its engine or preferably replacing it with a lighter unit. But essentially, it is a good design.'

Which backed up what James had told me yesterday.

Everyone started to speak at once. David's voice cut through the others, restoring order.

'What do you say to this, James?'

James smiled suavely, 'I'm flattered Dr Phillips approves. Of course, if we'd had a larger budget, any issues with weight distribution could easily have been ironed out but Roderick's economy drive put a stop to it all. As for faulty components, I have to say, not guilty; our beloved chairman found some tinpot manufacturer in the Far East who could knock out pressings cheaper than we, at Berrington, could sneeze.'

'Dad's not here to defend himself,' said Allen.

Phillips cleared his throat once more, 'There must always be rigorous adherence to quality control. Procedures will need to be reviewed before you recommence manufacturing.'

James stood. 'A statement of the toothachingly obvious. Do we really have to listen to this?'

'We're simply considering how best to move on from this badly-managed event,' said David, reasonably.

'Will this be a problem on all of the Sirens, James?' I asked.

'I'd need to investigate,' said James.

David cut in, 'How long before we can correct the fault?'

James didn't respond.

'What about it, James? We need to get on and rectify all of the affected cars,' I persisted.

James looked around the room. 'Would anyone else like to tell me my job?'

'Stop feeling sorry for yourself and answer the question, man,' said David.

James looked dubious. 'I'll need to examine the drawings. We'll be able to fabricate replacements at Berrington but it will take time to design and manufacture the tooling.'

'How much time?' I asked.

'Six to eight weeks at best.'

Dr Phillips interjected, 'If I may comment? I have taken the liberty of examining the critical components and with only minor modifications, which could be carried out by any competent toolmaker, the set from your Vixen motor car can be substituted.'

James's face was now the same shade of pink as his tie.

'Well. If you'll excuse me,' he said, 'I believe my interests are best served elsewhere. And so, this is goodbye not au revoir. But before you proceed upon this doom-laden path, you should probably know your guide is not what he seems.'

With this, he passed a folded paper to Carina. 'I believe you have some explaining to do, dear boy,' he said to me, quietly. James walked calmly from the room without looking at any of us.

'How are we supposed to carry on without a chief engineer?' asked Carina angrily.

'What did he mean, Jake?' asked Helen.

'Yes, do tell, Jake. We're all waiting.' A broad smile played across Carina's full lips as she unfolded the paper. 'On second thoughts, let me.' She scanned it quickly. 'Apparently, you signed off on some questionable accounts which were at the centre of a big fraud case,' she said.

This can of worms wasn't done with me yet. I'd better come clean. 'It was my last project whilst working for David; Marlowe's Bakeries, the owner was recovering from heart surgery. I carried out a review without realising most of the assets I was shown were already mortgaged to the hilt. Marlowe had found a neat way of defeating the standard checks we do. On the basis of this new business plan their bank agreed a substantial overdraft facility. But he never intended to rebuild the business. He cleared out the account and did a runner.'

'But there's more, isn't there, Jake?' asked Carina. 'The police raided your offices and took you away. It seems there was talk of a commission payment from a grateful client.' She couldn't resist a laugh at my expense.

'Marlowe fled abroad and the prosecution argued I should be detained or I might run too.'

'How much was your commission, do tell?' asked Carina.

'I took nothing. I was as much a victim as anybody.'

Carina didn't try to disguise her amusement with my discomfort. 'The really juicy part is the manager who signed off on the loan is now at our bank. And he's pissed at Jake.'

Hysterical. Thanks Carina. 'Adrian Keating approved the loan application. Next thing I knew, there were blue lights flashing outside my office,' I confessed.

'I wish you had told us this before, David,' said Helen.

'Then you'd never have hired me,' I said.

'Nothing was ever proven against Jake and it was entirely his decision to leave Lansdowne & Partners,' said David.

'Is there anything else we should know, Jake?' asked Allen.

'Nothing at all.'

Carina was quick to come back, 'Really? How come there was a Detective Sergeant waiting for you in reception yesterday morning?'

My coffee was cold. I put my mug down untasted. 'He came to enlist my help,' I added.

Carina frowned.

'Help, how?' asked Helen.

'He's on the team investigating your husband's death,' I answered.

'How could you possibly help?' asked Carina.

'He's hoping my work here might uncover something useful.'

'That's nonsense. We should leave it to the police. We've enough to do,' said Carina tartly.

'Do they think Rod's death was in some way connected to the company?' asked Helen.

'He didn't say,' I responded.

Allen came out of his trance, 'Carina's right. The police must deal with this. We need to get on and save the business. It's Dad's legacy.'

We took a short breather. Time to grab a fresh coffee. Helen's question was a good one. Could Race's death have been connected to Race Engineering? And if so, how?

After further discussion, Dr Phillips agreed to step in as interim production director, to scrutinise factory stock, update procedures and push on with the replacement of the faulty components. We agreed to modify six Sirens, initially, for extensive testing. Phillips left the meeting to make a start.

As the door closed, Carina shifted impatiently in her seat, 'Our chairman's dead, our chief engineer's quit and our business consultant is a jailbird. We'll be a laughing stock if we try to relaunch the Siren.'

'Where's your sense of adventure?' I asked. 'There's now independent evidence to show the Siren's a good car. Once we have the approvals we need there's nothing to stop us going to market with a suitably upbeat message.'

'Everything's simple in your world, isn't it?' Carina responded.

'Saving the Siren will save this company.'

'Let's hope you're right,' she responded.

Allen passed his papers around and took us through the numbers, speaking confidently. 'Even before we see any sales contribution from the Siren, we'll be able to manage our cash within existing limits, providing everyone pays us on time.'

David congratulated us on producing a workable plan and asked for comments from Helen and Carina.

'I can't help wishing you had been more open about your recent past, Jake,' said Helen.

'Now we know why you were so keen to look like a hero,' added Carina.

Allen watched them both thoughtfully. 'I'm sure we all have things we regret. Dad promoted me before I was ready. None of us can change what's happened but we can choose a more promising future. And with Jake's help that's what we are doing now.' he said.

Convincing Carina wasn't going to be so easy. 'Putting numbers on a spreadsheet doesn't make them true,' she said.

David adopted a conciliatory tone, 'Your caution is noted, Carina, but I agree with Allen, I believe this plan is both realistic and achievable. All we have to do now, under Jake's direction, is to take action and deliver the desired results.'

Carina shook her head, 'It's blind optimism in my opinion. Naïve in the extreme. What do you think, Mother?'

'What alternative is there? We must be pragmatic,' said Helen.

David asked Allen to record a directors' vote, noting James' absence. Predictably, Helen and Allen were in favour and Carina grudgingly made it unanimous.

I reflected on the outcomes of our meeting as I walked back to my office. The Marlowe moment was awkward but we'd got through it. Good news about the Siren and a loose consensus on the way forward. And James would no longer be sniping from the side-lines. As I reached the door, I heard my phone ringing.

7: Up through the Gears

I lifted the receiver and said my name.

'Now then, lad, this is Ken Matthews. I'm Wyvern Motors and chairman of Race Engineering Dealer Council. They tell me you're running things at Race. I've just had a note faxed to me from Race's offices. It says you're causing chaos, laying off staff and rocking the boat down there.' He paused briefly to draw breath but picked up his thread again rapidly, his voice went up an octave as he became more emotional. 'Just who do you think you are? And why weren't we told about your appointment? I've summoned the council for an emergency meeting today and I demand you attend and give us some answers.'

This was trouble I hadn't anticipated. Dealers bought cars from the factory and sold them to the public. Race financed the cars held in stock until they were sold, meaning that at any one time the dealers owed Race a huge amount of money. If the dealer council kicked off, things could turn ugly. I'd better go careful until I'd figured this out. 'Good morning to you, Mr Matthews. I'm very surprised to hear about the fax, can you tell me who it's from?'

'Doesn't give a name.'

'What a shame. We held a staff meeting yesterday to share the situation and give everyone the opportunity to ask questions. I'm baffled as to why they would share their concerns with you when it would have been simpler to speak with us.'

'Be that as it may, I have a right to know what's going on,' said Matthews petulantly.

'I'm sorry we haven't spoken sooner but I was only appointed on Monday evening and things have been a little hectic since. I'd really welcome the chance to meet with you and the council and explain the current situation.'

'Aye, well, good to hear, at least. But I have to tell you unless we get satisfactory answers to our questions, we'll be withholding payments to the factory.'

'Ok. I'll bring the council up to date with the recovery plan the board signed off this morning. But let's understand each other. We need everyone to pay their bills as they fall due. Otherwise, we'd have to stop supplying cars. None of us would want that, would we?'

Matthews named a hotel at the National Exhibition Centre complex near Birmingham and we made an arrangement to meet at four pm. I replaced the receiver and then picked it up again. Time to share the pain. I summoned Carina and Allen to my adopted office.

Carina reached me first, arriving in a dense cloud of Chanel's COCO. The hair had received further attention. She sat in one of the guest chairs and gave me a big, beaming, freshly lipsticked smile. I was having trouble keeping up with her magnificent mood-swings.

'I don't see why we need to get everyone in for briefings like this morning, Jake. You and I could work together more closely. I wouldn't mind a few all-nighters with you. I'm sure we can...'

I never found out what we could... She stopped speaking as Allen put his head around the door, her face freezing in a steely gaze.

'Join us, Allen' I said. 'I've had the chairman of the dealer council bellowing down the phone at me, suggesting the network will withhold payments to us unless I attend a meeting this afternoon and explain myself.'

Carina's expression went into neutral as Allen's exclaimed, 'Just what we need.'

'He's wound up about a fax sent from this building in the last few minutes. I want to nip this in the bud. Do either of you know who it might be?'

They both shook their heads.

'What can you tell me about Matthews?' I asked.

Carina crossed her arms. 'That old misogynist? He's a bully and a trouble-maker. We should ignore him. Call his bluff.'

Allen was more cautious. 'We need to go carefully here. Between them, the dealers owe us over three million pounds and their regular payments are factored into our cash flow. Any interruption could bring the whole thing crashing down.' He frowned. 'I can't say I know Matthews well. The only conversation I've had with Wyvern Motors recently is with their accounts department to confirm how much money they owe us. I personally rang all of the dealers yesterday to ensure we knew the exact position.'

'Well done, little brother,' said Carina.

Allen ignored her. 'I do know Matthews has been with Race pretty much from the start and he's been tremendously loyal over the years.'

I smiled, 'Ok. I'm not about to do anything which could jeopardise our cash flow. I'll attend the meeting this afternoon but we have to show a united front which is why, Carina, I want you to come with me.'

She pulled a face and the green eyes flashed, 'I'm supposed to wreck my day on the whim of these old men, am I?'

'What could be more important than guaranteeing we're able to collect all of the money we're owed?' said Allen.

'I insist, Carina. I need you there.'

'Well, if you *insist,* then of course I will *obey,*' Carina smiled sarcastically. 'How exciting to see you be so masterful.'

Carina left the office once we'd made arrangements to travel to Birmingham together. Allen remained seated.

'Do the police really have no idea what happened when Dad died?' he asked.

'If they do, they're not telling me,' I responded.

'Who would do such a thing?' he said, half to himself.

He sat quietly, something still on his mind.

'What is it you want to say?' I asked.

'When you arrived, we thought you were just some consultant David knew. We had no idea that you'd been through such an awful time. I wish you'd said.'

I reflected. Allen was right. It'd been dreadful. I'd tried hard to lock it away in a thought-proof container. Maybe it would always stay with me. All I'd been able to do was keep my head down and focus on each problem as it occurred. Working with my lawyer to refute the charges. Finding somewhere to live when I lost my house. The constant worry about where the next pay cheque would come from. Saving Race was now my main goal. My route back to restoring my reputation as an honest, hard-working and reliable finance man. Maybe, in time, I could put Marlowe behind me, even though it had ruined my life. 'Once the initial shock wore off it was bloody boring. Moving beyond it all has been the real problem.'

'What do you mean?'

'I lost everything. And no one wanted to know me.'

'What did you do?'

I looked at him frankly, 'Do you remember that old Billy Ocean song? "When the going gets tough"?'

'Doesn't everyone?'

I smiled 'I made up my own choice lyrics and sang them out at full blast, most nights. Kept me sane through the darkest times.'

Allen grinned. 'Thank you, Jake, for all you are doing.'

He closed the door behind him.

I looked at my watch and wondered where the day was going. I was hungry. Maybe I could find a sandwich downstairs? In the canteen, I joined the queue for the counter. The first group from the production team were on their early afternoon break. Selecting a ham salad roll and a mug of tea I looked around for somewhere to sit. It was busy but I found a space at a long table in the middle of the room. Noone spoke at first but the silence was broken by a man in his mid-thirties with a dark beard and a mop of unruly black hair.

'Slumming it with the lower classes today?' I looked up to see his big, friendly grin. He was one of the fitters from production. I read his name and job title off his badge.

'Thought I'd come and see where the real work is being done round here. Any ideas where I might find some, Paul?' I smiled back.

He laughed. 'Hah, good answer. Seeing as we're on first name terms, how're you getting on with saving us, Jake?'

'Making progress,' I said between mouthfuls. 'The thing is, there's a ready market for the cars you build. The company deserves to prosper.'

Gradually others around the table came into the conversation and I found myself in an informal "Q&A" session, drawing out all of the anxiety left over from yesterday's staff meeting.

'We heard you'd been around the proving circuit with Mike R – how was it?'

'Really good. Showed me what sales potential there is in the Vixen. We had great news about the Siren this morning as well, so I hope we can turn things around pretty soon.' I filled them in on Phillips' report.

To be greeted by silence around the table.

'I'd have thought you guys would have been a bit more excited about getting the new car back on sale – what's up?' I asked.

Paul looked at each of his colleagues.

'Go on, tell him,' urged one of the team.

'Thing is; the Siren's a disappointment. It's not what we expected. It's pretty enough, a soft top and quick in a straight line but to be honest, if you want a fast, well-handling sports car, you're probably better off with a Vixen.'

'But it wasn't supposed to be like that, was it?' piped up one of the others.

Paul grinned at his colleague. 'You're right, Steve. We'd heard it was going to be really special, to see off the competition.'

Steve chipped in again, 'There was a toolmaker, Bill something? They brought him in from outside and he was here for about six months, making all sorts of things – what happened to him?'

Paul took a bite of his sandwich and looked thoughtful. Swallowing quickly, he piped up, 'Bill Somerton. Yeh, kept himself to himself. He was got rid of just after the old man died.'

'What was he working on?' I asked.

Paul put the lid back on his sandwich box and prepared to get up.

'Didn't it have a fancy name?' asked Steve.

Paul stood by the table for a moment, deep in thought. 'What did they call it? Project something? Archimedes, wasn't it?'

'It was summat like that,' said Steve.

As the guys returned to their shift, I finished my snack and reflected. Something my new buddies had mentioned had jogged a thought. What was it?

I walked over to the bin, threw my rubbish away and stacked my plate and mug with the other dirty items. I was thinking about the upcoming drive with Carina up to the NEC when it came to me. Roads. Guardian of the roads. Not Archimedes, Artemis. James' inspiration. There was something else. I'd almost reached the top of the stairs before I'd worked it out. Before he died Race had told James to cut costs and get the Siren to market but Bill Somerton had only been got rid of *after* Race died. By then, James could have kept him on, so why make him leave? Carina wouldn't have objected and no-one was listening to Allen.

Back in my office, I called James's mobile. No answer. I left a message, conciliatory, friendly. I wondered if I'd hear back. An idea struck.

I went next door into Allen's office. He looked at me enquiringly.

'Have you ever heard of Project Artemis?' I said.

He shook his head, 'No. Why?'

'Not sure. It might be something. Can you find the time to do me a favour?'

'Anything. What?'

'Well, you were telling me your dad's office has hardly been touched since he died. Can you get someone to go through everything discreetly and see if they can find any reference to Artemis? It's supposed to be something James and your father were working on for the Siren. I've left a message for James but who knows if he'll bother to ring back.'

I was on the point of leaving his office when I remembered the toolmaker Paul had mentioned. 'And can you see if you can track down an ex-employee, Bill Somerton. He was let go, just after your dad died.'

'I think he retired early. What are you thinking?'

'I'm not sure yet. Let's just see what we can find out. And keep it quiet.'

'I can see there's something else on your mind, isn't there?'

I thought back to our first meeting on Monday night. It would have been so easy to dismiss him as being too green to do the job but he'd shown me what he was made of these last two days.

'It's like I'm driving along and there's a banging noise coming from under the bonnet.'

'What do you mean?' said Allen.

I counted down on my fingers. 'Too many coincidences, One, our mystery photographer at the crash scene determined to make trouble for Race. Number two, someone tipping off the police that I was working here. Why? Were they hoping to get me fired? Then, Ken Matthews and his anonymous fax. And all of this after your dad's tragic death.'

Allen looked thoughtful. 'D'you think it's all related?'

'We need to keep an open mind until the truth comes out.'

Allen persisted. 'Why would anyone get in the way of trying to save this place? We all have so much to gain.'

'Agreed. Could it be a rival?'

Allen shook his head. 'I can't believe anyone hates us that much.'

'So, what have we got to work with? The Courier's a dead end. I'm just glad they hung on to the full set of photos. They were the clincher for Phillip's investigation.'

Allen spoke decisively. 'Ok. We're not going to get very far with an anonymous tip-off to the police but I could get someone to look at the reports for our two fax machines. We can check which one it was sent from and see if anyone remembers who was using it at the time.'

'Good thinking,' I said.

'Just before you go,' he said, 'I've been thinking about your dealer meeting and working on some ideas to get them on side. May I talk you through it?'

'Where did you find the time?' I joked.

'I've been learning from you. Set priorities and delegate, delegate, delegate,' He grinned.

'Let me borrow your notepad.'

An hour later, I walked out of the building to find Carina already there, waiting for me in her distinctive white car with its drug dealer's wheels. I opened the passenger door and climbed in.

She pressed the starter button and we were rewarded with the throaty rumble of the Vixen's exhaust. 'You're late,' she said.

'Sorry. I got held up talking to Allen.'

'Boy talk? Oh, hang on, we're speaking about my brother. Anything I should know about?'

'Just some ideas to fire up our dealers.'

'Nothing important then.'

I smiled. 'You'll hear it soon enough.'

'I see.'

I didn't feel like explaining. 'Nice car', I said, surveying the sumptuous, quilted red leather interior.

'Glad you like it,' said Carina. 'I had the boys in the trim shop create something special for me.'

'Funny really.'

'What is?'

'I can't decide which describes you better, Siren or Vixen?'

Carina threw back her head and laughed, tossing her loose mane of auburn hair. 'I'd say, I'm a little of both. You know, irresistibly alluring but wild when you get to know me.' She did her best to look coquettish but only got as far as predatory.

We lapsed into silence as we drove towards the motorway, leaving me free to mull over the current situation. She turned on the cassette player. It was D: Ream again. "Things Can Only Get Better". I turned it off. There's only so much baseless optimism one man can stand.

Carina stared at me for a moment but didn't comment.

I let my thoughts stray over recent events. Under Phillips' supervision, the reworked Sirens would be available for testing within a couple of weeks. I wondered if Allen would be able to turn anything up on our mysterious fax-user. And what about our motorcycling copper? Was he on the level? How could anything I might come across help him and how could he influence my Marlowe nightmare?

Carina interrupted. 'This is the quietest I've known you since we met.'

'I was just trying to work out what I'd got myself into by agreeing to help Race.'

'Meaning?'

'Nothing here has gone right since your father's death.'

'Noone's going to mourn his loss. He'd upset a lot of people over the years.'

'Do you really think so?'

'You know what they used to say about him on the circuits? Check your wallet after you shake hands with Race,' continued Carina conversationally. 'So, what's on your mind?'

Time to share my frustration. 'Why is it that whatever I say, you never believe we can save this business?'

She took a moment to answer. 'You have to realise we're a minnow in this industry surrounded by sharks and whales. If one doesn't eat us for breakfast, then the other could well roll over and squash us.'

'I love your optimism.'

'If any of little brother's assumptions don't work out, we'll run out of money. Why aren't we pushing our bankers for more support? Surely, given their exposure, they would see the merit of protecting their position with some hard cash? But you dismiss any suggestion I make. I can't tell you how frustrating it is,' she said animatedly.

'Our borrowings are already at the red line,' I said.

'A little more cash would buy us more certainty. Why not bluff them?'

'You mean lie? After I was hoodwinked into overstating the assets at Marlowe's? I don't think so.'

'Just seems like a lower risk than taking our chances in the market,' she grinned.

'I can't do that. But I can promise to try to keep you up with my thinking. My job would be much more challenging without your support.'

'What else is bothering you?'

'Why does it feel like someone's trying to stop us saving Race?'

Carina drove on in silence. 'It's just a run of bad luck,' she shrugged. 'It must be.'

'Too many coincidences, surely? But we'll know in a couple of hours, your brother's chasing down the sender of Matthews' fax.'

Carina concentrated on her driving for a moment before speaking again.

'I don't know why you are bothering with all of this. You're smart and good-looking. You could easily find something more suited to your talents.'

I smiled. 'Glad you approve. And once Race Engineering's on the road to recovery, I won't be a Jakey No Mates anymore.'

A smile played around Carina's lips.

'Maybe I shouldn't tell you this but you were a big hit with Kat last night. It must have been your impeccable manners.' She laughed. 'I'm seriously thinking Kat and I should make a start somewhere fresh and you should come with us.'

Now what?

'South America,' she said. 'Opportunities there for someone like you. Loosen up your ideas and I predict a bright future for us both. And Kat of course.'

This sounded like fantasy island stuff to me but now was not the right time to challenge her, after all, I'd only just got her on side again. Change the subject.

'How did you meet her?'

'She was working in the Bloomsbury Square Hotel in London. I was there for a meeting but when I saw her, I booked in for the night and persuaded her to come to my room. We've been together ever since.'

'Do you two always carry on the way you did last night? I mean, when you don't have an audience?'

'I can't think what you're implying,' she laughed. 'We have highly compatible needs.'

'Really?'

'The only thing she has to worry about is me. I make the rules and all she has to do is guess what they are.' Her big green eyes bored into me and she licked her lips. 'I can be quite capricious, you know.'

'Too complicated for me but great, if it works for you both.'

'You sound jealous. You're perfectly welcome to join us any night, for a little rehearsal.'

'I think I'll pass, thanks.'

She laughed. 'There's nothing in this world for those that don't ask.'

'You really don't believe we can save Race, do you?'

'I like you, Jake. Really. But why take the chance it will all end in disaster? Kat and I could make all of your dreams come true.'

Was she teasing me again? I couldn't fathom her out. It seemed like she would only be happy when she had everyone under her control.

We hit the M40. Carina floored the Vixen's accelerator, snapping up through the gears.

'You like to drive fast, then?'

She shot a sideways glance at me again, 'Love it,' she responded, speaking loudly over the increased exhaust note. 'Better than sex. Almost.'

'Good for you. Tell me, what do you know about Project Artemis?'

Silence, for a full minute, whilst she overtook something, then, 'Nothing. Why do you ask?'

'I'm surprised. I would have thought you'd know all about a major project to improve the performance of your cars?'

She spoke angrily, 'Never heard of it. I told you before, Rod kept everything close. It was deeply frustrating.'

'Maybe. But James was working on it too and there was a full-time toolmaker, Bill Somerton, alongside them until just after your father died.'

Carina's driving became more aggressive. The engine snarled as she moved up and down the gears, her left foot stabbing at the clutch and her right pushing on the accelerator. Her eyes shone and cheeks flushed as she focussed on zipping through the dense traffic. I steadied myself on the central armrest as we raced up behind cars in the fast lane and she flashed the headlights to move them out of our way.

'Interesting. Your father nearly broke the company investing large sums into innovative engineering and yet you know nothing about it?'

'What my father gets up to is his business.'

That was an interesting slip of the tongue. Why was she so riled? We'd hit another rough road in our relationship and were enveloped in stony silence for the rest of the surprisingly brief journey. We came off the

M42 and drove into the NEC complex, reaching the hotel car park a few minutes later. Thanks to Carina's aggressive driving, we were in good time, the reception clock showing ten to four as we walked through the door.

The hotel had been refurbished over the last few years, now claiming to be the largest conference venue in the UK and its swanky reception had been laid out to impress. We walked through several acres of polished marble and shiny steel to reach the desk and ask directions. Carina made a brief pit stop in the ladies, returning with fresh lipstick and immaculate hair. The long trek through the deeply carpeted corridors led to a wing containing smaller meeting rooms. A sign outside our destination indicated this was the Brace Engineering de la Council.

Carina looked at the sign and shook her head. 'Those old buggers didn't even bother to correct it.' She snarled a sarcastic smile at me. 'I offer you the world and you accuse *me* of keeping secrets. I'm going to enjoy watching them rip you to pieces in there,' she whispered angrily.

'You first, Carina,' I said, politely as I opened the door for her.

Inside, a group of middle-aged men in suits and ties were sitting around a large table, each with a notepad and pen in front of them. Some had their jackets off and their sleeves rolled up. Carina wrinkled her nose in distaste. The room was stuffy and had the unmistakable tang of stale males. The remnants of a buffet lunch lay on a side table, oval tin foil platters containing a few quartered sandwiches with curling crusts and a stack of dirty plates, forks, used napkins and chicken bones. Dirty coffee cups were scattered in front of the delegates. The door closed behind us, suppressing the sound of the hotel's insidious background music.

'Ah good. You're here.' A portly character with receding grey hair and a walrus moustache stood to greet us, displaying the full majesty of his generous figure. Powerfully built and generously padded, he made a commanding presence in the room.

'Now then, Carina. Come and sit,' he said, indicating the two empty places next to him.

Turning to me, he introduced himself as Ken Matthews. Some of the others around the table acknowledged Carina whilst I was ignored. We took our seats. After a brief, tight-lipped introduction from Carina, Matthews took over as my chief inquisitor.

'So, Mr Elderfield, I have two questions for you; what the hell have you been up to at Race's? And why have we not been consulted before this?'

'Good afternoon, Mr Matthews, Gentlemen. Thank you for making the time to meet with us today, we really appreciate it. May I call you Ken? And Ken, I'm glad you've asked me such direct questions – it will save a lot of time if we are up front with each other.'

I paused for a moment and looked around the table. I saw the debilitating angst of worry and anger on the lined faces there.

'Rod Race was a rock star of the motor racing world and a great loss to this business. But when any great legend dies, there's always a wave of interest in his latest work and back catalogue.'

There were guarded murmurs of assent around the table.

'When Carina and the team announced the launch of the Siren you must have been flooded with interest.'

'Of course,' acknowledged Matthews.

'It must have felt like the good times were back. Lots of visitors to your showrooms, interest in the Vixen and orders flooding in for the new car. And then disaster. But, you know, there are only two things in the way of our mutual success. First, is the issue with the Siren. I have here some copies of the report I commissioned to look into the crash.' I passed the papers around.

'There are enough copies for everyone. The bottom line is the whole problem was caused by a single component which we can easily replace. As we speak, the engineering team at Race, now led by the highly respected Dr Jan Phillips of the Technical University of Delft, are replacing the defective components and will re-test the car.'

'What does Jim Bishop have to say about this?" asked Matthews.

'He's chosen to focus his efforts on his own business.'

'Ah,' said Matthews knowingly.

The atmosphere began to thaw as the attendees assimilated the contents of the report.

I turned to Carina. 'I know you're planning to put out a press release this evening announcing these results, Carina. But there's more isn't there? Would you like to tell the meeting about the publicity planned to emphasise the safety of the car?

She recovered her composure very quickly. Her mouth mimicked a warm, encouraging smile but her eyes sparked angrily. 'Oh no, Jake. This is very much your story and you should tell it.'

'Thanks, I will. Race Engineering will announce a twenty-four-hour endurance challenge at Silverstone Circuit. We'll make available six Sirens and field some of the top drivers from our international Vixen race series. Arrangements are being made as we speak. All the trade press will be invited and gentlemen, you and your teams also. This represents a huge statement of confidence in the new car by everybody and a significant financial investment in the future by Race Engineering.'

A question came from the far end of the table. 'We hear the company's bust. How the hell will you pay for all this?'

'Glad you asked me. We've completed a reforecast for the entire business. By making savings elsewhere, we're able to focus our funds on activities to grow and support the business.'

'You mean redundancies, don't you?' someone piped up.

There were angry murmurs from around the room. Carina smiled her vixen's smile.

'Absolutely no redundancies, just the minimum lay-offs until we can get the sales line to where it needs to be,' I responded, beaming a big, confident smile around the table. 'And that's where you gentlemen come in.'

Carina's expression hardened and a sarcastic note had crept into her voice. 'Go on, tell them how you are going to wave your magic wand and get customers flooding through their doors again.'

I ignored her cynicism, focusing on my audience, 'I said there were two things in the way of our success. We all need sales, desperately. The endurance race will rekindle interest in the Siren but it might take some time to feed through into hard cash. So, in the meantime we need a second string to our bow.'

I paused and took a long hard look around the table. Carina watched me closely, her face betraying nothing.

'Over the last two years, Race has sunk every penny it could into research and development for the Siren. As a consequence, the Vixen has been starved of investment and frankly, it shows. So, here's what we're going to do. Working together, the finance and sales teams, with the support of our lenders, are going to place a bonus of two thousand pounds on every Vixen that you, our dealers, register in the next three months. We want you to use the money to create "Dealer Limited Editions", where you choose from a range of options to specify your version of the car. We are also creating a cooperative advertising fund, where Race will match every pound you spend on promoting your cars.'

There was approval around the table and even some smiles.

'Carina and her fellow directors have agreed to not draw a penny from the company until it's turned the corner. Like the pig, we're committed.'

Matthews looked puzzled. 'The pig? What do you mean?'

I smiled. 'Consider the traditional English breakfast, bacon and eggs. The hen might be involved but the pig …'

Matthews' frown dissipated and he roared with laughter. 'That's a good 'un I've not heard before.'

The dealers' body language had completely changed over the course of the meeting. As they relaxed and talked amongst themselves, Carina became quieter and more introspective. She turned to me and asked a question in a low voice.

'Despite everything you've said, you and Allen are planning to spend your way out of trouble. I thought you said we were already at the red line?'

'On his own initiative, Allen's done the risk analysis and shared it with the bank. It's self-funding. They're relaxed.' I responded.

Carina shook her head, 'Are you sure he's done his sums right?'

'He has a real talent for strategy. You shouldn't underrate him.'

Carina frowned. 'I certainly won't do that again.'

I addressed the group. 'Gentlemen, I only need one thing from you in return. Between you, you owe Race a considerable amount and we need to keep the cash flowing. If anyone holds up their payments it could cause us a significant problem and I expect you to come down very hard on any trouble-makers.'

Spontaneous applause broke out, just as two members of hotel staff arrived with a trolley laden with fresh cups, cream cakes and pots of coffee and tea. Everyone stood, grateful for the chance to stretch after the intense discussion. Matthews slapped me on the back and muttered something about "Bloody Santa Claus."

Over the clinking of cups, there was a buzz of informal chat between the small groups standing around the room. I heard snippets of history and enthusiastic discussion of Race's prospects for the future. There was a buzz of commitment and enthusiasm for the company and its cars in the room. Once we were back on track, a much tighter relationship could be built with these guys.

Matthews came up to me, stirring his coffee. 'Where's Carina?' he asked, dunking a custard cream in his drink. 'I wanted to congratulate her on what a smart move it was to hire you.'

When I told him I didn't know, he drifted off to talk to his contemporaries.

Carina slipped back into the room and poured herself a coffee. She was relaxed, her earlier anger reduced from boiling to a steady simmer she hid well from our hosts.

'Where have you been?' I asked as she came up beside me.

'Checking up on Kat,' she said.

'I love your caring side.'

Carina was on the point of laying into me once more when Ken Matthews wandered back over.

'I was just saying to Jake, I'm as excited about the business now as I were when we started. Well done!'

Carina offered him a tight-lipped smile and muttered an acknowledgement. After he'd gone, she started on me. 'Pleased with yourself? I bet you are. Don't relax just yet. Like I said, once you've been around the car business for a while, you'll find plans can unravel very quickly. I would watch where I was treading, if I were you.' With this, she drained her coffee cup, put it down on a nearby table, turned on her heel and headed to her car.

I followed her out. Unlocking the driver's door with a single blip of the key fob, she climbed in. I reached for the passenger door handle but it was still locked. She started the engine. I gestured to her and she pressed a button, lowering the passenger window and leaning across.

'Two clicks for both doors but one gets you just the driver's door. Things aren't always what they seem, are they, Jake?' she said, as the window closed again and the car shot out of the parking space.

I stood uselessly in the car park watching the tail lights of the Vixen disappear into the early evening haze. Better call a taxi. I reached into my pocket for my mobile phone, hitting the power button and waiting for a signal. Two men came out of the hotel and walked towards me. They moved with an easy, discreet confidence. Identically dressed, in black jeans and zipped-up bomber jackets, they were both about my age with short military haircuts. As they walked past me, the one closest lifted his elbow, knocking the phone from my hand. It fell to the ground with a crash.

'Sorry, friend, didn't see you there.' He put his heel down hard on the phone and I heard the screen crack. 'Look at me, I'm so clumsy.' He reached down, picked up the shattered phone and handed it to me with a grin on his face. The grin melted to a look of rage as he came in close. 'What did you say?' he said.

I felt the blow to my stomach before I'd even realised what was happening. I reeled as his right fist caught me on the chin and I went down, face first, to the ground.

The second man helped me to my feet and made of show of dusting me down. 'Are you alright? You should be more careful. It's amazing how easily accidents can happen. I'd go home if I was you. Think about getting yourself another job before something worse happens, eh, Jake? There's a good chap.'

They walked off slowly, casually, leaving me standing there, with the useless mobile phone still in my hand. Unreal. Here I was standing outside one of the poshest hotels at the NEC in broad daylight and I'd been warned off. The damage report read as follows; one phone–destroyed, one pride–dented, everything else–pretty much intact. Gained–one valuable piece of knowledge–someone definitely wanted to put an end to Race Engineering's recovery.

I walked back into the hotel and found the gents. I washed my hands and face, peered in the mirror over the sink and used a hand towel to mop at a graze over my right eyebrow. I dusted down my jacket as best as I could and straightened my tie. The dead phone went into the bin, its SIM card into my pocket. I looked back in the mirror. I'd had worse. Tempers tended to fray around dying businesses. Back in reception, I found Ken Matthews settling the bill for the meeting room.

'Can't bear to leave us, Jake?'

'Do you know if anyone's going near Stratford?'

'What happened to your face?'

'I tripped when I got outside. No harm done.'

'Are you sure? Well, aye, I can drop you. I'm heading back to Oxford so it's no trouble. Fallen out with Carina, have you? I'm not surprised. Bit of a handful, or so they say.'

'Thanks, I'm very grateful.'

'It's fine, lad. And I'm grateful for all you are doing for the business. I'd hate to see it fail after all these years.'

We walked out to his car. Another Vixen. Matthews unlocked the car doors and we climbed in. He nosed the car out gently and we were soon settling down to a steady seventy miles per hour on the motorway, heading towards Stratford. Unlike Carina's driving, Matthew's confident, steady manner translated to smooth acceleration, slick gear changes and gentle braking, keeping respectful distances from other vehicles – just what I needed after a stressful day.

'You've been involved with the business for a long time?'

'Oh aye. I got to know Rod and Jim well. After I moved down from Yorkshire, I used to race a bit meself – only in an amateur way, like, but I would often be in the pit lane giving the lads a hand. 'T'was great fun. Then, when Rod started building his own cars, I thought I'd have a crack at selling them rather than the Jags and I never looked back. I've had a good living out of Race Engineering and there's no doubt about it.'

'How would you say Rod and James got on?'

'Well, they had their moments. Rod could be a difficult bugger, very full of himself but Jim ain't the easiest man in the world either. Rod always thought he knew best and he'd never credit Jim for his ideas – and some of them were bloody good! I don't know how he stuck it all these years really.'

'I'm not sure James had a lot of choice in the matter.'

'Money, was it? I'm not surprised, Rod was generous to a fault but only with himself - tight as a swan's arse when it came to anyone else. Always a challenge to get him to put his hand in his pocket.'

As we pulled off the motorway to turn towards Stratford, Ken paused and thought hard.

'Mind you,' he said, 'They both came to a dinner with us, we'd won an industry award, week before Rod died. Jim hardly spoke a word to anyone and when we went to our table, I saw that he'd moved his place card so he didn't have to sit anywhere near Rod. I don't think they exchanged two words all night.'

Ken dropped me back in Stratford on Bridgefoot near the Royal Shakespeare Theatre. As Allen had paid my first invoice promptly, I decided to treat myself to dinner. I crossed the road into Bancroft Gardens, walking past the Swan Fountain before crossing Waterside. I could hear the swans, geese and ducks calling to each other and settling down for the night on their little island under Clopton Bridge. I walked up Sheep Street, peering through restaurant windows. What did I fancy? All the early diners who were going to the theatre would have moved on by now, so I should be able to find a slot somewhere in this busy street. The Opposition looked full, maybe The Vintner would have a table? As I reached the top of the street, I saw a familiar, metallic blue shape parked amongst the cars on the single yellow line opposite. The registration plate, S11REN, leapt out at me. All the Sirens were supposed to be grounded. Who would be driving this one? I could see Carina's white Vixen parked behind it.

As I walked in, I saw a familiar couple sitting at a table in the bay window to my left. They were deep in conversation. I kept going, to where the waitress who was acting as receptionist was standing.

'Can I help you?'

'I thought I might eat with you, but perhaps I'll take a glass of wine in the bar first?'

'Certainly.'

I left my name with her and ordered a large glass of peppery South African Shiraz, taking a seat on a high stool at the end of the long counter opposite the bar. The entire wall in front of me was covered by a large mirror, affording a great view of James and Carina but without putting me in their line of sight.

I could see Carina's emphatic gestures and blazing eyes as she spoke. I couldn't quite hear all she was saying over the noise of the busy, vibrant restaurant, but with her unusually deep voice, the odd word carried to me. I caught "Jake" and "Dealers". It was clear Carina was bringing James up to speed on the day's events. She said something I couldn't make out and then she put her hand on James' arm and they both laughed. She put down her empty champagne glass and got up to leave. James also stood and gave Carina a long, intimate hug and a lingering kiss on the cheek. Carina left without looking in my direction.

My attractive waitress chose that moment to come back over and I saw James' eye follow her profile admiringly as she walked towards me. A spark of recognition and a flush of anger swept across his face as she stopped beside me.

'Mr Elderfield? Your table is ready, if you'd like to follow me?'

'Thanks. Something's come up. Another time.'

I carried my wine glass over to where James was still standing, frozen to the spot and staring at me.

'Hello, James. I left you a message earlier but as you're here now, perhaps we could have a chat?'

James picked up his glass and tossed the contents down his throat before placing it back precisely onto the table. He looked at me coldly.

'Elderfield. Been fighting? I'd expect nothing less of the lower classes.'

'Shame Carina had to dash off,' I said, 'It looked like an interesting conversation.'

'She was just filling me in on your pointless pitch to the dealers. When will you ever learn? I've had it with you. Out of my way.' James tried fruitlessly to push me aside, muttering a swear word as he failed. He stepped around me and left the restaurant, walking briskly across the street without looking, causing a passing car to come to a sudden halt. He unlocked the Siren and got in, revved the engine hard and cut into the stream of traffic to the sound of screeching tyres and angry horns.

I paid for my wine and walked back towards Old Town, stopping off at the chippy in Ely Street before continuing towards home. As I walked, I picked at my dinner and considered what I'd witnessed. Were they having an affair?

As I put my key in the door, I could hear the phone ringing. I dropped my fish and chips onto the dining table and answered the call.

'Jake. I'm glad I've finally got hold of you. I missed you at the Metropolitan and left messages on your mobile, where have you been?'

'Sorry Allen. My phone met with an accident and it won't be making any more calls.'

'We have a major problem. I took a phone call earlier from the sponsorship manager at Nalco. You remember? The North American Lubrication Company, the people who are sponsoring the American race series for the new car. He's been told the authorities in the States are going to hold their own enquiry into the crash. It means the race series is unlikely to run this year, if ever.'

'That doesn't sound like good news.'

'It gets worse. Nalco want their money back now or they'll sue.'

'Pay them. When we were at the circuit, Mike said he's holding the cash in the account.'

'There's a problem. They say the first payment was one and a half million pounds and Mike is only holding a quarter of a million.'

'What? That doesn't make sense.'

'I went back to Nalco and requested all of their documentation. It seems they signed an agreement with a sponsorship agency we use, Beckmann Turner. The contract was valued at one-point-five million per year for five years. The agency invoiced for the first year, weeks ago, just before Dad died. Once they'd received payment, Beckmann Turner transferred a first instalment of two hundred and fifty thousand pounds to Racing.'

'So, Beckmann Turner are sitting on most of the cash?'

'Talking to Mike, it's not uncommon for the intermediary to release chunks of cash as milestones are met.'

'How come we didn't pick this up before?'

'I'm sorry, Jake but I had no knowledge of it. Of course, I knew about the money Racing had received but until I received Nalco's fax, I was unaware of the contractual details.'

'Well fine, if we pay up what we're holding, Beckmann can cough up the balance.'

'That's where we come unstuck. I can't raise Beckmann Turner and Nalco's contract makes us liable for the full amount.'

I couldn't believe this. 'They can't have just disappeared, can they? What does Carina say? She knows something about the sponsorship side of things.'

'I've not been able to get hold of her.'

'I've a feeling you will if you try her now.' I looked at my watch. 'Get her to meet us at the office in half an hour.'

I said a wistful farewell to the considerable remains of my supper, thinking I could re-heat it in the microwave later. I called a cab to take me back to Race's office.

Twenty minutes later, we three gathered in my borrowed office. Carina had changed from her daytime outfit and was now wearing a short, tight, black leather skirt and close-fitting, studded black leather jacket. Black nylons and over-the-knee, high heeled boots completed her outfit. Her hair was scraped back into a severe pony tail and her make-up made her look dark and dangerous. She marched into my office and sat on the edge of the desk, dangling one stockinged leg over the side, rocking it backwards and forwards.

'What happened to your face? Your aim must be considerably off if you cut yourself shaving,' she said.

'I experienced some turbulence after you dumped me.'

She grinned evilly. 'Sorry, but you do seem to have a way of getting my back up. Still, all friends now. This won't take long, will it? I'm all dressed up with someone to do.'

'I'm sure Kat will wait patiently, whatever bind you have her in right now,' I said.

Allen raised an eyebrow.

'I can't leave her alone for too long. Who knows what trouble she might get into?' grinned Carina.

'If you can drag your mind back to business matters, Carina..., Allen and I need your expertise.'

She frowned.

Allen summarised the situation for her benefit.

'You know the ins and outs of the sponsorship business, Carina, what do you make of the situation?' I asked.

'Rod must have set this up the with Andy Turner. They were old pals.'

'Who's Beckmann?' I asked.

Carina smiled, 'Turner's invisible friend. It makes his agency sound like it's more than just him.'

'And what do you know about the Nalco deal?'

Carina looked me straight in the eye. 'Absolutely nothing. Turner's a slimy bastard but he knows everyone on the international circuit. Rod used him to set up opportunities. He'd only call me in to mop up the detail after a deal was done.'

'How come you didn't know about this one?'

'I'm not a mind reader. Those two must have cooked this up between them and kept it quiet. Sounds to me like Turner has taken advantage of the situation and slipped off with the cash.'

'Yes, but where to? How can we find him?'

'How would I know?'

'This could sink us, Carina. We need to find him.'

Carina grinned mirthlessly. 'I did warn you. This is how it goes. What do you want me to do about it? You're the one who's supposed to save us – I think you'd better get on with it, don't you?'

'Tell me everything you know about Andy Turner.'

'He's a fixer. Spends his life at the circuits, chasing down the next deal, lives offshore somewhere. He'll do most things for a percentage. Like you.'

'So, you can't tell us where we can find him?'

'Have you tried phoning?'

'I've phoned, faxed and emailed,' said Allen ignoring her acid tone. 'The numbers came up as unobtainable and the email bounced back. It's like he's vanished.'

Carina stood and smoothed down her skirt, laughing, 'Well, Jake, little brother, this has been lovely but as I can't see how I can possibly help you with this mess, I'll go and get on with my evening.'

'You met James earlier,' I said. 'What was all that about?'

Carina laughed in my face. 'A private meeting. You understand private, don't you?' She stared angrily at me, then left, slamming the door closed behind her.

'What now? Are we finished?' asked Allen quietly.

I ignored his questions, determined to find a way out of this, impossible as it looked. 'What do we have to work with?' I asked.

Allen opened a file, laying out a series of documents on the desk in front of me. 'A copy of the contract signed by Randy Parks, Nalco's CEO and Andy Turner, on our behalf. A copy of the receipted invoice from Beckmann Turner to Nalco, marked paid and a copy of the remittance advice from Nalco to the agency. From Mike, I have the remittance advice from the agency to Racing.

I've had someone I trust, from our local dealership, go and visit Turner's office in Bristol but it's all closed up.'

'We'll ring David and fill him in.'

'Lansdowne.' David's clipped tones came through the speaker phone.

We talked through the positive outcomes from the dealer meeting and then spoilt his day with the Nalco update.

'Any ideas, David?'

'It's hardly original but there is only one thing to do in a situation like this.'

'And what's that?'

'Follow the money.'

Allen looked at me enquiringly as I terminated the call.

'Time for a day out tomorrow,' I said. 'I can't think of a better reason than locating a missing one and a quarter million.'

'Before you go, I've something you might find useful.' Allen reached into his drawer and brought out a box.

It was a mobile phone.

'I ordered it for Dad but he never had the chance to use it.'

He handed it over. I read "Motorola Star-tac" off the lid. The picture made it look like a communicator off Star Trek.

'It's the latest thing,' he said. 'It's tiny, truly pocket sized. It has the optional longer life battery and I'll be able to send you text messages.

'Great,' I said. 'Can it make phone calls?'

'I'll show you,' he said. I watched him flip the lid up, switch on, dial and press send. I heard my answer machine pick up the call. Allen left a message and pressed end.

'Easy,' he said. He looked at the display as he handed it over to me. 'It could do with charging up.'

'Thanks,' I said, 'That'll be useful.'

8: Thursday: Change Down

Allen picked me up at some unbelievably early hour, in, you guessed it, a Vixen. This one was black, with a piano black dash and black leather seats. When I asked him where the coffee machine was, he just laughed. At least he was lightening up a little, despite our difficulties.

For all of his quiet demeanour he'd clearly inherited his father's competitive driving skills, although he was much less aggressive than Carina.

The rush hour traffic, as we got into the Bristol, was nose-to-tail and our progress slowed to an intermittent shuffle as we crawled around the Bear Pit roundabout and up past the main hospital complex in Perry Road. The centre could best be described as a work in progress, with smart shops just across the road from areas where I wouldn't like to leave any car of mine overnight. We parked in the multi-storey at Trenchard Street.

We passed a guy sleeping rough on the stairs as we exited the car park. It all felt very inner city. Not grubby, not posh, but somewhere in between, The mix of Victorian shop fronts offered many things to many people. Bicycle repairs, Chinese herbs, piercings whilst you wait and fancy flowers were just a few.

We turned into a passageway running between an ironmonger's and a second-hand dress shop into Hobb's Yard. Not all of the doors were numbered but once we'd located one and five it was a pretty safe bet number three was the one in between them. Paint was peeling away from the door in generous helpings. Four screw holes and a mark in the remaining paintwork showed where a name plate used to be. Peering through the grimy, opaque glass we could make out some stairs leading straight up. Allen tried the door. It was locked.

'What now?' said Allen.

'At least we know we're in the right place.' I had reached down amongst some discarded newspapers and turned over a brass plate with four screws still rusted into place. "Beckmann Turner Marketing" was engraved in bold italic script.

I tossed it back amongst the detritus on the floor. Allen looked at his watch.

'We passed a café back there,' he said, 'Why don't we split up and ask around for information. You could work your way around the yard, and I'll try the street. I'll meet you down the road in half an hour. Last one in buys the bacon sandwiches,' he said.

I grinned. Nice to hear him taking charge.

Allen was already there when I arrived, sitting at a window seat, a mug of coffee in front of him, peering at a small screen in his hand.

'What have you got there?' I asked.

'It's a Palm Pilot,' he said. 'It's the latest thing from the States. It synchronises with my desktop and lets me manage my contacts, emails and to-do list.' He smiled, 'After our conversation the other night, I decided I'd better do everything I could to get on top of my game. They say this will keep me productive even when I'm out of the office.'

'Does it make good coffee, though?' I asked.

He laughed. 'How did you get on?'

'I checked around the yard and no one had anything useful to say, except they rarely saw anyone go in and out of there. You?'

'The office belongs to the chap in Bennett's, the ironmonger's, next to the yard entrance. The rent's paid until the end of June but he hasn't seen Turner for over two months now.'

'Is there any forwarding address?' I asked.

'No. Bennett said if we pop back in half an hour, when his assistant gets in, he'll show us around upstairs.'

'Very public spirited of him.'

'He's gagging for gossip.'

We walked back up the street and met a man standing in the alley, a bunch of keys in his hand. Allen introduced us. Bennett was unremarkable. Medium build and height, with carefully-combed heavy brown hair and horn-rimmed glasses. In his freshly washed and pressed mid-brown warehouse coat, with three pencils in the breast pocket, he looked ready to grace the stage, cast in the part of "First Ironmonger".

'Gordon, Mr Elderfield. A pleasure to meet you.'

'Jake,' I said, shaking hands, oddly formal in the grubby little alley.

'I do my best to keep this clean but the kids are always hanging around. You find all sorts,' he said apologetically.

'What can you tell us about Andy Turner?' I asked.

'Not much, really. Sharp dresser. Very full of himself. Always paid prompt in cash.'

Allen and I exchanged glances.

'Did he spend much time here?'

'Hardly ever saw him. Rarely any visitors – I remember a VAT inspector once who came into the shop looking for him,' he added helpfully.

Bennett fitted his keys in the door's twin locks and led us up the stairs. He opened the door at the top and ushered us through. The office smelt musty and unused. The blank, soiled cream walls yawned back at us. The place was empty apart from a single desk and chair, a small brown sofa and a filing cabinet. A telephone stood in the middle of the desk. I lifted the handset, confirming the line was dead. Allen pulled out the drawers and checked underneath. Nothing. Next, the filing cabinet. Empty.

We thanked Gordon and went back downstairs and into the yard, leaving him to mourn the loss of his paying tenant.

'Our man has shown us a clean pair of exhausts, then?' said Allen.

'Looks like it.'

Allen kicked at the papers lying on the ground. 'Now what?'

'Let's take David's advice and track down the cash. The agency's bank details are on their invoice to Nalco. We know they made the payment to Racing, we're after the balance. Time to see if it's a listening bank, wouldn't you say?'

'They'll plead client confidentiality, won't they?'

'There's only one way to find out.'

It was a still only mid-morning as we walked across the centre of the city to Corn Street, where Beckmann Turner's bankers resided. It was pleasant to be out in the sunshine amongst the modest numbers of strolling window shoppers and tourists. At lunchtime, all of the sandwich shops and pavement cafes would be full of office workers, escaping the daily grind for a few minutes of shared gossip or solitary tranquillity before returning to their desks. On arriving at the bank, we went to the enquiry desk and I asked to see the manager. It was nearly half an hour before we found ourselves seated in front of him.

'Good morning, gentlemen and what may I do for you?' he enquired politely.

A plastic sign on his desk displayed his name.

'Well, Mr Smith, it seems a customer of yours entered into a contract on our behalf without our knowledge. He received a payment for which we are now liable. The company who made the payment would like their money back and we would like to help them get it. They are threatening to sue us unless it's returned. Mr Race, here, is the finance director.'

'You make a serious allegation; can you substantiate it?'

'Yes, I believe we can. The problem is your client has disappeared.'

'So far, everything you have said would appear to be a matter between you and this individual. I fail to see how it affects the bank.'

'My primary concern at this stage is to trace the missing funds. If, as I hope, the money is still in his account at this branch I can have our lawyers take steps to recover it.'

I smiled pleasantly and handed over a piece of paper with the details on. Smith was comfortable-looking, grey-haired and bespectacled. Middle-class and middle-aged.

'You must see my position in this. I'm not sure what I can do to help,' he said.

'I hear the banking industry is set for big change in the next few years,' I said tangentially. 'The internet is going to transform everything. Branches will close and customers will access everything on line. I should think there'll be massive redundancies, wouldn't you?'

Smith frowned. 'I don't see the relevance.'

'Simply this, Mr Smith. You see, the most vulnerable employees of the bank will be those senior managers, say in their mid-fifties, with plenty of years of service. They must be in line for early retirement with generous benefits, don't you think?'

'I really don't know what you're trying to say …'

'How old are you? Fifty-four, fifty-five? Are the people upstairs already talking to you?'

'That's my business, Mr Elderfield. I think it's time you left.'

Allen shuffled uncomfortably. I kept my seat.

'Just a few more years to a generous pension,' I said. 'Unless anything gets in the way.' Time for the uppercut. 'I wonder what might happen if I publicly accused this bank and your team of sitting on your hands whilst your client committed fraud? You'll probably still get asked to leave but possibly not with the benefits you were expecting.'

He was emphatic, 'You can't prove any such thing.'

I persisted. 'How do you know? The allegation might be enough to queer your pitch. Is it worth taking the risk?'

For the first time, he hesitated before replying. 'Give me a moment,' he said through pursed lips. He left the room.

'I really feel you appealed to his better nature, I'm sure he's on board with us now,' grinned Allen sardonically.

We sat admiring the décor for some minutes before Smith came back in followed by a young man bearing a tray. Smith seated himself behind his desk whilst his assistant poured coffee for Allen and me. Smith smiled ingratiatingly, waiting for our coffee monitor to leave.

'Mr Turner is no longer a customer here. He closed his account almost three months ago.' Smith placed a folder on the desk between us. 'I have all of the details right here.'

'So?' I asked.

'I have no wish to see the bank associated with any fraudulent activity.' He paused, looking at his watch. 'My goodness, I'm running late for my next meeting. Perhaps, if I could leave you both here to finish your coffee. I'll have someone show you out, shall we say in ten minutes? I do hope you can resolve this situation satisfactorily. I will bid you a good morning.'

As he left, he tapped the folder on his desk absent mindedly, as if to remind us of its location.

Allen looked at me curiously.

I smiled. 'Should we?' I asked.

'Definitely.'

He watched as I reached across the desk and removed the thoughtfully stapled copies of Beckmann Turner's bank statements, folded the papers and placed them in my inside jacket pocket. We sat like a couple of guilty schoolboys, finishing our coffee, until we were shown courteously from the building.

Back in the car I studied the sheets we'd liberated.

'Well?' Allen asked, unable to contain himself any longer.

'These go back three years. The earlier pages show money coming in and smaller payments out to the Racing team's account with a difference of...'

'A staggering thirty percent,' exclaimed Allen, peering over my shoulder at the papers on my lap.

'And payments out, roughly one third, two thirds, going into two other accounts.'

'Ten percent into one and twenty into the other,' said Allen, his fist clenched. 'Bloody hell.' He shook his head. 'Thirty percent creamed off the top of every sponsorship deal we've had in the last three years. How does the racing team ever show a profit?'

'I agree. I'd expect a trade agency fee to be no more than fifteen percent. Someone's been enjoying a nice flow of cash at Race's expense for some time.'

Allen looked like someone had pee-ed in his porridge. I went through the statements again. 'But the last set of transactions just before the account closed were different. One point five million came in from Nalco, with two hundred and fifty thousand going out to Race Racing. Then a few days later, a hundred and fifty thousand goes one way and the rest...'

'One million, one hundred-thousand...,' interjected Allen.

'...followed the larger slice of the commissions into the other account.'

'Do you think Turner cooked this up all by himself?' asked Allen.

'Not sure. Both accounts have the same sort code. Maybe one's a trading account and the other is rainy day money? But your dad would have sussed it wouldn't he?'

Allen spoke slowly, thinking out loud, 'How could Dad not know about these excess commissions? He had to be in on it.'

'Fits the facts, doesn't it? Could your dad have been tucking a slice away, planning to put it back in later?' I mused.

Had Rod deliberately pulled money out of the company to stop James spending it on Artemis? Helen's words came back to me; Rod had planned to exploit James in every way he could. How could I tell Allen his dad sounded like a complete bastard?

'But he wouldn't have kept the Nalco money, would he?' I asked.

Allen examined the statement dates carefully. 'The last payment was made just a few days after he died. But I suppose it could have been instructed beforehand?' he suggested.

Could make sense. If Rod had wanted James to believe things were tight, the last thing he'd want would be an extra million plus sloshing around the company's account. Was it that simple? Just an elaborate scheme to short change James?

Allen shook his head, 'Why would he screw his own company?'

So, Allen didn't know the history between Rod and James then. What if Rod never had any intention of putting the money back into the business? His slice of the commissions plus the lump sum from Nalco was a major chunk of cash. Was this Marlowe's Bakeries all over again? But this time, all of the money would be in a bank account in the name of a dead man. All I had to do was find it.

Allen looked despondent but resolute. His chin had taken a firm set. 'We have to get it all back, Jake. How?'

I thought hard. 'If Turner was getting the ten percent and your dad was taking the rest then Turner could argue he's done nothing wrong. He was simply doing as directed. If we can track him down, maybe he can help us understand your dad's plan.'

'But we don't know where Turner is or how to get hold of him.' Allen's frustration was understandable.

'Not yet. But we do have the details for both of the accounts where the money went.'

'So, what's next?'

'Our own bank will be able to interrogate these codes and find the account names and the branch. Once we have those details, the courts can force the other bank to confirm the beneficial owners and we can freeze the cash in both accounts. Without access to his money, Turner is going to be very keen to get in touch and explain what's gone on.'

I took out the mobile phone Allen had given me and rang David, bringing him up to date.

As soon as he knew it was us, he cut in. 'There's been a development. I've had a call from Trevor Woods. The bank knows about Nalco's claim.'

'How?' I asked.

'A tip-off,' said David, drily. 'It's gone right to the top and the decision has been taken to place Race's account with your friend Keating. He's on his way over. You need to get back to the office as soon as you can.'

Allen proved to be more than equal to the challenge of a fast drive back to Stratford. Seventy-three blistering miles. He checked in with his team, whilst I confronted Keating.

As I walked into my office, he was lounging in the chair behind the desk, looking through my papers, smirking to himself.

'How lovely to see you again, Jake. And so soon!'

'Did you miss me, Keating?' I asked.

'Not much. Forty-eight hours must be some kind of record, even for you.'

'It's customary for visitors to stay on this side of the desk. Move.'

'I have every right to be here. I represent my bank to whom you owe money you can't repay.'

'I'm not going to ask you again.'

Our loud voices brought Allen into the room. He leaned against the office wall with his arms folded.

'What's going on?' he asked quietly.

I gestured at Keating. 'He's about to move out from behind my desk before I make him,' I said.

Keating put his hands up in a placatory gesture. 'OK, Elderfield, but the fun is over. I'm glad you're both here. It'll save me repeating myself.' He resettled himself in one of the guest chairs, crossed his legs and looked relaxed. He was enjoying this far too much. 'It seems there's a substantial debt you didn't tell us about. Naughty, naughty. Fortunately, a well-wisher got in touch and brought us up to date. Race Engineering are insolvent. And,' his oily smirk returned, 'I have no choice but to call administrators in to salvage what I can for the bank.'

I thought fast, making an effort to appear relaxed. 'You know as well as I do it's for the directors to decide a company can no longer trade. Of course, you could apply for a winding up order but you'd better make sure you have your facts straight before you go ahead or you could find yourself with a substantial bill for damages.'

Keating sat staring at me. Had he expected me to just roll over? There was no way I was going to let him win this, whatever I had to do.

His crocodile smile was back. 'I applaud your attempts to save this business, really, I do, but you don't have the funds to cover what you owe Nalco, do you?'

'What if I could get the money back, Keating? Just imagine how much egg you'd have on your face if you kick things off and I clear the debt. Just how stupid would you look then?'

He shook his head. 'You're just playing for time. You haven't a hope in hell of recovering it.'

I stayed silent.

'Have you?'

Got the bastard. 'I know where the money is,' I said.

Allen glanced at me sharply. I silenced him with a look.

'There's a big difference between knowing where it is and getting it back,' said Keating.

'True, but if you leave this office still threatening to wind us up then I'm going to tip off the Americans and you can see who gets to pick over the bones first. Remind us, Allen, whose is the bigger debt…, Nalco or the bank?'

'Nalco,' answered Allen.

'Then I think their expensive, sharp-suited lawyers would probably win, eventually, but in the meantime your bank would be tied up in a very expensive High Court action for months. Can you imagine how pleased your new bosses would be with you then?'

I waited. Keating cracked first.

'My responsibility to the bank is clear.'

'Have you been listening to anything I've said? Let's keep it really simple. I'm on the trail of the missing money. This business is viable and makes a real contribution to the local economy. It provides an income for a hundred and ten families and will make money for your bank for many years to come. Let us finish the job and get Race back on track.'

Keating's glare was hostile.

'If you don't back me on this, I am personally going to make sure everyone in the West Midlands knows what a shit you really are.'

He held my angry gaze for what seemed like minutes, then he seemed to deflate. 'Be reasonable. If I don't act now, how's it going to look? Especially after last time. I can't just sweep Nalco under the carpet. What would you have me do?'

'I've got the account numbers and sort code for the missing money right here. If you can help me get my hands on whoever is behind them, I'll find a way to get our money back.'

'Easy enough to get names and branch details.' Keating thought about it. 'And I can trace it back to the account holders' addresses too but I'd have to break a few rules to pass the details to you.'

'That would be really helpful,' said Allen, thinking, I'm sure, there was just a chance it hadn't been his dad who was responsible for the missing cash. And finding the money might help us solve some of our other riddles. Those two blokes warning me off yesterday. Race's death and the Siren crash.

I looked at Keating. 'So?'

'You'll have to make it worth my while.'

I couldn't believe what I was hearing.

'What do you have in mind?' Allen asked.

'Let's be clear,' said Keating. 'You want me to help you trace the missing funds and buy you enough time to track it down. Shall we say ten per cent of the monies you recover with a minimum fee of a hundred grand? I'll increase your overdraft to cover it.'

I stepped forward and grabbed him by the lapels, pulling him out of his chair. 'You conniving bastard,' I yelled into his face. 'I always thought you were on the take. You took a bung from Marlowe, didn't you?'

Frightened faces appeared at the office window. Allen stepped between Keating and me. He looked intently into our faces. 'Please remember where you are,' he said quietly. I let Keating go, stepped back and took a deep breath. He sat down. And his silence was telling. Allen opened the office door and spoke to the small knot of anxious staff who had gathered outside. 'It's all ok. Just a misunderstanding. All sorted out now.'

Muttering voices acquiesced, 'Well, if you're sure.'

Keating sat quietly, collecting himself.

Allen took the other guest chair and I perched on the edge of the desk.

Keating stared at me malevolently. 'Typical of you, Elderfield. Maybe I should think about a charge for assault. After all, I have a witness.'

'I saw nothing,' said Allen. He looked at me and gave a decisive nod. 'Ok, Mr Keating. The company will accept your terms.'

'This is blackmail – we can't possibly agree to it.' I was outraged.

Allen stayed calm. 'I don't see that we have a choice.'

'Where are the account numbers?' Keating asked.

'One more thing,' I said. 'I'm going to need forty-eight hours to follow up whatever you find out.'

Keating thought. 'Twenty-four is my best offer.'

'Done.'

I jotted the details down on a piece of paper and handed it to him.

'You can use the phone in my office, I'll take you through,' said Allen.

Allen came back in and closed the door. 'Will that give us enough time?' he said.

I looked at my watch. 'It's after five on Thursday. Late afternoon tomorrow? All the big chiefs at the bank will be packed up and dusting off their golf clubs for the weekend. Nothing will happen until Monday morning and even then, it will take all day before the smelly stuff hits the twirly thing.'

I looked across at our corrupt banker through the glass partition separating my office from Allen's.

'I'm amazed you agreed to bribe the bastard,' I said.

Allen shrugged. 'I'm learning. No witnesses to the conversation and if this works and we recover the money – what's he going to do, sue us?'

I laughed. 'Smart move.'

Allen grinned.

Keating was standing over Allen's desk, using the speaker phone. We watched as he made his call. We could hear voices but couldn't make out any of the words. He started writing and looked up at us, his face grim. He terminated the call and came back into my office.

'Got it,' he said. 'Both accounts are with the Isle of Man branch of The Royal Argent Bank. The one account is in the name of Andrew Turner,' Keating placed a piece of paper on the desk. 'At this address in the Isle of Man. The other is in the name of Legerdemain Ltd, whose registered office is in the heart of the financial district in Douglas.'

'Legerdemain. Doesn't that mean sleight of hand?' said Allen.

I studied Keating's paper.

'You can leave now, Keating. I'm on this,' I said. I didn't try to disguise my contempt for him.

'Before you go, Mr Keating, there is one question I would like to ask,' said Allen. 'When did you receive the tip-off about Nalco?'

Keating grinned.

'The call came in late yesterday afternoon.'

More evidence that someone was out to stop us.

'Good luck, Jake,' said Keating, 'and remember, this time tomorrow, I'm alerting the bank's lawyers. Good evening gentlemen, I'll see myself on.'

Keating picked up his briefcase and walked smartly out of the office, closing the door quietly behind him.

'Who are you ringing?' asked Allen, as I picked up the phone.

'The man who got me out of trouble with the Serious Fraud Squad.'

I'd come to rely on Dean Channing in those dark days and I was sure he could help us now. I checked my watch;

it had just gone six. I hoped he was still in his office. The answer machine cut in. Dammit. I started to leave a message asking him to ring me when I heard him pick up the phone.

'You just caught me, Jake. What can I do for you?'

I quickly explained the situation and he focussed in, asking pertinent questions and, knowing him, making detailed notes on a legal pad as he did so.

'Right,' he said, suddenly business-like, 'We can certainly go after Turner.'

'What about the other account, Legerdemain? Most of the money went there. Without which we are truly sunk.'

Allen watched my face intently. He mimed pouring and drinking a beer. I smiled an acknowledgement and he retrieved two cold cans from the fridge and placed them on the desk. Just then, there was a knock on the office door and he went to greet a young man, whom I recognised as one of his team. The guy nodded at me and handed Allen a folder. Allen took it and, closing the door, came and sat once more.

'Give me Legerdemain's address again,' said Channing.

I did so.

'Right, I'll call you back. Will you be on this number?'

I confirmed and we hung up.

I swigged my beer. 'What have you got there?' I asked Allen.

He closed the folder and handed it to me.

'Take a look. Whilst we were out today, I had Jeremy turn out this office.'

'Remarkable. It doesn't look like it's been touched.'

'He's very discreet.'

The slim blue folder had one word on the cover, "Artemis."

'You found it!'

'It was hidden inside a bundle of old news clippings.'

The file contained photocopies of sketches, notes and scrawled calculations on hotel notepaper.

'That's James's writing,' Allen said.

The drawing showed various mechanical components.

'What am I looking at?'

'I think it's some kind of turbo.'

'This looks really interesting.... Did you find the toolmaker?'

'Somerton. It seems he and his wife bought a camper van and went touring across Europe. We've been trying to trace him but there's been no luck so far.'

'Is Jan Phillips still in the building?'

Allen picked up the phone, 'I'll check.'

Ten minutes later, Phillips joined us.

'Good evening, gentlemen, what can I do for you?'

I handed the folder over, 'Take a seat, Dr Phillips. We'd like your opinion on these papers.'

Phillips sat, took out the half-moon spectacles from his breast pocket and put them on. He slowly worked his way through the folder, studying the pages carefully.

'This is most interesting, most interesting indeed.'

We waited impatiently for his methodical examination to run its course.

He stood and slowly spread the drawings out over the desk. He used his propelling pencil to point at the illustrations as he spoke about them.

'I'll keep this simple,' he said, looking at me. 'Current thinking is there are two approaches which can be used to create more power from an internal combustion engine of a given size. A turbocharger and a supercharger. But each device has an implicit weakness. A turbo only works at high revolutions per minute, a supercharger at low revs. Engines fitted with a turbo display a notable lag before the power kicks in, whilst a supercharged engine runs out of power as the engine turns faster. In combining the two, the challenge is to derive the benefits of each without magnifying their weaknesses.'

'Didn't Lancia do that years ago with one of their rally cars?' Allen went to the top of the class.

Phillips smiled. 'They were the first people to apply the principle successfully in their Delta S4 Group B rally car fifteen years ago. Others followed, of course. But petrol engines generate a lot of heat which can cause premature failure. All of the major vehicle manufacturers have been spending a fortune looking for an effective solution. It is the key to maintaining reliability whilst increasing power output from our old friend, the petrol engine. Its success would make a real difference to the environment…'

He turned from the drawings to face us. 'You will know of greenhouse gasses,' he said confidently.

I smiled, 'Are you telling us this could cut pollution?'

'Half of the oil consumed in the world goes to power private cars. If we could double engine efficiency, global oil use would be cut by a quarter.'

'And cars would be cheaper to run,' I said.

'Their number will only grow. New technologies will eventually replace the fossil fuels used today. In the future, we will use electric vehicles. For now, we need devices like this one to buy us time, so we can keep innovating and find sustainable long-term answers...' He turned back to the drawings. '...This concept is inspired. The designer has shown a way in which the surface area and orientation of the propelling vanes can be varied, which will relieve the temperature stress in the system. The new metal alloys now available can make this work.'

'What would the effect be?' I asked.

'A significant boost to efficiency and power right across the engine's range with no reduction in reliability. If, for example, such a device was fitted to the smaller, lighter engine from the Vixen sports car and used to replace the heavy - forgive me - outdated engine in the Siren, this would propel Race Engineering into the twenty-first century. You would be the talk of the industry.'

Philips took off his glasses and polished them on his handkerchief.

'I would say the ideas represented here are certainly unique.' He looked thoughtful, 'There is sufficient novelty and a clear inventive step.' Phillips paused, then nodded decisively, 'Yes, definitely enough to justify a patent application.'

Allen picked up the first drawing, 'Could we make one of these?'

'A working prototype would require significant time and investment.'

I took the sheet from Allen, 'Look at the date on this – two years old. Just before some of the biggest spend on the Siren development.'

Allen was animated, 'You're right. It looks like James was working to make this a reality.'

Phillips watched us. 'You need to be very careful about taking this public until a patent application has been filed, so this idea has the full protection of the law.'

'What would we need to do?' I asked. We resumed our seats.

'First you should make sure you have an agreement in place with the inventor, permitting your use of this invention.'

Allen got up from his chair and went to the filing cabinet in the corner. 'Dad kept everyone's personnel files in here.' He pulled open the second drawer and took out a file, placing it on the desk. Opening it, he leafed through until he found the document he was looking for. He nodded his head decisively, 'Yes, I thought so, James had the same clause in his employment contract as everyone else who works here. Any inventions he makes in the course of his work for Race automatically belong to the company.'

'That was very shrewd of your father,' said Phillips.

'Please continue, Dr Phillips,' I said.

'The next step is two-fold, on the one hand you need to undertake a search of existing patents so you understand what others have claimed as their own. This will allow you to make sure no one else has thought of this or something similar before you spend any serious money. You can then draft your patent application in the certain knowledge the inventive steps you claim are not protected by anyone else's granted patent anywhere in the world.'

'What happens then?' I asked.

'When your application is filed, a priority date is set and once your patent has been examined and granted, your invention is protected as of that date and published for all to see. Anyone who wants to make use of your idea must agree a basis for its legitimate use with you, perhaps a royalty, or you would be able to use the full force of the law to prevent them copying your invention and to sue them for loss of earnings.'

'That sounds straightforward enough,' said Allen. 'What would it cost?'

'It's an expensive business. You will need to engage a Patent Attorney, who will help you through the search and examination of prior art stages. You will then need to draft your application and submit it to the relevant

Patent Authority for every territory where you seek protection. Each office, in each country, will examine the idea, raise their own objections and will need to be satisfied by the answers from your Attorney, before they grant the application.'

'So, we have to go through this process for each and every country separately?' I asked.

'Pretty much, yes,' admitted Phillips. 'It is not a small investment. It will cost several hundred thousand dollars at least but this idea could be worth millions, if it works.'

'You mean it may not work?'

Phillips agreed with me, 'No, Mr Elderfield, it may not work. No one will know until it has been built, tested and proven to be safe, reliable and effective.'

'How much?'

Phillips shrugged his shoulders, 'Who knows? By the time it's approved, maybe half a million to a million dollars?'

Allen and I looked at each other. 'There's no way we could consider that sort of spend at the moment, Jake,' he said.

'Agreed. So, as Dr Phillips has just said, we need to put this away and keep it quiet until we can find a way of investing in it.'

Phillips took off his glasses once more and put them back in his pocket, before launching his parting shot. 'All I would say, gentlemen, is don't wait too long. Others in the industry have been searching for answers for quite some time. I would also say to you, as a matter of form, I should have signed a non-disclosure agreement with you before you showed me these drawings. We will take it as read. I will pull out a standard one, sign and drop it off to you.'

Here was another dimension to the puzzle. An invention with the power to make the Siren the supercar Race had intended. Killed off by the running battle between Hot Rod and James. So many ifs to consider; if Bishop hadn't been so precious with his ideas, if Race hadn't been such a bastard, if the money hadn't been stolen…

Phillips left the office to get back to his role, supervising the work to rectify the Sirens for testing. I looked at my watch, seven pm. I couldn't question his commitment to us. After an all-nighter and two full days he was still eager for more. I gathered up the drawings and put them back into the folder.

'You'd better put these in your safe,' I said, passing them to Allen.

'If James had this great idea two years ago, why is it still a secret?'

'Maybe it didn't work?' I offered, 'We've seen how sensitive James is to criticism. Maybe he just wanted to bury it rather than risk further embarrassment? With your dad no longer around, it's easy for James to blame him for cancelling it.'

'Could be,' agreed Allen, thoughtfully, 'But where are the prototypes and the test reports? And why did they get rid of Somerton?'

'Was James making sure no one could ever point the finger at him for wasting company money?'

Our train of thought was interrupted by the telephone. It was Dean Channing calling back. I put him on speaker phone.

'I've spoken to an old colleague of mine, Anthony Peters, who is the managing partner at a law firm in the Isle of Man. There is a flight every day from Birmingham and the good news is he's booked you onto tomorrow's, departing at seven ten in the morning. There'll be a ticket in your name at the Manx Air sales desk. You'll need to check in by five thirty. He'll pick you up when you land at Ronaldsway Airport.'

'A nice early start. Thanks. How do you think Anthony can help with this?'

'I've had him do some digging around Legerdemain this evening. He'll brief you when you get there.'

'Inspired, well done.'

'Let me know how you get on. Have my mobile number in case you need it.'

'Thanks, Dean, I'll be in touch.'

I turned to Allen.

'We'd better update our shareholders on the current situation.'

Allen looked at his watch, 'Good idea. It's just gone seven thirty – I'll set up a conference call for eight.' He went back to his office and got on the phone.

I pondered the current situation. The plan I'd started with; to cut costs, boost sales and manage the bank's expectations, now looked naïve in the extreme. I'm hardly a one-size-fits-all merchant but, to be honest, everyone thinks their business is unique. The same worn-out record wherever I go. The names might be different but the problems are the same. But this was really something to get my teeth into. Tip-offs, a warning off, someone's hand in the till and Race's death. I wasn't going to give up this one chance to get my career back on track for anyone. I'd just have to be very cunning and ultra careful.

I looked down over the Sirens calling to me from the car park. I had to find that money. Unless. I checked my watch. New York was five hours behind us – the CEO at Nalco was probably just back from lunch and I had his direct line number. I'd jotted it down in my Filofax just in case. I picked up the phone.

I heard the comforting thrum of an American ring tone down the wire. Three rings then a voice,

'Parks?' A statement and a question all in one.

'Mr Parks? I'm Jake Elderfield at Race Engineering. It's my job to untangle the situation we find ourselves in with you. I hoped we might talk about our relationship.'

'Call me Randy. It's mighty simple, Jake. As far as we're concerned Race made a deal for the Siren to run in a race series here in the States and we agreed to be main sponsor. It's not going to happen and so I want my money back.'

'I totally understand, Randy. Unfortunately, as I think our finance director, Allen Race, has explained to your sponsorship manager, the agent who made the contract, Andy Turner, has disappeared. So has most of your money. We have two hundred and fifty thousand pounds sitting in Race Racing which we could pay you immediately and we are pursuing the balance.'

'I'm not interested in a down payment. I want to know when the heck I'll get my money?'

'You have my absolute commitment we will get all of your money back.'

'Look, Jake. None of this is my problem. Can you repay us?'

'With a little time, yes.'

I heard a growl on the other end of the phone. 'But you don't have any time. I want my money now or I'm going to reach for my lawyers and drag you guys through every court in your land. You got twenty-four hours. Have my home number in case anything changes.' The line went dead and I heard a transatlantic dial tone.

I looked at the phone. Well, it had been worth a try and at least his deadline was no shorter than the bank's.

Allen came back in just as I was replacing the receiver.

'The call is on for eight but I can't get hold of James – he's not answering his mobile or landline and he's not been in the factory today or at Berrington Pressings.'

Allen and I sat together in my office; Allen ready with his notepad. He looked at me quizzically,

'Should we tell them about Artemis?'

'Not right now. Our immediate need is to recover the missing money. Once we've got the business back in the black, we can talk them through it.'

Allen nodded brusquely. 'Agreed.'

He dialled us into the conference call and we summarised the situation for David, Helen and Carina. I didn't bother mentioning my brief, unsuccessful call with Randy Parks.

'Let me see if I have this straight,' said Helen. 'You believe my husband had been helping himself to our sponsorship money for the last three years and it's now sitting in a bank account in the Isle of Man? How much is missing?'

Allen responded, 'Over two million pounds.'

'Unbelievable!' said Helen bitterly. 'I wonder if he ever had the intention of making a success of the Siren? Perhaps he was just planning to run off, leaving us holding the bill?'

'We can't be certain that he took it, Mum. Not until we have unravelled the situation with Legerdemain,' said Allen.

'Good luck with that,' said Carina, 'I'd say your chances of getting your hands on any of the money by the end of the weekend are zero.'

'It seems to me it comes down to a straight choice; we bring this to an end right now or we ask Jake to go to the Isle of Man,' said David.

'Won't the police help? It is our money after all,' asked Helen.

'Until we can show it's been taken illegally and rightfully belongs to Race and Nalco, they are not going to be able to act. The Isle of Man is a separate jurisdiction, which will only complicate matters further,' said David.

'What about this Andy Turner?' asked Helen, 'Will he help us?'

'This is hopeless. Shouldn't we just take a vote to close things down now? David?' said Carina impatiently.

'Let's do this formally,' said David. 'I will now ask each of the directors in turn as to your views on our course of action. If you believe the company no longer has a viable future then you have a duty to appoint administrators. If you think we can meet our obligations as they fall due by keeping trading, then you have a responsibility to all shareholders, customers and stakeholders to battle on. Allen would you please record a minute of this call as a board resolution. Please note James' apologies, and with three directors present, the board is quorate. The proposition is, "does the board believe they should appoint an administrator immediately". Carina, what do you say?'

'I vote in favour,' said Carina

'What a surprise,' muttered Allen, next to me.

'Allen?' asked David.

'As long as there is a chance of success we must keep trying. I'm against.'

'Helen?'

Helen paused, then, 'I agree with Allen. I vote against.'

David came in again, 'The resolution is dismissed. We must ask Jake to go to the Isle of Man tomorrow to get back our money.'

Allen went to his office to sign some papers. I deliberated, then made one quick, private phone call to David. David's phone rang then went to answer machine.

'It's Jake, David,' I said. 'Keating demanded a bribe to help us track down the missing money. I thought you and Trevor Woods should know.'

I was feeling the pace again and I had a very early start tomorrow. Allen had thoughtfully arranged for me to borrow a pool car, another Vixen, which I could use to get me home tonight and to make the trip to Birmingham airport tomorrow. We left the building together, Allen locking up behind us.

'Bad news about the Matthew's fax,' he said.

'What's the story?' I asked.

'We went through all the fax logs. Someone was very clever. They'd set the machine to send the fax on a pre-timed programme. They didn't need to be present.'

'A dead end then.'

'I'm afraid so.'

He dropped the car key into my hand and walked me across to a Silver Vixen parked just a few slots away.

'It's just come out of the factory. It has all the swanky new options fitted.'

'I'll try not to break it.'

He got into his car and made his way towards the exit, where the security guard opened the gate to let him pass through. I took a good look at the immaculate car in front of me. It might not have the cutting-edge styling of the Siren but it still looked great. Its classic lines suited it well. I blipped the button on the key fob and the lock on the driver's door shot up. I slotted myself in behind the steering wheel and looked around the plush interior. The seats, dashboard and inside of the doors were trimmed in dark grey leather with contrasting orange saddle stitching at the seams. The instrument binnacle in front of me was simply laid out, with a speedo, rev counter and the usual ancillary dials and warning lights. A low panel, below the radio/cassette player, contained a bank of expensive-looking polished aluminium switches which, according to the icons next to them, would control heated seats, traction control, lights and so on. Unusually, the lock was positioned on the centre console. I inserted the key and pushed the red start button set into the middle of the bank of shining silver switches.

The engine burst into life with a loud roar before settling down to a low rumble. I clipped in my seat belt, put the car into gear, took off the handbrake, released the clutch and pressed on the throttle. The car moved slowly forward as I edged my way through the car park. Although everyone had left for the night, almost every space was still occupied. The staff would have to make do with parking in the road for the time being until we could make a dent in the unsold stock. I approached the main gates but the guard was nowhere to be seen. Must have nipped off somewhere.

I got out of the car, leaving the engine running, opened the gates, jumped back in and moved forward. I left the gates standing open, figuring it would give the guard something useful to do when he got back.

There was little traffic at this time in the evening. I turned right as a dark blue BMW saloon pulled out of an entrance on the other side of the road, tucking in behind me. Everything inside the Vixen was sparklingly clean and smelled new. The fuel tank was full. I looked at the Beamer in the rear-view mirror. I wondered if the two men sitting there were admiring the Vixen? I couldn't see any change in their expressions and they didn't seem to be speaking to each other. Maybe they didn't like flash blokes in sports cars? I grinned to myself. I was going to enjoy this. I looked behind me again. Could have been two soberly dressed shop window dummies, judging by their lack of animation. I turned left at the end of the road and they stayed with me. We pulled up at the traffic lights and they came up close to the back of the Vixen. It was incredible. I had never seen two people remain still and silent for so long. They looked like hard men; the sort you'd find cast as the bad guys in Mission Impossible. I saw the driver in the car behind the BMW flash his lights and wave his arm at me. I looked forward again. The lights had changed. I put the Vixen in gear and moved forward, turning right. My minders stayed close behind, causing an oncoming car to have to brake. This was starting to feel wrong. As the next junction approached, I timed it to the last possible second before turning left, then a quick right and another right to bring me back to the main road. The BMW stayed with me as if glued there.

I didn't feel tired any more. My pulse raced faster. I took a deep breath and sat up straight, looking in my rear-view mirror warily, between glances at the road.

They were big lads. Much beefier than the two stooges in the hotel car park. I didn't fancy them following me home. Did they already know where I lived? I was approaching the big traffic island at Bridgefoot. I took a quick left, onto the old Warwick Road and accelerated out of town, sweeping around the long bends, accompanied by the restless note of the Vixen's engine as I climbed through the gears. The BMW dropped back a couple of metres but stayed solidly with me as we picked up speed. I headed towards a place I knew well, via the dual carriageway. If I put my foot down, perhaps I could lose them in the back streets of Coventry. I pressed down harder on the accelerator.

The BMW closed up behind me. Was he going to ram me? I watched the two impassive faces in my mirror, feeling the adrenalin pumping through my veins. Two blue lights started flashing in the BMW's grille. Well, at least I wasn't going to get a beating. What were these two playing at? Were they trying to drum up trade on a quiet night? They pulled out alongside me and the officer in the front passenger seat instructed me to pull over.

I stopped on the hard shoulder and they tucked in behind me. The passenger got out, put on his flat cap and came up to me. He signalled for me to lower my window and bent down alongside me.

'Is this your car, Sir?' he said.

'No, it's on loan from my employer, Race Engineering.'

'And your name?'

I told him.

'Thank you, Sir. Wait here, please.'

I saw him climb back into the Beamer, confer with his colleague then speak into a handset. A few moments later, he came back to me. He leaned down again but this time he looked a lot more relaxed.

'Ok, Mr Elderfield. DS Cooper has vouched for you.' There's been a spate of car thefts recently. Usually nice two seaters. And with the trouble at Race Engineering, we thought we'd better check you out.' He grinned,' But you might want to have them repair your faulty speedo. It seems to be reading slow.'

I thanked him and closed my window, breathing a sigh of relief. Enough excitement for one day. I carefully mirror, signal, manoeuvred my way back onto the carriageway, driving like a granny going to church. The BMW took off and accelerated past me, the officer in the passenger seat grinning and saluting me. I wasn't sure how long it would take for my heart rate to recover. At the next exit, I swooped up onto the junction, swung the car around the roundabout at the top and back in the direction of home. Bollox, I thought, flooring it.

I accelerated out of the slip road, hearing the throaty roar of the engine and feeling the back end of the car squat down as the tyres delivered the extra power to the road surface. Home. Time to eat, take a shower and have an early night.

Back in Old Town, I parked the Vixen in a quiet side street where it could rest undisturbed until early morning. I blipped the key fob and the lights flashed in acknowledgement. There was a smooth metallic click as the locks slid into place, securing the car from intruders. I couldn't help grinning as I walked away. I could get used to having a beast like that in my life.

Inside my place, I switched on the lights, dropped my document case on the sofa, took off my jacket and tie and made my way through to the kitchen, curious as to what I might find lurking in the freezer. Frozen peas, was the answer. I was just weighing up the merits of yet another take-away when the doorbell rang.

Curious, I made my way to the front door to see a shadow through the glass. The profile looked distinctly female.

9: Diversion

A familiar petite figure stood there; her short, severely cut black hair framing her pale face. Dark eyeshadow and black eyeliner emphasised the slight, cat-like, upward tilt of her eyes and her ripe lips were precisely delineated by bright red lipstick. She was wearing a long, black, mackintosh-style coat buttoned up to her neck and carrying a heavy-looking, zipped cooler bag in her right hand.

'Your poor eye, what happened?' Kat reached up to touch my face.

I smiled. 'I tripped and fell. Don't worry, it looks worse than it is. What can I do for you?'

'Carina asked me to bring you dinner to apologise for being such a bitch to you.'

'Carina said that? Really? Are you sure she hasn't poisoned it?'

She laughed. 'It's a peace offering. She hopes tomorrow goes well.'

Her use of English was a world away from the Kat I'd first encountered on Tuesday evening. But what intrigued me more was how Carina's switchblade personality had flipped again. Still, Kat was a great cook and I had nothing in the house.

'Well, you'd better come in then.'

I stepped back in the room allowing her to enter. The light caught the sheen of silk in her coat.

'Let me help you with the bag.'

She gave a brief smile before turning serious again. 'Thank you but it's fine. Where is the kitchen?'

I indicated the back of the house. 'Can I give you a hand?'

'Relax. It will only take a few minutes.'

I decided to go with the flow. 'Ok, thank you. I'll take a shower and get changed. I'll be twenty minutes.'

'Perfect. See you.'

Intrigued, I towelled myself dry, putting on a clean casual shirt and a pair of jeans, and barefoot, came downstairs.

It was dark now but the main light was turned off and my two small table lamps in the sitting room were on. One of my favourite cassettes was playing quietly and as I looked through to the back of my cottage, I noticed all of my papers had been cleared off the dining table and it was now set for one but with two waiting wine glasses. A single candle sat at the centre of the table, giving off a low light and casting shadows around the room.

'Good timing. All is ready.' Kat was coming out of my kitchen carrying a bottle of white wine and a corkscrew. I made a conscious effort to close my mouth and take the chilled bottle from her without dropping it. She had removed the long coat and was wearing a short, stylish red dress and heels. But the big surprise was her closely-cropped blonde hair. The coat and wig lay on the sofa.

'You look very different,' I said, stupidly.

'I know. It's confusing, isn't it? Sometimes, even I forget who I am playing,' she laughed. 'Please to open wine,' she put on the heavier accent, teasing me.

Life was full of surprises. I filled the two glasses as Kat took dishes and plates from the oven and placed them in front of me.

'Eat, whilst it's hot,' she said.

I took the lid off the casserole dish and spooned goulash onto my plate and then turned to the other dish, taking creamy mashed potato and baby carrots.

'This is delicious, thank you.'

She sat and sipped her wine whilst she watched me. When she put her glass back on the table, a heavy blush of bold lipstick decorated the edge of the vessel.

'It's good to see you eat. You are too thin.'

'Eating well has not been a big priority lately.'

'You need to look after yourself. Sleep good, eat good and have fun.'

'Excellent advice. Would you like to be my life coach?'

She took another sip of from her glass and gave a toothy grin. 'Life coach, I like it.'

'A glamorous life coach that makes house calls.'

She did the accent again. 'I think you like me, Mister Jake? Maybe just a little bit?'

'And I think, more than just a little bit Kat, definitely much more.'

'Dessert now?'

'I couldn't eat another thing.'

'Good. Shall we take the wine upstairs?'

She kicked off those trademark heels with their red soles and climbed the stairs in front of me. She moved slowly, seductively, swaying her hips gently. At the top we kissed, she on tip toe, pressing her mouth hard against mine. I felt the tip of her tongue slip tentatively into my mouth. I reached around her and unzipped the dress. It dropped to the floor, leaving her naked. We fell into my bed together and she wrapped her warm, lithe, silky body around me.

Some hours later, I crept back downstairs. I filled the kettle and switched it on, putting coffee in a mug. I thought about pinching myself but as the kettle boiled, I decided a mouthful of hot black coffee would be less painful but just as effective. No, definitely hadn't been dreaming. What just happened? Apparently, Kat's relationship with Carina was less than exclusive and my luck was in. The smell of her musky perfume hovered around me, dragging me back to the sensual delights of last night. After a bout of passion, we'd relaxed, drinking wine, lounging entwined in a nest of warm, comfortable bed clothes, secure in the half-darkness.

Prompted by Kat's gentle questioning, I'd shared my recent history; the very moment when the story of my life had imploded. Sirens wailing in the street outside. Insistent masculine voices in the main office, the sound of heavy footsteps outside my door. Disbelief and incredibly, my amusement, as they started to talk. The long hours of questioning in dingy rooms, appearing in front of a judge, then the sharp smell of disinfected detention, bunk beds and uniforms. I had been sure that Ella, my then partner, would believe I was innocent and do everything to support me. But the disbelief on her face when she visited me in that place told a different story. She only came to see me the once. I used up my one phone call every week trying to track her down. I even wrote to her parents but received no response.

The ache of disappointment was still with me even now, months later. Hadn't we meant more to each other?

'When I got back to Stratford someone else was living in our rented house and my things were boxed up in the garage. My love, my reputation, my home, all gone.'

Kat listened to me without interruption, quiet, patient, the gentle reassurance of her touch a constant presence as I explored my despair. I ran out of words and wallowed silently, overcome by the renewed sense of betrayal.

Kat's soft, delicately accented voice took over, filling the dark, silent void inside of me and taking me on to another place. She described her early life in Communist Prague. The repression, the secrecy, the greyness which had been her everyday existence. As a child, she'd dreamed of escaping to something better, had fantasised about coming to the England of her childhood story books, Buckingham Palace and London streets paved with gold. Her relationship with her parents became more distant; her weak father, who found favour with his masters by informing on his friends and her bitter, domineering mother who determinedly steered her daughter towards the career as a ballerina she had always wanted for herself but never achieved.

And then, overnight, the Velvet Revolution became reality. People gathered in the streets and marched for their freedom. The authoritarian regime's violent response simply melting away when their Soviet masters failed to come to their rescue.

'I found love.' There was wonder in her voice. 'With my dance teacher. She drew me to her. I was so young. When we made love my drab little life burst into glorious colour and after, whenever we danced, I wanted her. She was so wise, so beautiful, so strong.'

'You thought it would last for ever?' I couldn't keep the note of bitterness out of my voice.

She sounded wistful and sad. 'Her ambition was one of the things I found so attractive at first. She was so sure about everything. But I soon realised she would do anything to get what she wanted. And her business partners were very bad people.'

'What happened?'

'A friend died tragically. I couldn't believe the reckless, selfish stupidity of it. So, I did something, whilst my blood was still boiling.' She sipped more wine. 'It wouldn't have been safe to stay in Prague.'

Did they threaten you?'

'They didn't get the chance.'

'What did you do when you got here?'

'I waited tables. And I was an au pair for a while. Then I worked in hotels.'

'Which is where you met Carina.'

'She made a play for me and I thought, well, why not?'

'What are you doing in my bed if you prefer girls?'

She laughed, 'How can I say what I prefer if I've never tried the alternative?'

'So now what do you think?'

'I'll let you know,' she teased.

How could my life get this complicated this quickly? 'Why Carina?' I asked.

'She wanted me and she had plenty of money.'

'That simple?'

'I was bored with working dead-end jobs and flattered by her attention.'

It was dark and I couldn't see her face but I could hear the rueful smile in her voice.

'And her good looks helped, of course,' she added.

'What would she say if she could see us now?'

'Who cares? It's my body and I'll sleep with whomever I choose.'

'So, tell me what Tuesday night was all about? I thought I was there for dinner and a business discussion but it felt like I'd been dropped into the middle of a play.'

She laughed. 'Did you like my act? It was fun, wasn't it? And you're a man. Carina was sure she could manipulate you in the most obvious way.'

'I suppose I should be flattered that you two went to so much effort.'

She paused, sipping wine. 'Beyond reason and beyond doubt. That's what you said love is.' She sounded thoughtful.

The kitchen clock said 3.30 am. Finishing my coffee, I picked up the abandoned plates and dishes from the dining table and took them through to the kitchen. Running hot water into the sink I made quick work of washing and drying everything before placing it back in Kat's voluminous bag. As I went to close the zip, I noticed a bulging pocket on the inside. Curious, I took out a fat brown envelope, untucked the flap and removed the contents. A pristine wedge of fifty-pound notes and a small, anonymous-looking clear plastic tube containing a viscous liquid. No labels. It reminded me of the sort of container you might find holding shampoo in your hotel bathroom. Except there was nothing written on it. I turned my attention to the cash, counting it quickly. Ten thousand pounds. Why would Kat be walking around with that kind of money in brand new fifties? Did she even know she'd got it? I looked at my watch. No time to sort this out now. If I didn't get moving, I'd miss my plane. And unless I found the missing million plus before the weekend, Race was finished and so was my career. I scrawled two quick notes; one I wrapped around the money before stuffing it back in the envelope, adding the bottle and sealing the flap. I wrote Allen's name and "Private and Confidential" on it. The other note was for Kat explaining that I was passing the money to Allen for safe keeping. I placed the bag on the dining table and put the note against it.

I carried my clothes through to the bathroom, where I showered and dressed. I couldn't resist peering around the door at Kat before I left. She was beautiful. I walked in and kissed her gently on the forehead, despite my concerns.

'Bye bye, beautiful man,' She murmured sleepily.

I smiled, 'Bye Kat, see you soon.'

She was asleep again almost before the words "see you," were out of her mouth. What the hell was I going to do with her? One to think about at the weekend, once I'd got Race's cash back. I smiled to myself, well there's nothing like being an optimist, ask those D: Ream boys.

Downstairs again, I grabbed my things and picked up the car key from where I had deposited it on top of the sideboard. And then I was out of the house, walking under the lit streetlamps. A van came slowly towards me and stopped outside the Bull's Head to unload supplies. I heard the landlord unbolt the door and put his weary head around it, greeting the driver in a loud whisper.

Climbing into the Vixen, I experienced the tingle of exhilaration once more at being let loose in this car. I fired up the engine and with a low rumble of the exhaust, drove sedately through the slumbering streets. I made one detour on my way to the motorway, to hand the envelope to the security guard on the gate at Race Engineering with instructions to pass it to Allen as soon as he arrived.

10: Friday: Double De-Clutch

A spectacular sunrise lit the M40 as I blasted up the empty motorway towards Birmingham. My note to Allen asked him to put the cash in his safe and have the contents of the little bottle analysed. Maybe I was completely wrong and I'd have to eat humble pie with Kat but I had a funny feeling about this. Had last night been an actual apology from Carina? Had Kat just taken advantage of Carina being out to take me for a test drive? Or could it have been some devious scheme of Carina's? Maybe the cash was Kat's payment for seducing me?

I smiled, maybe ten quid, definitely not ten thousand. For now, it would be safe with Allen and in his usual efficient way, he'd find someone who could tell us what the liquid was. I'd have to square things with Kat, one way or another, when I got back from Man.

The Vixen snarled its way to the exit for Birmingham Airport and pretty soon it was climbing the ramps of the multi-storey car park. I searched the packed floors before tucking the purring beast gingerly into a vacant space. Dashing into the terminal, I used my most winning smile to extract my ticket from the sales desk as quickly as possible, reaching the check-in three minutes before the deadline.

At the top of the escalator, I had my boarding card examined before joining the queue for security, where, after the usual checks, I reassembled myself; phone, keys, wallet back in pockets, document case under my arm. I went over to a coffee bar, where a surly individual grudgingly handed me a scalding black coffee in a stupidly thin cardboard cup and a bacon roll on a bendy paper plate. I took a seat at a nearby table. After a quick examination of the shrivelled, plastic-looking bacon in the soggy microwaved bun, I focussed my attention on the coffee.

A voice, just behind me, broke into my thoughts. 'Jake. This is a surprise.'

A pair of wide-set blue eyes smiled back at me from an innocent-looking face. Today, the tousled mop of curly brown hair was tumbling over the collar of a smart three-piece suit and Detective Sergeant Cooper was carrying a cardboard cup like my own in one hand and a raincoat draped across his other arm. Cooper took the chair next to me and placed his cup on the table.

'Is the coffee any better than the tea?' he asked.

'Shouldn't think so.'

'Where are you going today?' he asked.

I was reluctant to be too candid, given David's reticence about involving the police at this stage. I decided to keep it simple. 'I'm heading to the Isle of Man, chasing money. And you?'

'Official business, also in the Isle of Man.' He lowered his voice, even though there was no one near us. 'There's been a suspicious death which has links to the Race case. Too much of a coincidence I'd say.'

'Should I be worried?'

'What you should be is careful. Are you flying back this evening?'

'I am.'

'Good. You can buy me a drink at the airport and I'll update you. Any news from your side?'

What to tell him? 'A pair of toughs took the trouble to warn me off on Wednesday and there's been a number of tip-offs against us,' I said.

'A conspiracy against the company and a second suspicious death then. Things are getting interesting. Anything more on Race's death?'

'Nothing. Any clues from your side?'

'A blank so far but where I'm going today might help.'

With time to kill, we fell into easy conversation. I asked him about the motorcycle meet he'd gone to the other day. He spoke animatedly about the event, providing a lap-by-lap account of the key race of the afternoon.

'And of course, that's why the boss is sending me today rather than going himself.'

'Oh, how so?'

'Because in just a couple of weeks, the Isle of Man plays host to the infamous TT, billed to be the most dangerous motorcycle race in the world. Should be huge as it's the ninetieth anniversary. They say there'll be ten thousand bikes there this year. And where will I be? Back here, doing my job like a good copper. It's how they torture "fast trackers" in the force, find out what you like and make sure you don't get to do it.' He smiled ruefully.

Two sips later, they were calling our flight. I put my half-full cup and the untouched roll in the nearest bin as we made for the gate.

Cooper looked at his boarding pass, 'Where are you sitting on this thing?'

'I'm in 5B,' I said.

'Ah, 19A. Well, I'll see you in the Isle of Man.'

We joined the long, straggling queue to have our paperwork checked. Endless corridors and two staircases brought us out onto the tarmac. The small, white plane, its twin propellers gleaming in the sunlight, waited patiently for us as we steered through a cordoned maze and across a road. I waited at the foot of the steps, watching a handler load baggage from a trolley into the plane's fuselage. The cool, early morning breeze tousled everyone's hair. Close up, the shining metallic propeller on this side of the plane looked like a dangerous medieval weapon, displayed behind a line of Tensabarriers. The queue shuffled slowly forward, creeping up the steps and through the cabin door.

I searched for my seat number. I was next to an unfurled copy of the Financial Times with a pair of pinstriped legs beneath it. I sat down, pushed my document case under the seat in front of me and turned my phone off.

The plane was going to be full. DS Cooper was standing awkwardly in the aisle towards the rear of the plane, having to crouch to avoid hitting his head, whilst folding his raincoat and placing it into the overhead locker.

There was a brief announcement from the pilot followed by the usual "mime with voiceover" safety demonstration from the crew. Then, like an ancient smoker first thing in the morning, the turbo-prop engines coughed noisily into life. We taxied along the runway, performing several left and right turns and shuddering to a halt, allowing another plane to go ahead of us. The pilot hit the loud pedal and the engines roared, the brakes came off and we accelerated forward, the little plane vibrating until the wheels came clear and we reached up into the skies. Above the clouds, we levelled out, cruising through the early morning sunshine. My neighbour seemed to be asleep behind his newspaper, the pages having fallen back over his face. I left him undisturbed, purloining his coffee ration from the cabin staff as well as taking my own. Holding the spare cup in my left hand, I sipped steadily from the one in my right. Well, if he woke up in time, I might share, but then it was quite decent coffee. I fell to contemplation.

It would be interesting to hear what Cooper had to say later. This evening might also be the right time to level with him about the missing money. Were Race's death and the stolen cash related in some way? I wondered what Anthony Peters had discovered about Legerdemain. Was it someone's idea of a joke to name a company after a conjuring trick? Would I be able to use this trip to get the missing money released in time? I'd have to be very persuasive. I put my two coffees on the little table in front of me. Maybe I should take up Helen's suggestion and go and see Turner whilst I was on Man? I might get something out of him which would speed things up. I had his address in my Filofax, jotted down after Keating's phone call.

Despite the coffee and with only the inflight magazine and the banks of cloud we swept over as distractions, lack of sleep and the early start caught up with me. I slipped into an uncomfortable doze. I was back in my house, walking barefoot down the stairs. The dining room was illuminated by candlelight and bloody D: Ream's "Things can only get better" was playing softly. Kat was handing me a bottle of cold white wine but as I went to open it, it became a small bottle of clear liquid. I woke abruptly with a crick in my neck just as the captain was putting the seat belt sign on and telling us to prepare ourselves for landing.

We dropped down through the pregnant cloud, shaded by a gloomy sky. A thin rain was falling, welcoming us to the Isle of Man's small airport. The landing was fast, the pilot hitting the brakes pretty firmly and those of us who were unprepared found ourselves jerked forward in our seats. My companion - the Financial Times with the pinstripe legs - was clearly a frequent flier on this route. His only reaction to the bumps and thumps was a slight drooping of one corner of page three, revealing an ear and the upper left side of his face. I braced myself and watched as my fellow travellers were thrust forward twice more, before we trundled sedately across the runway towards the old-fashioned terminal building, coming to a surprisingly gentle halt near the door marked Arrivals. A chorus of clacking seat belt buckles was followed by lots of passengers standing prematurely, making the interior of the plane feel smaller and darker. Everyone's need for release now seemed more urgent. The minutes passed, punctuated by impatient shuffles and the opening and closing of overhead lockers. Through the nearest window, I saw the steps move towards us. The door opened and I took my turn politely in the slow, synchronised process of exiting my seat and then the plane. It was such a pleasure to stand on the top of the steps for a moment and take a lung full of fresh, moist air. Until the chap behind me put up his umbrella and caught me between the shoulder blades with it.

'Sorry. Didn't hurt you, did I?' He shouted cheerfully as we stumbled down the steps together.

I trudged across the unprotected open space to the terminal, shrinking inside my jacket to try and make myself impervious to the steady drizzle. DS Cooper caught up with me, within a few metres of the door.

'No one warned you to bring a raincoat?' he said.

I shook my head. He opened the door for me and we went in. My light grey travel suit was now pockmarked with darker grey splodges of rain water, like an urban leopard wearing the right camouflage for the mean streets.

Judging by their almost ubiquitous business attire, most of the passengers were fellow commercial day trippers, here for a meeting or two but unlike me, they were armed for the local weather. The few weekenders amongst us made their way to one side of the Arrivals Hall where a conveyor belt appeared out of one hole in the wall only to disappear into another further along. They stood patiently waiting for the luggage fairy to make it happen for them.

'Well, it looks like my ride is here,' said Cooper, gesturing towards the uniformed constable waiting near the exit.

Cooper's face broke into a grin, 'See you in the bar this evening. Good hunting.' I wished him a successful day. He exchanged a formal greeting with his colleague and was led from the building.

Dean had told me to look for a red Morgan sports car waiting on the double yellows outside the terminal and sure enough it was there, its tan canvas roof doing a sterling job of keeping the rain from the cream leather interior. As I approached the sports car, I saw Cooper climb into the front passenger seat of a spotlessly clean squad car, also parked illegally. Its bright horizontal stripes like the war paint on the body of a fierce ancient warrior.

I opened the passenger door of the Morgan and dropped into the seat, collecting a dribble of "liquid sunshine" down the back of my jacket collar.

Behind the steering wheel, Anthony Peters was the least formal lawyer I'd ever met. I'd guess he was in his mid-forties and his lean figure, bright check shirt, fleece and worn denim jeans signalled "outdoorsy" but his neatly-trimmed dark hair and inquisitive face suggested an intelligence honed on the challenges he experienced across a desk. He flashed a friendly smile and squeezed my hand in greeting.

'Jake? Tony, Good morning,' he said.

'Is it?'

'Late night and an early start?'

Peters looked at me sympathetically as I grunted an acknowledgement and wiped the condensation from my side window. I looked back regretfully at the terminal building, wishing I didn't have to be here in this miserable, wet place. I sighed. I had a job to do.

'Welcome to Man.'

He started the car and put it into gear.

'Do we have time to slot in another meeting whilst I'm here? There's a guy I need to see.'

'There's an old saying in this land. "Traa dy-liooar" – time enough. The meeting I've organised for you isn't until later on this afternoon and so, other than making sure I give you a decent lunch, which admittedly, could take several hours, there's plenty of time to spare.'

'Then how come you got me here on such an early flight?' I whined.

Peters smiled, responding with irritating patience, 'It's that time of year I'm afraid. All of the later flights were full and Dean did say this was urgent.'

It clicked. 'The TT,' I said. I looked gloomily out of the window. 'Fantastic. I've been made to get up in the middle of the night because of a bloody motor cycle race that hasn't even started yet.'

Peters was unflappable, his smile resolute 'Our population goes up by a third for the next two weeks.'

'Next you'll be telling me it's the most dangerous motor cycle race in the world and this is its ninetieth year.'

Peters laughed. 'I knew it. You're a closet fan, aren't you? You know, the motorcyclists are only the latest tourists to come here. It all started with the Vikings over a thousand years ago. They liked it so much they decided to stay. They established the Tynewald, the oldest independent parliament in the world. Apart from the TT, this place has been peaceful ever since.'

Great. I'd found myself a bloody tour guide. I leaned forward and eased myself out of my sopping suit jacket, not easy in the Morgan's confined interior. Peters carried on, his enthusiasm, unlike my jacket, undampened.

'You know, last year, a couple of policemen on foot patrol had to chase two totally naked men riding motorcycles along the promenade in Douglas. Not so much as a helmet between them. These guys kept moving just fast enough to keep the coppers running behind them.

They escaped up a side street to wild cheers from the crowd.'

Peters turned sideways to study my face. 'That was hard work.'

I looked at him.

'But I finally got a smile out of you,' he explained. 'You need to relax. Like it or not, you're here with me until the evening flight so you might as well enjoy it. What's the address for this extra meeting?'

'A place called Andreas, to see a guy called Turner.' I pulled out my Filofax.

'I know it. Up in the north of the island. I've a pal who uses the glider club there.'

We moved off and joined the small stream of traffic leaving the airport. We turned right towards a place called Ballasalla.

'It's going to take us about an hour to get there but it will give me a good chance to show you why so many people love this place.'

'Can't wait,' I said. I was beginning to wonder what the hell I was doing here, trapped in a car with a man who seemed determined to sell the Isle of Man to me.

'What have you eaten this morning?'

'Nothing.'

'No wonder you're in a mood. The first task of the day is to get a decent breakfast down you and I can brief you on Legerdemain and our meeting this afternoon.' He grinned, apologetically, 'I often have clients come out from the mainland who are contemplating becoming resident. By the time I drop you back at the airport, I guarantee you'll be booking your holidays here.'

We drove in silence until we arrived in a damp village and Peters brought the Morgan to a halt in front of a café in the High Street.

'Come on,' he said, grabbing something from behind his seat and jumping out of the car. 'Time to feed the inner man.'

I shivered as I put on my damp jacket and followed him quickly through the rain. Inside, it was warm and welcoming. An aroma tinged with freshly-ground coffee and frying bacon lingered in the air. About half the tables were already occupied, leaving plenty of choice as to where to sit.

'Take a seat and I'll order. Anything you don't eat?'

I shook my head, heading for a large, round farmhouse table in the window. I sat on the Windsor chair and pulled myself up to the clean, polished pine surface already set with cutlery and condiments.

Peters sat down next to me and a cheerful, middle-aged woman followed him across with a tray containing a pot of coffee, milk and mugs. 'Your breakfast will be with you in just a tick, my loves,' she said.

Peters handed across a dark blue cable knit sweater he'd brought in with him. 'Do us both a favour and lose the jacket. You look like I'm interviewing you and it's going badly.'

I took off the sorry-looking garment and hung it across the back of my chair, pulling on the jumper. It was cashmere, obviously expensive, a good fit, not bulky but warm. I realised how cold I was.

Peters poured the coffee, looking thoughtful. 'What do you hope to get from Turner?' he asked.

'I don't know if he's the ringleader in a conspiracy or just the guy who's made it possible for someone to trouser a lot of Race's money. Either way, he must know the truth of the matter, so, I hope to learn a lot more about what's gone on. Your turn. Tell me about Legerdemain.'

'It's a nominee company. A trust which is both offshore and blind. In this case, it was set up by a character called Richard Wilberforce who runs an outfit which specialises in questionable offshore entities. You know the type. Most of his clients are UK residents illegally sheltering their earnings through such trusts. Wilberforce sets up a company and acts as trustee. The identity of the beneficial owner stays a secret. The UK resident parks their cash, taking advantage of the Isle of Man's low tax regime and privacy laws. Wilberforce pockets a fat fee and the customer's tax bill shrinks. Wilberforce is the sort of character who gives us tax specialists a bad name.'

'Sounds lucrative.'

'For him, yes, but as I'm sure you realise, less so for his clients if they get caught by HMRC.'

Our breakfast arrived. Two plates, loaded with bacon, sausages, fried eggs, tomatoes, mushrooms and baked beans. 'I'll just get your toast,' said our waitress.

It was some minutes before we spoke again.

'I don't know how you stay so slim, if this is the way you normally eat,' I said.

Peters smiled, 'It'll set you up for the day ahead.'

I returned his smile, warming to his company.

'Tell me about the Legerdemain meeting?' I asked.

'We're seeing the man himself. You're a new client and I've offered to introduce you, for a fee of course,' he grinned. 'I implied what you were asking for was more in his line than mine.'

'Anonymity and a low tax bill? Sounds perfect.'

Peters paused with a piece of toast in his hand, the thickly-spread marmalade losing its battle to adhere to the generously-spread butter. As he spoke, I saw gobbets of marmalade dribble off the edge and fall to the table.

'That's right. But, it's the old and familiar story – too good to be true. Tax evasion is illegal, whereas avoidance is just plain common sense. Anyone domiciled in the UK is required by law to declare the whole of their worldwide earnings and pay the appropriate level of tax on them. Avoidance is about using all legal means to reduce your tax bill. Evasion means hiding things and telling falsehoods.'

'You're a tax adviser, don't you do the same thing?'

He smiled, 'I could say the same about you accountants. In my defence, I always ask new clients a lot of questions so I can understand their financial circumstances and life plans. Then I set out a regime to help minimise their tax legitimately. It might mean a move offshore, becoming non-domiciled or just using the available tools to stay on the mainland whilst paying as little tax as legally possible. As far as I can see, Wilberforce just ignores the law.'

'So, if you're both tax lawyers, how do I tell you apart?'

'Easy – he's the baddie so he has to wear a black hat.'

We pushed our empty plates away and finished our coffee.

Peters stood. 'Ready to make a move?'

'Absolutely. I'll just use the bathroom.' I found the door at the back of the café and used the facilities. Washing my hands, I reflected on everything that had happened since David came to my house on Monday morning. Just five days ago. It felt like a lifetime. My pale face stared back at me from the mirror over the sink. A bruise had appeared around the graze above my eyebrow. I used my damp hands to straighten my hair, neatened up my shirt collar and pulled the borrowed sweater down properly. Good. Slightly less piratical.

Walking back through the cafe, I unhooked my jacket from the back of the chair and bundled it into a damp ball before re-joining Peters in the Morgan. He took the sorry item from me and stuffed it behind my seat. 'My butler will work his magic on this later.'

'Right,' he said as he turned the ignition key. 'Andreas here we come.' He gave me a look I could only call cunning. 'And on the way I can tell you about all the glorious things we'll see as we drive.'

I learned Man was thirty-three miles long by thirteen miles wide, some two hundred square miles in total. Roughly half of the island was inhabited and with much of it given over to farming, the place was a fantastic habitat for wildlife, with wooded glens, high hills, uncrowded beaches and dramatic coastlines.

As we waited at temporary traffic lights, Peters told me about the place we were in, Ballasalla. 'In old Manx, it means a "place of willows". The river below us is the Silverburn.' Gesturing to my left he added, 'It's crossed, over there, by a thirteenth century packhorse bridge which was built by the Cistercian monks from Rushen Abbey. The abbey's a ruin now, of course. It's reckoned to have provided building materials for most of this place.'

The lights changed and we moved off. Leaving the village, we drove through a lush green wooded valley. 'This is Silverdale Glen. All the streams you can see used to feed the old ochre and umber mills.' He looked wistful. 'I used to bring my family here. The kids loved it but my wife wasn't so keen. The old mill pond is a boating lake now and there's a Victorian water-powered roundabout and loads of places to have picnics.' He shook his head slowly. 'She was always complaining about something,' he said, half to himself.

We turned right at a junction, climbing as we headed inland.

'Where's this?' I asked as the road wound its way through a coniferous forest sitting alongside the base of a high hill.

'South Barrule – the highest hill in the south of the island. The forest runs to around one hundred and thirty hectares and it's a great place for mountain biking. And on the very top is the remains of a fort they say was the home of old Manannan himself.'

'Who's Manannan?'

Peters grinned. 'Legend has it Manannan was God of the sea, lord and protector of this land and he gave this island his name. They say he still exerts his influence today. Next, you'll be telling me you came here never having heard of Manannan's Cloak?'

'I can't say I have.' I returned his grin. 'Should I be wearing it?'

He laughed. 'They say it's a natural phenomenon and a mythological mechanism. A shroud of grey and purple mist rolls in from the sea and envelopes the island, protecting it from enemies and unwelcome visitors in times of trouble.'

'Sounds like I'd better watch out for it. You talked about mountain biking. Is that something you're into?'

'Most weekends in fact. Keeps me sane.'

'Stressy job?'

'Ah, the job's fine. It has its moments, but it's ok.' Peters hesitated before saying more. 'Ever been married, Jake? No? I was about your age when I came here. Fell in love with the boss's daughter, his little princess. At first it was great but after a while, nothing I ever did was good enough, or so it seemed. It's taken us a long time to find a way of working together, for the children's sake.'

As we pressed on, the Morgan's ancient suspension introduced me to every bump and pothole in the road. Old Manannan chose this moment to turn up the taps, and the drizzle became proper rain, falling in overripe drops bursting against the low, slit-like windscreen. Peters flicked a switch on the steering column and the miniature, chrome-plated windscreen wipers performed a comedically rapid, synchronised dance across the glass in front of us, smearing the heavy watery droplets into a continuous blur.

'Those work well,' I remarked. Peering out of the rain-streaked side window, I saw a sign on my left, "Foxdale".

Following my gaze, Peters went back to his commentary. 'That's "Forsdale" in Manx. It comes from the Norse and means "the dale of the waterfall". Until the early twentieth century this was lead mining territory. They used to dig out around three hundred tons of ore every month. And where there's lead, you'll generally find some silver, about twenty ounces for every ton around here. Some people made a fortune. Most of the miners emigrated when it came to an end. It took decades for the place to recover.'

'Do they make you learn all this stuff when you move here?' I asked.

'Oh yes, it's compulsory,' Peters grinned apologetically. 'People think it's just some obscure island sitting in the Irish Sea but there's so much history and romance here. I've come to love it.'

We reached a sign for St Johns and I learned about Tynewald Day, set here, on a hill, celebrating the long-standing Parliament each year with an elaborate ceremony. Officials read out summaries of all the island's laws passed in the previous year and the whole thing ends up in a big party. After the next junction, my driver announced we had joined the track of the TT course.

'Go on then. I can see you're dying to tell me,' I said.

Peters couldn't suppress his grin. 'What?'

'The TT. Spill.'

'In 1903, the Motor Car Act passed into law on the mainland, restricting automobiles to twenty miles per hour. The Automobile Club of Britain and Ireland approached the authorities in the Isle of Man for permission to race on the public roads here. There's been racing here since 1904. In 1907, the Tynewald passed an Act to close public roads for a "time trial-style" motor cycle race and the TT was born. Each year, there's a week of practice followed by seven days of racing.'

'Feel better now?' I grinned.

Peters looked sheepish. 'Much.'

With just over a week to go, the transformation of these public roads into a racetrack was already starting, with filled sandbags piled by the verges, ready to be put into position. We saw several crews putting up advertising hoardings as we drove along.

Peters continued his lecture, 'As you now know, some of the fans arrive quite early and many of them ride the circuit. There's even a special day, "Mad Sunday", between the practice week and the racing when they can do it officially. The locals put out welcome banners and flags and the bikers often wear fancy dress.'

'And it really is dangerous?'

'Over two hundred riders have been killed since it began. Six fatalities last year.'

'Have you ever been tempted to have a go?'

He laughed. 'I think I'll stick to sliding down muddy slopes on a mountain bike. Much safer.'

The roads were narrow, the straights short, and the bends severe. I remembered a family friend telling me about a neighbour of his who'd raced bikes in the nineteen-fifties and his drum brakes had got so hot he'd experienced "fade," where the brakes ceased to work, and he'd used the gears to slow himself. All the bikes of that era would have suffered the same difficulty. Peters cut into my thoughts.

'We have the Red Arrows coming this year, adding to the publicity. A lot of people follow what we're up to. Those in the know say there'll be half a million visitors to the new website before it's all over for another year.'

I looked around us at the empty, rural landscape. It was rugged and barren, with gloomy, drizzle-laden skies.

'Where are we now?'

Peters took his eyes off the road for a second, 'Pretty much in the middle of the island. You see the high peak on your right? That's Snaefell. It's the highest point on Man. We'll get a closer look at it later, on our way back to Douglas.'

We travelled east, then north, turning left and heading straight through St Jude and on to our destination, Andreas.

As we approached the village, Peters turned to me, smiling, 'Almost there,' he said. 'Do you notice anything different about this place?'

I considered for a moment, 'The roads seem wider.'

'Correct,' he said. 'The Royal Air Force built an airbase here during the war and they had to make some adjustments so they could move their planes around. They also took the spire off the local church so they could get a clear flight path.'

On the outskirts of the village, newish semi-detached properties gave way to terraces of stone-built farmworkers' cottages with generous sized gardens, greenhouses and potting sheds. Many had precise rows of vegetables and canes, evidencing the fertility of the ground and the diligence of this hard-working farming community.

Peters chimed into my thoughts again. 'There's a film coming out soon. Next year, I think. The Brylcreem Boys. All about the RAF pilots in Ireland in the war. It was shot a couple of years ago on the airfield here and up the coast at Jurby. One of my clients was an investor.'

The rain had eased off and there was just a hint of a break in the clouds by the time we reached the centre of the village. We pulled up outside the Post Office and Peters went in to ask for directions. We were sent out along the Ramsay Road and took a left turn at the edge of the village.

'There's your airfield,' I said, looking out of my window. I could see a tower, some huts and a scattering of light aircraft a hundred meters away.

A thought struck me. 'I know you said it's a glider club now but do you think they would let small planes come and go from here?'

'I should certainly think so. Provided it's safe and for the right fee, of course.'

'Interesting. I was wondering why Turner would choose to live so far from Ronaldsway when his job would call for so much international travel. I guess that explains it.'

'More discreet than going in and out of the main airport,' said Peters.

We drove a short way down to the end of the small no-through lane and pulled up outside a detached, stone-built, double-fronted cottage. The walls were coated with a grubby lime-wash and the paint on the window frames was flaking. A rambling rose, planted in more serene days, with the idea, no doubt, of adding colour to the front of the house, had gone unchecked for some years, reaching the guttering in some places and making overt attempts to steal in through the windows.

The picket fence along the front of the property, with patches of faded white paint still sticking to it, was mainly naked, greying, decayed wood. The driveway was simply a gap in the fence with two well-worn ruts in the lawn.

On this occasion, a police squad car was occupying some of the space, mud spattered over its otherwise immaculate wheel arches.

We came to a halt on the opposite side of the lane, with open fields to our left and in front of us.

'I wonder what the Peelers are doing here?' said Peters.

'I've a feeling I'm about to see a familiar face,' I responded.

Leaving the Morgan, we walked across the lane.

'What a state,' said Peters.

'No prizes for the best kept garden here,' I said.

The front door opened and DS Cooper peered out, ducking under the low beam.

'Hi Jake, I did wonder if you might find your way here.'

I opened the rickety front gate and walked up the weed-strewn path, Peters following me. I introduced the pair of them and we went inside. I was still having trouble reconciling the figure I'd first met, dressed in motorcycle leathers, with the serious-faced, suited and booted individual in front of us.

The modest sitting room was spartanly-furnished. Small, overgrown windows allowed little light to penetrate the space. A couple of landscape prints each side of the fireplace provided the only decoration against the rough, whitewashed walls. There was an absence of knick-knacks and the uneven flagstone floor boasted a faded red rug, softening the austere decor a little. It felt unloved and infrequently occupied.

'If it's Turner you're after, I'm afraid you've arrived too late,' said Cooper.

'He was your suspicious death,' I said.

'The housekeeper found him yesterday morning.'

First Race, now this. How the hell could I make sure I wasn't number three? I knew the answer. Solve the puzzle. Quickly.

'I'd intended to ask him what he knew about a large sum of money owed to Race Engineering,' I said.

'The forensic boys have finished in here, so we can make ourselves comfortable.' Cooper gestured to the sofa and Peters and I sat down, Cooper occupying a solitary, seedy armchair by the fireplace. He listened intently as I explained the background to our visit, asking the occasional question and making a note.

'This money is critical to the company's survival?'

'Without it we're bust. What happened to Turner?'

'It looks as if he let a caller in, early yesterday morning. They went through to the kitchen and Turner was in the act of making them both a cuppa when he fell and cracked his head on the quarry tile floor. And that's how we found him. His visitor scarpered but not before he'd rifled through Turner's papers. No neighbours, of course, so no one to ask if they saw anything. The local boys will do a house-to-house in the village but I don't hold out much hope.' He brushed, absent-mindedly, at a patch of dust on the knee of his trouser leg.

'So how come you're here?' I asked.

'First officer on the scene's a car enthusiast and noted Race's name amongst the documents strewn all over Turner's office. He told his boss, who sent a message to my Inspector, who promptly told me to get my arse over here.'

'Looks like we've had a wasted journey.'

Cooper looked thoughtful. 'Maybe not. I'd be keen for you to take a look at Turner's papers to see if you can make anything of what's there.'

Peters chipped in. 'This afternoon, Jake and I are due to meet a lawyer who set up the company sitting on the stolen money. I'm wondering, Detective Sergeant, whether it might it be better if you attend in my place?'

Cooper considered for a moment.

'Good idea, Mr Peters.' He looked at me. 'I'd say between us, we should be able to lean on this character and get something out of him.'

'Then I'm going to suggest we all meet at a café bar called Stelladimes at four-thirty. It's at the corner of Athol Street in Douglas, about three doors down from Wilberforce's office. I'll wait there whilst you have your meeting,' continued Peters confidently.

Cooper jotted down the details in his pocket book. 'Excellent.'

'I'll take a look through Turner's papers,' I said.

'And I'll get the constable to put the kettle on.' said Cooper.

We went through the kitchen, ducking under the low doorway and reached a lean-to garden room at the back of the house. There was a cheaply-made desk, an elderly desktop computer and a pin board on the back wall with a few papers tacked to it. An empty shelf on the wall to the right-hand side of the desk showed, by the pattern in the dust, where the lever arch files had stood before someone had scattered them on the floor. Each file had been opened and the papers taken out and strewn in a disorderly heap on the desk. There was ash in the waste basket.

Cooper picked up the bin and examined the contents. He looked gloomy. 'Not sure we'll get much out of this,' he said. 'They've done a pretty thorough job of crunching up the remains. It'll take days to even try to retrieve anything.'

I spent the next hour going carefully through Turner's remaining papers. The other two soon got bored and retired to the sitting room with more tea. I could hear them chatting about the TT. Turner had spent his time courting and connecting with teams, sponsors, manufacturers and drivers on the international motor racing scene. Judging by his accounts, he was pretty successful until about three years ago when he'd become more reliant on Race, as other business thinned out. I searched through invoices and correspondence looking for anything about Legerdemain or clues to the missing cash. There was nothing.

Peters put his head around the door and suggested it was time for us to leave, so after confirming our arrangement to meet Cooper later, we climbed back into the Morgan.

'Useful?' asked Peters.

'Getting Cooper to come this afternoon was a great idea and now we know there was something in Turner's papers worth getting rid of.'

We headed down towards Ramsay, its panoramic horseshoe of a bay bisected by the historic Queen's Pier. The breathtaking view distracted me for a moment as I thought about the pieces of the puzzle. We were back on the TT course for the last leg of our journey to Douglas. The road skirted around the circumference of Snaefall, its peak still some two hundred meters above us. I took in the sweeping views of the coast, from Ramsay, now behind us, Laxey to our left and Douglas ahead of us. Old Manannan celebrated our progress by splitting the cloud, allowing bright sunshine to filter through, the blue-green sea shimmering in the distance.

Reaching into my document case, I took out the statements Allen and I had extracted from the bank in Bristol. The answer must be here somewhere. Time was running out.

Peters glanced across at me. 'What's on your mind?'

'In the last three years, Turner siphoned off exorbitant amounts of commission. No one at the company realised because their paperwork only showed the net amounts transferred after the commissions had been deducted. But I can't see how such a scheme could exist without someone senior in the company knowing about it. Rod Race had been buddies with Turner for a long time, so he has to be favourite.'

Peters frowned, 'What if Turner set the whole thing up as his retirement fund?'

'Then why bother with Legerdemain at all? Why not just put all the cash into his own account?'

I shook my head. 'Race must have been up to his neck in it with Turner. Hiding cash from the tax man and his business partner at the same time. The thing is; I can understand how he might have seen a share of the ongoing commissions as his right but taking the Nalco money would be impossible to cover up. His reputation would be ruined when it came out.'

'Perhaps he was planning to retire?'

'Man like that? He'd have believed he could go on for ever.'

'So, they were in it together but Turner decided to help himself to the Nalco money after Race died,' said Peters.

'There were two transfers from Turner's Bristol account after Race's death. The first was the hundred and fifty thousand into Turner's own Isle of Man account, and the balance, over a million quid, went into the Legerdemain account. It looks to me like the first payment was Turner's sweetener for closing down Beckmann Turner and tidying everything away. Race must have instructed both payments before he died.' I felt certain that must be it.

I frowned.

'What is it?'

'I'm lost. Race may have set this thing up but he's out of the running now. Since his death, we've had a questionable car crash and a series of tip-offs. And I've been beaten up. And now Turner's dead. Whoever's behind this now is very much alive.'

Peters looked glum. 'You've disturbed a ticking bomb. You'd better make sure it doesn't go off in your face.'

I didn't need reminding. Unless I cracked this, more than my career would be at stake.

'We're going round in circles. If the cash leaves Legerdemain before we can stop it, Race's creditors can whistle for it,' said Peters.

My thoughts whirled as Peters drove on.

'What about Wilberforce?' he mused. 'Makes more sense. Wilberforce and Turner could have been working together. They were both on the island. Let's say they saw Race's death as a once-in-a-lifetime opportunity. Why should they care if Race Engineering goes out of business? There's a falling out. Turner dies and Wilberforce weeds anything incriminating out of his papers.'

An interesting take on the situation. 'Doesn't explain the publicity around the car crash or this week's shenanigans,' I said.

'True. And Wilberforce wouldn't have the balls for the rough stuff. He's just a low-level confidence trickster making a living as a dodgy tax lawyer.'

My brain was buzzing. 'Ok. Let's try this. Wilberforce sets up Legerdemain for Race. Turner sets up all the sponsorship deals, takes his cut and passes the excess into the Legerdemain account. The Nalco deal goes live and Wilberforce sees his opportunity. He decides to keep the Nalco money for himself. He hires those two guys, the ones who warned me off, to keep his hands clean. They get rid of Race. He does a deal with Turner to keep him sweet and the two goons keep an eye on Race Engineering and drop a handy crow bar into the apparatus whenever it looks like I might be getting somewhere. In the meantime, he decides Turner has outlived his usefulness and sends his boys round for a visit.'

'That could work. With Race dead, his company out of business and Turner out of the way Wilberforce would have covered his tracks.' mused Peters.

'I've just thought of something else. There was no sign of Turner's bank books on or around his desk. Maybe Wilberforce took them to recover his share of the commissions?'

Peters nodded. 'He might just do that. He'd mop up every penny he could. I bet you're glad your Peeler's going with you this afternoon.'

'I think we've cracked it.'

'Good job. Let's hope your Sergeant has his handcuffs with him. You pair can wrap the whole thing up this afternoon. In the meantime, your tour of the Isle of Man is about to reach its conclusion.'

Part of me wished I could confront Wilberforce right now. But how much more powerful would it be to rock up with the law later on. In the meantime, I could feel smug and let Peters distract me with his tour guide act.

As we drove into Douglas, Peters told me about its history as a free trade port, a Victorian holiday destination and now, as an international finance and banking centre. He stopped the Morgan on the seafront to show me the fine old theatre, the Gaiety. Frank Matcham was responsible for designing ninety theatres in his forty-year career. This one had been saved from the wrecking ball by the Tynewald in 1971 when they resolved to buy it. Its ten-year refurbishment programme would see it back in fine form for both the millennium and its centenary.

'There's one last thing we have to do before lunch,' said my host.

We drove a short way out of town, to the south. Peters managed to look serious as he told me the legend of the fairies' bridge, where it's customary for visitors and locals alike to greet the fairies cordially so they don't experience their ire. I humoured him. 'You'll thank me later,' he laughed.

We circled back towards Douglas and motored along the promenade, before arriving at Peters' home.

Peters drove up to a set of tall timber gates. He slid open his side window and punched a code into a numeric panel.

'We're at the bottom of my old garden. The main house, BallaPeters – "the place of the Peters," after the Manx tradition, is where my ex-wife and children live and it's just over there. Madam has a beautiful Regency-style villa in a large garden facing onto one of the premier roads in Douglas. My kids go to the finest schools, go skiing every winter in St Anton, holiday somewhere hot every summer and I get to pay for the privilege. Not that I'm bitter at all, you understand.' He smirked. 'Actually, I don't mind. I love my kids and since I moved out of the house, Mrs Peters and I get on much better than we have done in years.'

The Morgan rolled forward onto the gravel driveway and crunched to a halt, the gates closing silently behind us. I plucked my jacket from behind my seat. It was in a sorry state after its soaking but maybe I could put it on a hanger for a while.

The drive ran to the side of a red brick, two-storey barn conversion. At the rear of the honey-coloured gravel was a terrace, formed from paving the colour of Cotswold drystone walls. Four raised flower beds, built of wooden sleepers, were inset in a square. Each bed was a riot of colour, with reds, purples and yellows tumbling over the edges. A heady scent lingered over the compact space. At the centre of the courtyard was a modernistic feature, sitting on a bed of cobbles. A loose jet of water bubbled up through a curved marble obelisk before showering down to be caught in a bowl at the base.

Peters stood admiring his garden for a moment. 'I'm still getting used to all this. The gardeners only finished it this week.'

To each side of us was a high brick wall and at the rear, the boundary with the main house was of a softer construction, a two-metre-high willow fence which closed off this haven of urban tranquillity from the villa's grounds. There was a gate in the willow.

'You're still on speaking terms then?'

'I'm sometimes even invited for dinner. Usually when she wants something. You wouldn't think this used to be the vegetable patch and compost heap, would you?' He looked at his watch. 'Lunchtime,' he said.

'After that magnificent breakfast?'

'We've got to keep your strength up.'

I followed him in through the front door, beautifully crafted in new oak. The double-height hallway, oak staircase and galleried landing created an atmosphere of what I could only describe as "artisan opulence," everything seemingly fashioned by hand from the best possible materials.

'Come through,' he said.

We entered an equally splendid, light-filled living space which was, at once, a contemporary kitchen, a dining area and a relaxed sitting room.

In the kitchen a slim young man in his early twenties was busying himself chopping salad. 'This is Neil. My butler.' The young man grimaced and then smiled. 'Ok, so his name is Neil Butler and he helps me around the place but it's a joke I haven't got tired of yet.'

Neil opened a bottle of red wine and pushed it and two glasses across the pristine wooden worktop towards Peters.

I placed my sorry-looking jacket over the back of one of the dining chairs. We helped ourselves to a generous selection of salads and sliced meat. The smell of herbs, oils and delicate seasoning conjured up an appetite in me that I hadn't expected. To follow, there were delicious cheeses with just out-of-the-oven crusty bread, hot dark coffee made from freshly ground beans and another glass of excellent red.

'Wilberforce will know I'm wrapped up with Race Engineering. Won't he cancel before this afternoon's meeting?'

'Relax. I'd already thought of that. You're in his diary as James Brown.' Peters held his glass up to the light and studied his wine, before taking another sip. 'Assuming you find the money, what's your plan?'

'You're the lawyer, you tell me.'

'Depends where it is now. If it's still in the Legerdemain bank account here in the Isle of Man, you'll need a barrister to apply to the authorities here to freeze the account. You'll then have to prove the money belongs to Race or their creditors and only if the court is satisfied will they release it.'

'How long will that take?'

Peters looked apologetic. 'The official way? Longer than you would like.' He smiled, 'But with any luck, Wilberforce will realise he can't win and voluntarily assist you.'

'You mean I have to bluff him or it could take weeks?'

'That's about the size of it, yes.'

'And what happens if the money has been moved?'

'It depends where to. Back to the UK might be a little easier.' Peters shrugged. 'If he's moved it somewhere else and denies everything it could take years.'

'So here I was thinking I was about to save the company and what you are telling me is unless Wilberforce rolls over, there's a good chance our creditors will run out of patience before we can fix things.'

'Bluntly, yes. That's why I suggested taking Cooper with you this afternoon.'

I grinned. 'No pressure then.'

'Jolly good drop this. More?' He topped up our glasses. After a few minutes, he looked at his watch and suggested we make a move. I looked around for my jacket but it had gone. I was just about to say something when Neil reappeared with my freshly-pressed garment looking like it had just come back from the cleaners. I returned my borrowed sweater and slipped the jacket on.

'Now you know why I have a butler,' laughed Peters.

A short drive later and we were back in town. We parked on a side street near the sea front and walked back up to the café bar in Athol Street. The attractive blonde woman behind the counter greeted Tony. He ordered a bottle of wine and three glasses. We took a seat at a table in the corner.

'Why do they call this place Stelladimes?' I asked.

'Stella serves behind the bar,' said Peters.

'Seriously?' I said, raising my eyebrow. 'I thought it was a take on a certain American coffee outfit.'

He laughed. 'Stella's the only star round here and she reckons she barely earns a dime out of the place.'

A squad car pulled up and DS Cooper climbed out of the front passenger seat and came in to join us. Without asking, Peters poured him a glass of wine.

He briefed us for our forthcoming meeting. 'Wilberforce is expecting a Mr Brown, played by Jake here, and me. He won't be too surprised if Brown brings his business partner along instead. You're a UK resident who wants to do something dodgy, which means a good fee for him. The appointment is for five o'clock. Jake's had some thoughts about how all this might be hanging together.'

I talked Cooper through our thinking.

'Where's your evidence for this?' said Cooper.

'It seems to fit the facts,' I reasoned.

'One step at a time.'

We sipped our wine and made small talk as the minutes ticked away. My phone rang.

'Well, Elderfield? Your time's up. You found the money?'

'Keating. Yes, I'm very well, thank you. No point asking after you, after all, the devil always looks after his own.'

'I'm waiting. What's the story?'

'I'm meeting the Legerdemain front man in fifteen minutes.'

'So, you don't have the money?'

'I'm very close, Keating.'

'Close doesn't count. Have you forgotten our deal already? You're out of time.'

I tried to restrain the anger I felt. 'You are so full of it, aren't you? It's four-forty-five on a Friday afternoon. Whatever you say, we both know nothing is going to happen now until Monday. So, make as much noise as you like. In reality, I have all weekend to come up with a credible plan for your bosses.' I held the phone away from my ear as Keating raised his voice.

Cooper, who was sitting next to me, could hear both sides of the conversation. He winked and gestured for me to pass him the phone. He put his hand over the microphone.

'I was going to tell you this when we met back at the airport.' He took his hand away and spoke into the phone. 'Good afternoon, Mr Keating. My name is Detective Sergeant Cooper of West Midlands Constabulary. You've been ignoring my messages. It seems we've received an allegation against you for soliciting a bribe from Race Engineering, which, as I'm sure you realise, is a very serious offence. We'll be in touch, but until then, answer your phone when we call and don't leave town.' He clicked the end button and passed the phone back to me. 'David Lansdowne relayed your message to the Chief Constable's office and they confirmed it with Allen Race. The whole investigation into Marlowe's has been picked up again. Mr Keating will be helping us with our enquiries.' He smiled and finished his wine.

I was about to put my phone away when it rang again. 'Jake? ... Jake?' I could hear music playing loudly in the background. 'Yes, Carina, it's me. Are you having a party there?'

'I hear you missed your flight? Did you oversleep?'

'I don't know what you mean. I'm sitting in a bar in the Isle of Man right now.'

'What? That's not possible.'

'I'm about to go and see the man who runs Legerdemain.'

There was silence on the other end of the line. I heard her put her hand over the mouthpiece and bark at somebody. Where had she got such a daft idea from? It can't have been Kat. I'd said goodbye to her before I left for the airport. 'You don't sound like your normal self, Carina.'

'I'm just fed up of all this nonsense with Race Engineering and the money. So, tell me, what's happening? Did you track Turner down?'

'He was dead when I got there.'

Carina stifled a laugh. 'What a pointless waste of time this trip is turning out to be. I did warn you.'

'My visit to Turner was incidental. The main reason I'm here hasn't changed and now I have the police on side.'

'The police?' she said.

'Yes. With two suspicious deaths and an intriguing fraud on their books they've become very interested in our problems. A Detective Sergeant's going to join my meeting.'

Cooper looked up.

Carina gave a short, sarcastic laugh. 'And what exactly do you think will happen when you get in there? Do you expect this lawyer, whoever he is, to gratefully confess everything and pay back the money? Time to grow up, Jake.'

Carina's voice became muffled. She'd slipped her hand over the mouthpiece again. I heard her say, 'Where do you think you're going? Come here. Sit. Don't move until I tell you to!' She came back on the line.

'I've got to go,' she said.

'Ok. Well, I'll keep you…' The phone line went dead.

'Time to go,' said Peters.

Athol Street was the hub of Douglas's financial district with major banks, solicitors and accounting practices either on this road or close by. Wilberforce's offices were in a slightly run-down 1970's office block, clad in slabs of grey marble and smoked glass. We signed in at the front desk and the uniformed receptionist opened the security barrier and directed us to take the lift to the fourth floor.

The lift doors swished open onto a small lobby of frosted glass. I pushed against the nearest of the double doors but it didn't move. DS Cooper gestured silently to a button in a perforated stainless-steel plate next to the door. Feeling stupid, I pressed it and heard a bleeping sound from somewhere on the other side. A voice squawked tinnily, at me, 'Yes?'

'We're here to see Richard Wilberforce. I have an appointment with him.'

The reception area was a chrome and black leather homage to nineteen-seventies financial glamour. The furniture must have arrived when the building opened. In a few years' time, collectors would be after this stuff. There was even a lava lamp on a "G Plan" glass and wood coffee table in the corner, between two black leather sofas.

An elegant young woman looked up from behind her keyboard, 'Mr Brown? Would you and your colleague like coffee?'

We declined. 'I'll let Mr Wilberforce know you are here. Please take a seat.'

Cooper and I took a sofa each. It was depressing. The seventies just weren't my period.

The receptionist summoned us. 'If you'd like to come this way.'

As his office door opened, Wilberforce stood to greet us. His three-piece suit looked like it had been made for someone of a much slimmer persuasion and despite the office's air conditioning being set to stun, his florid face looked clammy.

'Judy Garland's slippers but its hot today!' He pulled a red silk handkerchief from his top pocket and wiped his brow. 'Don't you think?' he added, when we didn't respond. He stepped out from behind his desk and showed us to a round meeting table in the corner of his office. We shook hands and he fussed over us as we took our seats.

'So, gentlemen, how can I help?' Wilberforce asked, an oily, ingratiating smile spread across his face.

'You're in a whole heap of trouble, Mr Wilberforce,' said Cooper.

The smile on Wilberforce's face froze. 'I'm sorry. I don't understand,' he said.

'I'm Detective Sergeant Cooper of the West Midlands CID. This is Mr Elderfield and he is working on behalf of the Race family to recover substantial monies which have been stolen from their company and placed in Legerdemain Limited, a company which you control.'

'Well, really. You come into my office posing as prospective clients and confront me with this? I should ask you to leave right now!' Wilberforce blustered.

'We could of course make this a formal interview at the local police station but we assumed you would prefer to keep things simple.'

Wilberforce looked flustered.

Cooper continued, 'I can't imagine your clients would take very kindly to a detailed investigation by Her Majesty's Revenue and Customs officers every time they return to the mainland, can you? I really think it would be in your best interests to cooperate with us.'

Wilberforce watched us sullenly and said nothing.

Cooper smiled, 'All we need are the answers to a couple of simple questions. Perhaps we should start with your relationship with Andrew Turner? How do you know him?'

I took Beckmann Turner's bank statement from my document case and placed it on the desk in front of Wilberforce. 'This money was invoiced to Nalco by Beckmann Turner. It was then transferred to Legerdemain. It belongs to Race Engineering and its partners and I'm here to demand its return.'

Wilberforce looked briefly at the statement and gulped nervously. 'Everything I have done has been in accordance with the laws of the Isle of Man and the wishes of my client. There has been no impropriety on my part. And I can promise you I don't know any Andrew Turner.'

'Where were you yesterday morning?' asked Cooper.

'I was right here in my office, all day. I had a client meeting. My secretary will tell you. She keeps my diary.'

This was not going the way I expected. Either Wilberforce was a better liar than he seemed or he knew as little as we did.

'We need to unpack Legerdemain as a matter of urgency,' said Cooper.

Wilberforce mopped at his forehead with the silk square once more. 'Gentlemen, please, I know nothing of these matters, please believe me. And you must understand, I can't reveal my client's identity without an order from the courts here in the Isle of Man.'

'That would take time we don't have, Mr Wilberforce.' Cooper continued, 'I could make a phone call and you could spend the weekend in a cell in Douglas police station, whilst the local force obtains a search warrant and looks through every paper in this office. Or....'

Wilberforce swayed backwards and passed a hand over his eyes. He silently mouthed the word, 'Or?'

I cut in. 'All we need to know is who is the beneficial owner of Legerdemain.'

He looked pained; as if someone had just licked all the frosting off his fairy cakes, 'But if I break client confidentiality, I won't have a business,' he whined.

'We need this information,' I said. 'But we don't need to say where we got it.'

'Umm. Let me think.'

Wilberforce ran his hand through his hair. A gleam came into his eye. He leaned forward and reached into a deep drawer in his desk, pulling out a file. He leafed through the contents until he reached a particular page.

'Here we are,' he said, looking up at us. 'About three months ago, I received a request to remit one million pounds to a UK-based engineering business.'

'What was the exact date of the transaction?' I asked.

'It was 17th February.'

'Two days after Race's death.' Cooper scribbled a note in his pocket book.

Wilberforce continued, 'In return for the funds, Legerdemain received a share certificate. The target issued new shares for the deal and verified that all pre-existing shares had been surrendered to the company for no value, leaving Legerdemain as the sole owner.'

'What company was purchased?' I asked.

'Berrington Pressings Ltd of Tyseley, Birmingham.'

'James!' I shouted.

11: Flat Out and Down the Straight

Cooper spoke urgently into his phone.

'We need to talk to James Bishop. Find him and put him somewhere safe until I get there. And tell the boss, will you?'

Wilberforce looked at both of us, blinking like an owl caught in the light, 'I'd like you to leave now. Will that do?'

'For now. Don't speak to anyone about this conversation. We'll be in touch,' said Cooper.

We left the building and headed back to Stelladimes to rendezvous with Peters, who promptly poured wine.

'How was it?' he asked eagerly.

'It's Friday night, where is everyone?' I asked.

'The weekend starts early round here. Come on. Fill me in.'

'I'll get David on the phone and we can brief him at the same time.'

David was with Allen, reviewing the day's figures. With my mobile on speakerphone, I brought them up to date.

David summarised. 'So, most of our money is now back on the mainland, in Berrington's account, which should make it easier to get our hands on it.'

Cooper leaned in towards the phone, ensuring he could be heard, 'If you see or hear anything from Bishop, please call the police straight away.'

Peters' mobile phone chirped into life. He looked at the screen and grinned. 'It's my butler. I wonder what he wants. Hello, Neil. Yes, ah, I see.' His expression changed. 'Ok, thanks for warning me. I'll tell him. Good job you checked. See you later.'

We looked at Peters expectantly. 'Not good news, Jake. Bad case of Manannan's Cloak.'

'What?' said Cooper, looking puzzled.

'Fog,' explained Peters. 'And getting worse. All planes cancelled until tomorrow morning.'

Cooper got up from the table. 'Excuse me, everyone, I'd better phone the boss.' He walked over to the far side of the empty bar.

'Cooper's on the same plane as me,' I said for Peters' benefit.

I resumed the call with David and Allen. 'We can't afford to wait for the legal process to run its course. There's no time,' I said.

Allen's voice came through the phone, 'But we have until Monday, Jake?'

'Once James has surfaced, we'll need to brief a QC and go before a judge to press our claim. That'll take days,' I said.

'We could seek an extension, now we know where the money is?' said David.

I was gloomy. 'We can't take the chance that he'll move the money whilst we're getting organised. We need to act.' I looked at Peters. 'I need to get off the island tonight. Is there a boat I can catch?'

He shook his head. 'The ferry won't run in this.'

'There has to be a way. I want to take a look around James' factory. Tonight. Before he has time to react.'

'There might be a possibility.' He tossed his head towards DS Cooper on the phone in the corner, 'D'you think he'll want to come with you?'

David's voice came over the phone, 'If, as I think, Jake, you are proposing a break-in, better not do it with the law looking over your shoulder.'

Peters nodded. 'Understood. I'll make a phone call,' he said, getting up and moving away from the table.

'Anything else we need to talk through?' I asked David and Allen.

'There's one thing, Jake. The sample you wanted analysed. It was Chloral Hydrate,' said Allen.

'What?' I asked.

'In the army they call it a Mickey Finn,' interrupted David. 'Take it with alcohol and it'll knock you out for hours.'

I closed off the call. Chloral Hydrate? It looked like Kat had declared her colours.

Cooper came back over as a squad car pulled up outside.

'My lift has arrived. I'll bring the team here and in Stratford up to date. You can track me down on one of these numbers if you need me.' He handed me his card; we shook hands and he left.

Peters came back over.

'Well?' I asked.

'We have to go now. Tide's turning.'

'What's the plan?' I asked.

'Explain on the way.'

He fired the Morgan up and we took off at break-neck speed through the empty streets, yelling over the screaming engine, 'A fast boat will ferry you to Liverpool for a flight back to Birmingham.'

'When you've had enough of being a lawyer you should try your hand at travel agency,' I shouted back.

He grinned. 'All part of the service. You're bloody lucky. Doubleday's boat is normally kept in the inner harbour and if it were there tonight, there'd be no chance – access is tidal. As it's in the outer harbour there's just time to get out.' He grinned, 'See what I mean about keeping the fairies on side.'

We passed the ferry terminal.

'Who's Doubleday?' 'A client. Did very well in mobile phones and came out here five years ago. Part of the consortium planning to rebuild the marina.'

We pulled up at the harbourside. Peters turned off the engine and looked at me, 'And luckily for you he owes me a favour.'

Sounded like a big favour. We climbed out of the Morgan.

'See that boat at the end of the pontoon?' Peters pointed to a sleek, black, low-slung cabin cruiser with two powerful-looking engines on the back. "Slowcoach" I read off the bow. I hoped that was ironic. An athletic-looking man, decked out in what I took to be boating gear, with a dark, weathered tan and greying crew cut was standing on the pontoon beside it, coiling a rope.

'I'll leave you here,' said Peters. 'George will see you safely across the water.'

I shook his hand. 'Thanks,' I said. 'I really appreciate your help today.'

'Go,' he said.

I ran down the steps onto the pontoon.

'I'll send my invoice on,' he yelled after me.

I waved my arm in acknowledgement, keeping up the pace as my feet clattered along the wooden decking.

'George,' I said, as I reached him. 'I believe you're expecting me.'

He grinned. 'Indeed. Let's get under way.'

I followed him onto the boat and into the cockpit.

'You'd better take this,' he said, handing me a waterproof jacket. 'You didn't come dressed for a sea trip.'

'Thanks.' I shrugged into the light but surprisingly warm garment.

Next came a life jacket which I slipped on.

'All set, then?'

'As ready as I'll ever be.'

'OK, here we go.'

George stepped off the boat, untied the remaining rope and jumped back aboard. Taking a seat at the wheel he spoke briefly into the radio handset, alerting the harbourmaster we were ready to leave and giving our intended destination. With his message acknowledged, he turned the key and pushed the ignition button and the twin engines fired up instantly before settling down to a reverberating bass rumble. Canting the wheel over, he pushed the throttle and we started to move away from the mooring.

We progressed steadily through the marina, George nodding to several people we saw pottering on their boats.

'Can't we go faster?' I asked.

He pointed to a sign. 'Strict speed limit,' he said, grinning, 'Don't worry, once we get out of here, I'll put my foot down.'

'Do you often go cruising in the fog?'

He smiled, 'The great thing about fog is it means no wind.'

'Great,' I said, none the wiser, 'But how do you see where you're going?'

'We have all the kit – a plotter which will keep us on course. Radar, of course. And there's also this,' he said, pointing to another high-tech looking screen on the console.

'What's that?'

He grinned. 'One of the new Automatic Identity Systems. Once everyone's using these, all shipping will automatically broadcast their identity and course. In a few years' time it'll be standard kit,' he grinned.

'How long will it take us to get to Liverpool?'

'It's forty-five miles. Under two hours.'

I looked at my watch. That didn't sound too bad.

George grinned, reading my thoughts. 'Don't worry. We'll get you back to your car in good time.'

I returned his grin with a token one of my own. I'd believe it when I was standing in James' factory tonight.

On the way out of the harbour we passed a tall building with full-width, plate-glass windows on its upper floor, from where the officials could observe everyone's comings and goings.

A bank of fog lay across the bay. George flicked switches on his instrument panel and screens came to life.

We kept to a path delineated by lines of buoys, their lights winking steadily. The dense wall of grey mist grew steadily closer.

'Don't worry,' he said, reading my thoughts. 'It looks worse than it is. According to the coastguards this is less than three miles thick.'

As we met the swirling grey wall, tendrils of cold, dense vapour enveloped the boat. All sound became muted and for a scary moment I wondered if the engines had died. I could no longer tell if we were moving at all.

'Are we ok, George?' I asked the ethereal shadow standing next to me.

'All good. We're bang on course. Just a few minutes and we'll be through this.'

I was gripping the rail in front of me so hard my hands felt like they were welded to the boat. I made a conscious effort to relax.

I'd never experienced anything like this before. Here I was, standing in the cockpit of an expensive, high-tech boat piloted by an accomplished sailor. I should feel safe, reassured, but this creeping cloud of dampness was truly unsettling, swamping my senses and chilling my bones. Was there more to the legend of Manannan's Cloak than I'd credited?

I looked at my watch as the fog began to clear. Twenty minutes. It seemed longer. I felt like I'd ridden the ghost train.

The sea beyond was flat and calm. As the last smoky wisps clawed at us, George checked the dials and pushed the throttles forward. The docile thrum from the engines became a deep-throated roar and the cruiser picked up its heels. The bow lifted and the boat started to plane comfortably. I felt the increased chill on my face and was glad of my borrowed jacket. I surveyed the empty sea around us.

'How fast will this thing go?' I had to raise my voice to be heard over the orchestra of sound.

'Flat out about forty knots but she'll happily cruise at around thirty.' He turned to me and smiled. 'We'll have you there before you know it.'

Although we'd come through the fog, he was keeping a close eye on the radar screen. He saw me watching. 'When we're travelling this quickly, other vessels can appear as if out of nowhere.' George looked towards the skyline. 'It'll be dark in a couple of hours.'

I was glad that George was being so diligent.

'Tell you what, if I turn the gas on, why don't you go down to the galley and make us both a coffee?'

I opened the cabin door and walked down a short flight of steps. It was a luxurious set-up with comfortable leather banquettes and a small kitchen area. A shower room with all of the usual facilities lay beyond that, in the bow and I guessed that the seating area would transform into a sleeping cabin. I found the kettle in the cupboard, along with a bottle of dark rum. I came back up top with two steaming mugs and took the seat next to George.

'Thanks,' he said, taking a swig. 'You found the booze then.'

'Shouldn't you say "shiver me timbers" or something?'

'No longer part of the training. These days it's more - would you prefer lemon or lime with your G and T?'

I checked my watch again, wondering how far we'd come.

'I heard you had a meeting with Richard Wilberforce?'

'Can't say I liked him. But then, he probably didn't like me much or the Detective Sergeant I took with me.'

George laughed. 'Oh, he'd have loved that. It's none of my business, but you really don't want to have anything to do with Wilberforce if you can avoid it. His clients usually find out the hard way that he hasn't done them any favours.'

'Sounds like you know him well.'

'He has a reputation around here.'

I hesitated. Hell, what harm could it do?

'Well, to be honest, I was after information about a business he's involved in.'

'Ripped you off, has he?'

He saw the confirmation in my eyes.

'Looks like his client has, yes. We put Wilberforce under pressure and he told us how the money's been used and where it is now.'

'And you're on your way to recover it?'

'If I can, yes.'

'I gathered you were in a tight spot.'

'A sponsor put up the money for a project which may not happen and they want it back'

'Can you get more time out of the sponsor?'

'I've tried but they're not biting.'

George remained quiet for a moment, studying his instruments.

'But you do believe you'll recover it?' he said.

'I'm pretty confident.'

George smiled. 'Want some advice from a simple sailor?'

'I'll listen to any good ideas.'

'You are totally focused on recovering the money, right?'

I nodded my agreement.

'Which means you're not thinking about it from the sponsor's point of view.' He paused to give me time to consider. 'How would you feel if you were him? That you were being fed a line, perhaps?'

He had a point. 'You're right. I'd be angry and suspicious. I wouldn't believe a word I was being told,' I said.

'What would convince you to accept the new terms?'

'I'd have to trust that the person I was talking to could actually deliver.'

'Put yourself in your sponsor's shoes. I mean, really understand his position and his point of view. He wanted the original deal because it worked for him. Now you want more from him. So, it's only right and fair for him to demand more of you. How will you reward him for the extra time and trouble you've caused? And, like you say, what's going to convince him you can deliver?'

I grinned. 'Thanks, George. You've made me think. I reckon I'll be in much better shape when I get the chance to speak to him again.'

'Good,' he said, smiling. 'You look all in. We've got another hour or so before we get close to Liverpool, why don't you go downstairs and relax for a while? I'll call you when we're there.'

I went down to the cabin, closed the door behind me and lay on one of the banquettes. I'd just close my eyes for five minutes.

Next thing I knew, George was waking me. He grinned, 'You might want to come up for this.'

'Who's driving the boat?'

'I will be again in two seconds.'

I went up top. The sky was growing darker with the approaching night and I could see shore lights in the distance to our left and right.

'Where are we now?'

'The lights on our port side lead down from Lytham, Southport and then Formby. To starboard is the coast of North Wales. Dead ahead is the Mersey; Wallasey is on the starboard bank. Here we get into the main shipping channel – the Crosby and then we move into the Queen's Channel for motorboats and yachts.'

'You seem to know your way well.'

'This is my home port. I've been around here all of my life.'

'Isn't it confusing to follow these channels?'

'All the channels are buoyed and numbered. Under the water there are revetments.'

'What's a revetment?'

George smiled. 'A wall. Back in the day, tons and tons of limestone were dumped into the water to form the channels. Sail over one of those and you'd know about it.'

'Why was it built up like that?'

'The Mersey has one of the highest tidal ranges in the UK – ten metres. Only the Severn has more. The revetments retain water in the channels as the tide goes out.'

We cruised on, still moving pretty fast as we headed into the river.

George spoke again. 'In a couple of minutes, we'll pass Bootle, where I grew up, then its ten minutes to the Liver Building at Pier Head. It'll be properly dark by then but you won't be able to miss it; they light it up like a Christmas tree. Then another mile further on, we go past the Albert Dock and on to Liverpool Marina.'

The banks on either side of us were high and the dark grey, slimy-looking walls showed their age. As we moved further down the Mersey the jumble of warehousing and factory units gave way to grander structures silhouetted against the night sky.

As we neared the mainland, I felt the tension start to mount inside me once more. This was all very nice but I was on a mission tonight. I had to thwart James' plans and get my hands on the stolen money if I was going to avoid being number three on the casualty list. In the meantime, I mustn't forget my manners. 'Thank you, George. I don't see how I can ever repay you.'

'Any excuse to get out in the boat is good enough for me.'

He concentrated, following the buoys which marked the channels we needed to stay in.

'This looks like a complicated business – where do we land?'

'We're heading for Coburg Wharf in the Liverpool Marina but we have to go through the Brunswick Lock to get in.'

'Will it take long?'

'It would do if we turned up at the wrong time. The lock can only operate two hours before and after high tide but fortunately we are comfortably in the zone. As long as there isn't anyone in front of us, it's pretty quick. About fifteen minutes.'

'You certainly know the routine.'

'Can't stay away from the place. We keep a berth here.'

The lights were coming on across the city.

'That's the Liver Building there.'

I looked up at the floodlit edifice.

'There's an old legend about those two Liver Birds on the towers. They say when a virgin walks onto Pier Head, the old birds flap their wings.'

George eased back the throttles as we passed Albert Dock. We motored briskly along through the dark, oily-looking water. George retuned the radio. I looked at him enquiringly.

'Need to make contact with the lock keeper.' He spoke into the microphone. 'Liverpool Marina, Liverpool Marina, this is Slowcoach approaching. Over.'

'Evening, George. We were told to expect you. You made good time tonight. Over'

'Should be with you in five minutes. Over.'

'One in front of you. Should be clear in fifteen. Over.'

George slowed the engines and pulled us in closer to the left bank. At first, it was difficult to make out where the lock was, among the tangle of steep, concrete banks clad with a geometric lattice of old timber.

He pointed. 'That's where we're headed.' I followed his gaze and saw two modest-looking gates, tightly shut, in front of us.

'Liverpool Marina, Liverpool Marina. This is Slowcoach. We are here and we await your pleasure. Over.'

'Roger that, Slowcoach. There's one in now. Stand off until we advise. Over.'

I thought about James. What was he up to right now? The sooner I got back to his factory the better.

I looked at George. 'How long?'

'Minutes.'

'Hope I don't miss my ride to Birmingham.'

'No chance. Everything's set up and waiting for you.'

I had a long night and a break-in ahead of me. I was tense, needed to relax. 'Tell me about this place.'

He smiled. 'These were old commercial docks built around 1830 but the ships got larger and the docks didn't. It all got closed down in 1975 and then reopened in 1987 for smaller boats. The yacht club started a year later and it's thriving. There's big investment here now.'

'You mean the Albert Dock?'

'Not just there. The trickle that started with Albert Dock ten years ago has become a flood. When I was a kid, this whole area was derelict. My mates and I used to hang around down here any chance we could get. Always hustling, trying to get onto a boat. But it's all changed now, the whole city and especially the docklands are getting a well-deserved makeover.'

George went to the rear of the cockpit. 'Keep an eye on things, I'm just going to get us ready.' He took four white bottle shapes from a locker and tied them securely to a line before putting them over the starboard side of the boat.

The radio buzzed into life.

'Slowcoach. Slowcoach. Are you receiving? Over.'

'Slowcoach here, Liverpool Marina. Are you ready for us?'

'Approach the gates, George. Are you heading for your usual berth, Slowcoach? Over.'

'Affirmative. Over'

'Understood, George. We'll let them know you're on your way in.'

George eased the throttles forward and the burble from the engines increased as we pottered towards the lock. The gates were already opening as we got underway. By the time we reached them, a line of three lights illuminated green and we made our way in between the high walls.

'How wide is this thing?'

'The gates are eight metres and we're five. Plenty of room.'

'Doesn't look it.'

'Relax.'

We slipped slowly between the open gates and concrete walls. The gap each side of the boat looked tight but George steered confidently on. Once inside, the walls opened out into a more generous space. George pulled the boat over to the right, stepping off onto the pontoon alongside us and tied off. The tall gates closed behind us and it felt like we were at the bottom of a large dark well, the illuminated night sky above us. I heard the water swirling all around us as the sluices were opened. Slowcoach, and the pontoon next to it, rose slowly towards the light. The inner gates opened whilst the level inside the lock was still below the inner harbour, water gushing through the ever-widening gap.

'Welcome to the City of Liverpool,' said George, looking proudly through the gates.

It was fully dark now and as the gates ahead of us opened, the whole illuminated city centre was revealed. It was magnificent. George untied us before easing the throttles forward once more. The big engines purred as we moved more slowly through the waters of Brunswick Dock to reach the waiting berth in Coburg Wharf. The boat slipped into its place. Leaving the engines idling, George moved out of the cockpit and stepped onto the pontoon, taking the mooring ropes with him. He quickly twisted the ropes around the cleats, making all fast at bow and stern before stepping back onto the boat.

'You can take off your life jacket now.'

I shrugged out of the bulky vest and handed it across. I reluctantly made to take off my borrowed waterproof. 'Keep it. Souvenir of your trip.'

I was grateful for the extra layer over my thin suit jacket in the cool night air. I went down to the cabin and picked up my document case and tucked it under my arm. George put both the life jackets back in the locker and, as we left the cabin, he made sure everything was turned off, locking the door behind him.

'This way,' said George. 'The car park is just ahead of you. You'll find Angela waiting in a black Mercedes. She'll take you on your way.'

'What about you?'

'I'll get Slowcoach refuelled. There's time for me to get under way again before they close down the lock gates for the night.'

'I'm really grateful for your help.'

'Don't mention it. Thanks for being a good excuse for a trip out.'

I walked the short distance in the direction George had indicated and quickly spied the car gleaming under the street lamps. A tall female figure in a smart, stylised, uniform-like outfit climbed out of the driver's seat. She opened the rear door for me. Her tailored, double-breasted jacket and matching black trousers looked chic. Wisps of blonde hair escaped from the array of pins holding most of her mane in check. Cool blue eyes appraised me as I opened the front passenger door instead. Her quick wide smile greeted me once I was inside the car. I'd unzipped my waterproof before I got in and as I made to throw it on the rear seat I noticed

"Slowcoach" embroidered in yellow across the back of the jacket.

She spoke in a rich Liverpudlian accent. 'You must have made quite an impression on Mr Doubleday.'

'How come?'

'Not everyone gets one of those y'know,' she smiled. She started the engine, looked in her rear-view mirror and reversed out of the parking space. We moved smoothly out of the car park and joined the Friday evening traffic.

'Hang on. George is George Doubleday? Tony Peter's client?'

She laughed. 'He's very unassuming. Some people might say eccentric but he's a great boss. He lets me get away with murder.'

'You work for him?'

'These last six years. Since before he listed Cell Phones Central and became even more wealthy.'

'Ah, that George Doubleday.'

'I'm his personal assistant. After he'd cleared it with George, it was me Tony rang to organise your trip tonight.'

'Then it's you I have to thank. What happens next?'

'I drive you to Liverpool Airport where you'll be rushed through without the usual rubbish. George's helicopter is on standby to take you back to Birmingham.'

'Wow. You make me feel like James Bond.'

She laughed. 'That makes me Moneypenny.'

'And George must be M.'

She drove the way I guessed she would do everything, quietly, competently and with great efficiency. We were soon heading down a dual carriageway along the bank of the Mersey towards the airport. The traffic thinned as we left the city centre behind.

'Do you see much of George, with you based here and him in the Isle of Man?'

'Oh, he's backwards and forwards for meetings all the time. Sometimes I pick him up and take him wherever he needs to go or if he's run out of days, I'll drop his visitor at the marina so they can meet on his boat.' She laughed. 'If I'm lucky, I'll get taken back over for the weekend. Perks of the job.'

'Run out of days?'

'He's only allowed ninety days a year on the mainland plus a day either side for travelling, in each tax year. Revenue's rules.'

'Of course. Why's his boat's called Slowcoach?'

The broad grin was back. 'His nickname at school. He was last in everything from the cross country runs to putting in his homework.'

The Mercedes slipped along through the sparse traffic, street lighting reflecting off the gleaming bonnet. Dark streets of terraced houses led away from the main road as we passed by unnoticed.

It was hard to resent Doubleday when he was such a nice bloke. So many entrepreneurs had the reputation for being difficult and demanding people and yet here was a man who'd built a successful retail empire by being insightful yet unassuming. I could see how this guy could command the loyalty and respect of his team. And here was bubbly Angela sitting next to me, cheerfully giving up her Friday evening for a favour her boss was doing. I found myself returning to the Kat conundrum. Which was the real Kat? Would she be a completely different person without Miss Feisty-boots in her life? Shame the way things were working out.

Angela broke into my thoughts.

'We'll be at the airport in ten minutes,' she said.

'Great.'

That charming smile again. 'You'll be back in Birmingham before you can say Slowcoach.'

The car phone rang. She picked up the call, suddenly ultra-professional. 'Yes. Say fifteen minutes to get through the formalities. You'll be ready? Good.'

She put the phone down. 'Your pilot checking we're on schedule.'

We swept into a reserved space in the short stay car park and exited the car. I put my "Slowcoach" jacket back on and Angela escorted me into the Domestic Departures building, where a member of airport security staff was waiting for us.

'Mr Elderfield? If you'd like to follow me? We'll soon have you on your way.'

Angela hugged me briefly and gave me a light kiss on the cheek. I caught a hint of her perfume. 'It was nice to meet you, Jake. Tony said you were alright. Take care.'

I did my best to keep up with my uniformed escort who set off at a casual gallop through check-in and up to an unprepossessing doorway in a side wall with a keypad next to it. My guide punched a passcode into the keypad, the lock buzzed and the door opened. We walked through and the door closed behind us.

On our right was a small desk mounted to the wall. 'If you'd like to sign in here?' I took the proffered pen and scribbled a signature next to the pre-filled entry in the book.

'This way please, Sir.'

I could get used to this VIP treatment.

The long windowless corridor was illuminated by strip lights housed within the ceiling. The plain grey walls betrayed no sense of place. I could hear faint traces of innocuous music playing for transiting passengers in the public areas. We turned right twice and left once before emerging, through a nondescript doorway, into the Duty-Free goods area, taking a path through the copious booze, fags and perfume displays, the glamorous sales assistants ignoring us and awaiting genuine customers they could besiege with their atomisers. We crossed the atrium before descending two flights of stairs, reaching another door where my guide punched in another security code. On the other side was the airfield, which we walked across quickly to the waiting helicopter.

'I'll bid you a safe and rapid journey,' said my guide. He opened the helicopter door for me and held my document case whilst I climbed up. He closed the door, stood back and saluted.

I shook hands with the pilot, whose precise movements inspired confidence as he moved switches and checked dials. I was the only passenger, the two seats in the back remaining empty. He spoke into the microphone curling to his mouth from his left ear and listened to the response that came through his headphones. There was a thunderous noise as the engine started and then we were rising into the air. More radio messages. My pilot was fully engaged in his task, which looked pretty complicated. I had no wish to distract him.

I looked at my watch and did a quick calculation. Angela had said the flight would be forty-five minutes. Allow a few minutes to get through to my car and then, say, half an hour to reach James' factory, which was in a place I knew well. My Dad had grown up in that part of Birmingham and the industrial estate where my destination lay had been populated by many famous names of the British motor industry. Before he retired, Dad had been a toolmaker in one of the many car component suppliers nestled in the area, feeding the remaining British car makers with parts. It still boasted a number of such companies despite the decline in recent years.

James' factory was waiting there for me. It had to hold the answers to some of the big questions. James had told me Race Engineering owed Berrington a ton of money and couldn't pay. So why would anyone spend a million quid on a metal basher that was bust? Unless Berrington had something worth investing in. And if that was so, why would James give it up for no return? Unless, of course, he was the one behind Legerdemain and he wanted to take the profits offshore? Had he made Artemis work?

Everything seemed so simple back on Monday. Just another engineering business skidding off track. In walks Jakey, desperate to redeem himself, proposing a simple, straightforward solution to an age-old problem. With just one nagging doubt. Rod Race's death before all this started. And pretty soon we're talking about the crash of the Sirens at the same place as Race died. Back on Monday, I'd been so focussed on landing the job I'd shied away from the idea they might be connected. Now? I wasn't so sure.

The pilot spoke into his radio again, checked dials and pushed buttons as the helicopter clattered its way through the inky-black sky.

That must have been a pretty sizable favour Doubleday owed Peters. And now I owed Peters. I grinned to myself. Recovering the money so I could pay his bill would be a good start.

So much had happened this week. I was struggling to keep up with all of the developments of the story. I took out my Filofax and compiled a list of headings, thinking about each one as I wrote them down. It looked less like a tale of disaster and more and more like a catalogue of conspiracy. James had a lot to answer for.

Rod Race's death.
Ned Drake was convinced Hot Rod's death wasn't an accident. Was it meant to put an end to Race Engineering? There was no hard evidence either way. Just a feeling…

The Commission Arrangement
Had Rod Race been raking off a private cash pile for the last three years? If not him, then who? Turner might have been able to tell us. Had Race's death been the trigger for Turner to transfer Nalco's funds to Legerdemain?

Who benefits?
A real brain teaser. It looked as if Race had planned to suck the Nalco money out of his company. Helen believed him capable of it. Those money transfers after he died though and the Legerdemain payment to Berrington – why would Race set out to buy Berrington when he thought so little of James? And why would James go through with the sale after Race was no longer around? Unless James now controlled Legerdemain. How could that be possible?

Artemis

A ton of money had been spent on R&D over the last two years, much more than was needed for the Siren as it stood. The difference must have gone on Artemis. According to Phillips, it wouldn't have been enough to complete it. What had they achieved? My confidence was growing that I'd find drawings, prototypes, whatever at Berrington tonight. If it existed, Artemis belonged to Race Engineering and I'd make sure the company benefited from it.

The Siren Crash
James claimed Rod's penny pinching was responsible. Was that true? Only someone who wanted to harm Race would take photos of the smash. Why had James been so adamant in his refusal to investigate? He claimed he'd be facing bankruptcy if Race Engineering went bust so why wouldn't he do everything he could to get the company back on track?

Turner's death
Why let Turner keep a hundred and fifty grand then kill him? And why then; on the day before I went to the Isle of Man?

Resisting the rescue
The crash photos, the tip-offs, my warning off and now Turner's death and the editing of his records; there was no denying that someone was working against us. Surely everyone would be better off if we save the company?

Kat, the Chloral Hydrate and the ten grand

Carina had really believed I'd missed the plane. I didn't want to believe Kat told her.

I looked back through my list; more questions. Following the money had led me to James. Could someone be working with him
?

Mike Rowe had the technical knowledge and access to the track. And David. Why had David put me in this situation? Was I meant to fail? With my recent dubious history, how perfect would it be to appoint me to "rescue" the company only to have it fold. He was the only one who knew of my tarnished reputation at the time of my joining and he'd wanted me appointed against Carina's will. Could he and James have a plan to carve up the carcass?

But no, that was ridiculous. David had reported Keating's bribe proposal to the police – why would he do that, if he was working against me?

What about Allen? He'd been involved in every step I'd taken since I arrived at Race. He was the first to know I'd want to question Turner about the missing money and could have tipped someone off to prevent that happening. Was his quiet, studious demeanour an act for public consumption?

And Carina? She and James seemed very close when I saw them at The Vintner. Carina's behaviour around me was a puzzle. One minute she was engaging and cooperative, even flirtatious, the next, aggressive and difficult. She wasn't close to her family, barely exchanging a word with her mother in my presence, despising her brother and seemingly very bitter about the way she'd been treated by her father.

Which left Helen. She'd told me how she and James had been close whilst Rod was away. She was tough minded and organised and she'd discovered the truth about her husband's affair on the night he died. Could she have been spinning me a line about refusing James' advances?

Even Race's bank manager was an old army mucker of David's. Did I think he was involved too?

Ridiculous. This wouldn't get me any closer to the truth. The only thing I was sure of was that James had a central role in this raging storm.

The pilot's radio buzzed and he spoke into the microphone. He gestured to me, pointing at his watch then holding up five fingers, twice. Ten minutes. I looked down at the line of the M42 below us. The headlights of so many toy-sized vehicles tracked along the black ribbon of road. The helicopter's progress was rapid and smooth despite the noise levels. I could see the illuminated terminal and ancillary buildings of the airport as they rushed towards us. A blank space of tarmac appeared below, next to a large hangar. Ground level lighting welcomed us as we hovered for a moment before we began our descent.

The helicopter's wheels kissed the ground gently. The rotors were still spinning as a uniformed official, clutching his hat and bending slightly forward at the waist, stepped up to my door.

'Good evening, Mr Elderfield. I'll take you through the airport. Do you have transport waiting?' I told him where I was parked. "No problem, Sir. If you pass me your ticket, I will get it validated and we will have you back to your car as quickly as possible.'

As before, I was hurried through service passages delivering me from airside to the entrance in the shortest possible time. Fifteen minutes later I was back at my car. I blipped the key fob to unlock the driver's door, slipped off my "Slowcoach" outer jacket and tucked it behind the seat, putting my document case and Filofax down next to me as I got into the Vixen. The rich smell of new leather upholstery enveloped me once again as I sank into the contours of the driver's seat.

I took hold of the steering wheel and glanced at myself in the rear-view mirror. This had been a hell of a week and it wasn't over yet. I needed answers and quickly. One final push should do it. I gave myself a morale boosting grin and gripped the wheel hard.

The neat analogue clock on the dashboard showed me it had been less than three hours since I'd left the harbourside in Douglas. I'd be at James' factory by about 11pm. Perfect time for a spot of burglary. The engine burst into life as I pressed the starter. I reversed out of my space and drove down the ramps of the now much emptier car park, before reaching the barrier, inserting my ticket and driving away.

Within minutes I was on the Coventry Road heading towards Birmingham. Sparse traffic was heading out of town and I imagined most of those cars would contain revellers heading for home after a night out. Such a life seemed a world away now. I wondered if I'd ever settle back into the work all week, party at the weekend pattern that I used to call normal? We'll see, as my mother would say.

I turned off the main road into the Hay Mills industrial area, driving slowly down the deserted street. I passed James' factory and turned right into the next side road, parking a discreet distance from the corner. A quick rummage in the glovebox produced a lucky find, a torch conveniently clipped into the lid. I turned off my mobile phone and slipped it and my Filofax into my jacket.

12: Passing on the inside

I closed the car door softly and blipped the central locking before walking back around the corner, towards James' factory. Pools of sodium yellow light radiated from the streetlamps, illuminating my route along the pavement. Berrington Pressings lay slumbering in the darkness. Single storey offices sat at the edge of the street, with the roofline of the double height factory behind. I came first to a large pair of solid-looking wooden gates set into the high wall alongside the main building. The right-hand gate had a pedestrian door set into it. A nearby sign stated "Deliveries Only".

I walked slowly past the building, looking for a way to access the place. All seemed quiet, with no obvious signs of life, either in this or the surrounding buildings. No tell-tale alarm box or cameras in evidence.

Peering through the first set of windows I came to, I made out the paraphernalia of a small drawing office. Beyond this, in the middle of the building, a pair of double doors led into a central lobby area.

With the streetlights behind me, I could see rows of lockers, a time clock and a rack of punch cards on the wall. The main doors were locked, unsurprisingly. Walking past the lobby brought me to another set of windows; an office with desks and half-a-dozen filing cabinets. I turned around and walked slowly back towards the side gates. I glanced up at the wall. There didn't seem to be any barbed wire or broken glass on the top of it. I guessed, at a push, I could get over and into whatever was on the other side.

I noticed that the pedestrian door in the gate was not quite closed. I pushed firmly, and it gave with little resistance. I stepped through and closed it behind me. The wood was warped, preventing the bolt that should have secured it from engaging with the frame. I picked up a piece of pallet wood lying nearby and used it to wedge the door shut.

The yard was large enough to unload a truck and a high-bay, roller-shutter door was set into the side wall of the factory for that purpose. I put my hand on the galvanised steel and felt the metal give a little. It remained secure. The door could only be opened by operating the electrical mechanism housed at the top, for which I would need to be inside. There was a door a little further along the building. I moved in for a closer look. It looked fairly solid. I put my shoulder to it but it wouldn't budge. I prepared to take a run up, when, looking to my left, I noticed a steel casement window. If I wrapped my jacket around my fist, I would be able to smash the glass. There was no one around to hear.

I got close to the frosted glass and shone my torch through. The latch wasn't properly engaged. I thumped my fist hard against the frame and saw the latch jump. Could I loosen it enough to open the window? I hit it again. This time the latch popped free.

I heard a noise from the road. Someone was whistling, and there was a repeated tap-tap noise. A night watchman? I made my way, as silently as I could, back to the gates. I eased the inset door open - just enough to take a look. I relaxed. A figure was moving slowly and unsteadily along the pavement, the stick in his right hand tapping the ground as he went. A Collie dog walked stiffly by his side; its grizzled black coat flecked with grey. As they inched their way slowly along, the man whistled a slow, sad tune. When they reached the next lamp post, they paused. I could see the old man's sparse hair and long, tattered overcoat picked out in the harsh light as he put out his hand and rested there for a moment. The dog sat patiently, looking affectionately into his face as he waited for the resumption of their walk.

I waited until they'd passed, then moved back to the window. Wiped my palms down my trouser legs, I calmed my breathing and examined the window closely. The latch was hanging free now but I still couldn't see how I could prise the window open. I was sweating, despite the cool night air. I looked again. There was a small gap between the window and the frame. If I had something small enough, I could wedge it in and lever the window open. Might there be a screwdriver in the car? The car. Of course, the car key. I took it from my pocket and inserted it, twisting the key against the frame, willing it not to break. The window moved just enough to squeeze a finger behind it. I prised at it. It moved a little. Just enough to take a proper grip. The window swung open reluctantly and I pushed it back against the wall, out of the way. I flashed my torch inside for a second and saw a sink under the window and urinals against the far wall. The space was just large enough for me to squeeze through.

I took hold of the top of the window frame in both hands, lifting myself up. I swung my right leg over the window sill and rested my foot on the far side of the sink. I then swung my left leg in alongside it. I squeezed my shoulders through the frame one at a time. To complete the manoeuvre, I would have to let go of the frame and drop onto the sink.

I lowered myself as gently as I could until I was sitting in the sink. A trickle of cold water leaking out of the tap soaked the back of my trousers. I let go of the frame and levered myself out of the sink to stand in front of it. I turned and reached outside, pulling the window closed. I ripped a wad of paper towels from the dispenser and pressed them to the back of my trousers, before depositing them in the waste bin. I used another handful to dab at my sweaty brow.

When I was done, I opened the door into the factory soundlessly to take a look-around. The factory was pitch black, the light from the streetlamps not reaching inside. I risked my torch, keeping the beam low.

Where to look? Ok, think logically. James would want to keep Artemis and his finances confidential. It would need to be somewhere where only he and perhaps a handful of trusted employees would have access. That eliminated the drawing and admin offices at the front. James would have an office. Where? Hesitantly, I shone my torch around.

The modest-sized factory was well organised. The floor was painted, marking out walkways and work places. I noted the loading bay on my right, at the back of the roller-shutter door. There were shrink-wrapped boxes awaiting despatch, loaded onto pallets. A forklift truck was parked next to these.

On my left, the beam from my torch fell across the painted shapes of presses, each as tall as one man standing on another's shoulders. These machines would transform sheets and ingots of steel into parts of cars through sheer force, making solid steel flow like water. A large wire basket stood on the floor next to each one, some half full of finished components. Moving further on I came to a tool room, where the machine tools that would force the raw metal into their new shapes would be finely honed by highly-skilled craftsmen. More than once, as a young boy, I had been allowed to accompany my dad on a Saturday morning when he went to do overtime. I would be given a quick tour of the factory floor before being taken back to the canteen for tea and toast whilst Dad did his shift. Memories of that time came flooding back and I could hear and see the ghosts of Dad's colleagues as they went about their work. Must stay focussed.

A large storage area at the side of the tool room held raw materials. Nothing there. I turned around and looked across the shop floor. A steel staircase led up to a mezzanine at the back of the building. James' office had to be there. I walked across the factory; my footsteps echoing around the unoccupied building and climbed the staircase. A pair of offices stood there, constructed from sheet steel partitioning with large plate glass windows above waist height. One office had cardboard boxes stacked floor to ceiling inside it. The other was in use. James' eyrie. Standing on the steel walkway, I shone my torch down into the gloom below. From here, he would be able to see most of the shop floor and his presence would be felt by every employee. I turned back to the office door, half expecting it to be locked. The handle turned smoothly and I went inside.

I kept my torch low, shielding it as much as possible. White-painted brickwork formed the rear wall. It was sparsely furnished, with just a desk and chair facing out towards the factory and three filing cabinets in the rear corner. A wallchart showed production quotas and performance for the last month. Completely different from his office at Race. Nothing to prove here. I hit the switch on the desk lamp and repositioned it so that it shined on the filing cabinets. I pulled at the top drawer of the first one. Just a couple of loose, suspended files inside, with some ancient paperwork. Nothing of note. Drawers two and three were the same. The second cabinet offered up all sorts of routine material. The third cabinet was locked. Damn.

The keys might be in the desk. I went through it, scattering an odd assortment of items from the drawers onto the desk top. Chewing gum, three pencils, a large reel of heavy-duty, black adhesive tape and from the deeper bottom drawer, a bottle of Scotch and a fine cut crystal whisky glass. The middle drawer held only a thirty-centimetre steel-rule which I left there.

I stopped to think. There was bound to be something in the toolroom I could use to force the lock. Turning off the lamp, I made my way out of the office and back down the metal staircase, using the torch beam to find my way. I missed my footing on the bottom step, falling forward. My torch went flying, skittering away to my left as I put out my hands to save myself. My body connected with cool concrete. I sat up, checking myself. Lucky fall, no damage. A low pool of light illuminated the centre of the storage area. My torch had rolled under the racking and was lying on the floor. Good that it still worked.

I crawled slowly towards it, feeling my way around a series of packed shelving units. I brushed accidentally against a stack of boxes which teetered and toppled with a crash. I froze, listening for any further sounds. Edging carefully forwards, I put my hand on the torch. As I stood, the narrow beam played across an intriguing tarpaulin-covered shape in the far corner of the stores. The boxes I'd knocked over would have screened it from view.

I squeezed through a gap between discarded machinery and pushed more boxes aside to get a closer look. Lifting the corner of the tarpaulin revealed the shapely rear wing of a classic car, painted in a deep burgundy colour. I tugged and the covering slid to the floor. I walked around to the front of the car. It was at once recognisable from the photograph on James' desk. The registration number, JB101, confirmed it. James' Bristol. Judging by the layer of dust on the cover it hadn't moved in weeks.

My torchlight caught a jagged reflection from the right-hand headlamp. Closer examination revealed a cracked lens and reflector. The chrome bumper below it was crumpled and smeared with something dark. My torch picked out more damage on the wing and bonnet. That was odd – didn't James say it was in for an engine rebuild?

I left the car and headed to the toolroom. I found a long, sturdy screwdriver and a heavy hammer and went back up to the office. Training the desk light onto the locked filing cabinet once again, I set to work. The lock yielded at the third blow, the blade of the screwdriver piercing right through. No percentage in being subtle, at this point.

I opened the top drawer. Personnel files. Second drawer held routine invoices. But the third drawer held what I was looking for. I lifted out a box file with one word on the outside of it, "Artemis", and took it over to the desk. I adjusted the lamp, flooding the surface of the desk with light and opened the box file.

There were a number of wallet files inside, together with an accounts book. In the first wallet, a slim file of correspondence related to a series of pressed steel components supplied by a factory in India. Amongst the quotations I discovered an interesting letter which queried the quality of the steel specified. The writer argued for a higher grade of material to be used in such a safety-critical component. I turned to the drawings at the end of the file and read the description. It was the part from the Siren's suspension that had failed. James had planned the crash.

The next file was bulky and contained engineering drawings, bills of materials and test reports for the Artemis Super/Turbo Charger. James had worked on his initial sketches and developed them into a series of prototypes. These papers documented the progression of the project, working in conjunction with a specialist lab in Cologne. Activity had multiplied in the last few months and, after initial failures, the results from the test house showed positive results from extended trials.

The third file documented correspondence with a London-based patent agent, starting less than two months ago. Having examined all of the prior art, she had seen little difficulty in obtaining patents. Later pages documented filing receipts for patent applications in most of the major markets for cars around the world.

James had been busy. I opened the accounts book and studied the flowing pen-and-ink writing. The descriptions and columns of numbers took a few moments to interpret but I realised I was looking at a list of project expenditure, starting from a date in late

February until now. Regular entries detailed the purchase of specialist alloys, invoices from metal fabricators, test houses and the patent agent. Almost all of the million pounds transferred from Legerdemain had been spent.

I turned back to the design file and looked at the engineering drawings. All had been issued since February in the name of Berrington Pressings. So here was the proof I needed. James had ignored the terms of his employment contract with Race and the stolen money had been used to complete the Artemis development.

In the bottom of the box file was a last wallet. Inside was an exchange of correspondence with a large German vehicle manufacturer. A faxed letter, dated Wednesday of this week, contained an indicative offer to buy out the rights to the Artemis Project for an eye-watering, eight-figure advance payment followed by a generous per unit royalty. Wednesday. That was the day James had walked out of Race.

Too late, I heard a noise behind me. I felt a sudden blow and sharp pain in the back of my head. Then, for me, the lights went out.

13: From the Commentary Box

I awoke with a dull ache across the back of my head and neck. I was groggy and had blurred vision. I was sitting in the office chair facing the desk. In front of me, illuminated in the pool of light from the desk lamp and lying next to the papers I'd been studying moments before, lay an unfamiliar object. A long, solid-looking, shiny, steel-bodied torch. There was a smear of blood and what looked like a small amount of hair around the rim of the broken lens. My blood, my hair. My own torch, which I had left on the desk, was nowhere to be seen. I was on my own. I tried shaking my head to clear it. Mistake. I made to get up from the chair but couldn't. My ankles seemed glued together, as did my wrists, which also seemed to be secured to the back of my chair.

The door opened and James came in. He was wearing a long, black overcoat, unbuttoned, over a black three-piece suit. The fedora hat placed on the desk was the one I'd last seen on Artemis' head in his office at Race. He was carrying my torch in his gloved hand. 'So nice of you to drop by, dear boy.'

He peered into my face. 'I must say, I am very impressed by your dedication. How on earth did you get back from the Isle of Man this evening? But how rude of me. How are you feeling? Bit of a headache, I suppose?'

He moved the head of the desk lamp, shining it directly into my eyes. 'Does that help at all? No? Good.' He gave me a broad grin and perched on the corner of the desk.

I screwed up my eyes against the light and lowered my head. I felt a trickle of blood run down the side of my face.

'Good of you to put the booze out for me. I could certainly use a drink after all this excitement." He picked up the whisky bottle I'd turfed out of his desk and studied it, before pouring a generous tot into the crystal tumbler. 'Laphroaig. One of my favourites. Lovely smoky flavour. Only one glass I'm afraid. Cheers.' He tossed the whisky to the back of his throat and put the glass back on the desk. 'I really didn't think you would be here before tomorrow. And so nice that you came all by yourself. Makes this discussion so much cosier, don't you think?' He poured himself another whisky, looking at me expectantly.

I pulled at my wrists experimentally.

'Oh, I shouldn't bother trying to get loose if I were you. Gaffer tape is excellent for this purpose and though I say it myself, I'm a bit of an expert with it.'

James reached inside his coat and took out his mobile phone. 'Nothing to say for yourself? No witty comments or acerbic one-liners? Perhaps, if we make a little phone call, it will restore your sense of humour.' He dialled rapidly. Clearly, a familiar number. 'Darling. You were a long time answering. Were you packing? Yes, I'm at the factory now and guess what? We have a visitor. Yes. How did you guess? I caught him going through the papers and I've had to inconvenience him somewhat. Would you like a word?' James held the phone next to my ear. I could smell the rich, peaty whisky on his breath. He tilted the handset so he could hear what was said. His voice was loud in my ear, causing the pain in my head to pulse, 'I've asked him how he got here so soon but he seems disinclined to answer. Perhaps he will speak to you?'

'Oh Jake. Things really aren't going well for you, are they?' Carina sounded relaxed. 'If only Kat had done as she was told, you wouldn't be in this mess now. But don't worry, she's been thoroughly punished for her misdemeanour. She'll think twice about disobeying me again. And it was delicious, the way she moaned and sobbed.' Her tone became brusque. 'So, tell me, what do you think you are doing at James' factory and how did you get back across the water so quickly?'

I stayed silent and she continued to speak.

'Still not talking? Never mind. When we heard about the fog, we expected to have everything neatly tidied away before you got back. Naughty boy. You have rather caught us out. Well, I must dash. Lots to do, you know. Hand me back to James now, will you? Goodbye, darling Jake. Such a waste.'

James leaned against the desk once more, with the phone to his ear. He listened as Carina spoke. 'What time is your plane?' he asked, 'Ok, good. My ferry to Calais is at five am. Yes, plenty of time.' He made eye contact with me as he was listening. 'What? Oh, its eight hours drive from there to Stuttgart. Yes, I'll enjoy a glass of champagne whilst we seal the deal and transfer all that lovely money into the Swiss bank account.' James smiled towards me. I wasn't reassured. 'What? Oh, nothing like that.' He looked at his watch. 'How would I ever get the blood out of my suit? No rush. Jake and I can have a little chat before I go. Yes, yes, he'll be staying here to, ah, oversee things.' He smirked, looking at me still. 'See you in Rio, darling. Safe journey.' James put the phone back into his inside pocket.

'Well, isn't this grand?' He sipped his whisky. 'I mustn't have too much; long drive ahead of me. I do hope you like smoke? You'll be seeing and tasting plenty of it soon enough.' James used the toe of his immaculately polished Chelsea boot to nudge a petrol can I hadn't noticed, resting on the floor next to his foot. I heard liquid sloshing around inside. 'I've made everything ready whilst you were taking a nap, just need to light the blue touch paper, as it were. But as we have a little time to kill before I leave, I thought we could swap notes. You see, I need to know how much you've found out and what you've said to your people.'

I stared at him.

'You're going to tell me one way or another but it would be so much more civilized if we can just have a talk. After all, what more have you got to lose? I can answer all your questions. Nice, eh? Just like old friends.'

I stayed silent.

'You're not going to be difficult, are you?' He took out a packet of cigarettes and a box of matches from his side pocket. 'I don't often smoke, after all, they are terribly bad for one, aren't they? But in this case, I think you'll find them a lot worse for you than for me.' He grinned, placing a cigarette between his lips and lighting it. He reached forward, pulled apart my tie and ripped open my shirt to reveal my chest. The tip of the cigarette glowed bright red. He wrinkled his eyes against the smoke. 'You don't really want me to do this, do you? After all, what's the harm in a little chat?'

It was tempting to tell him to go to hell. But unless I cooperated, I was going to suffer. Although David and Allen knew I was coming here, they wouldn't expect to hear from me for quite a while yet. The longer I could keep James talking, the more likely it was they would wonder where I'd got to. Seemed like my best hope of stopping James and getting out of this in one piece. 'What do you want to know?' I asked.

'That's better.' James flicked ash onto the floor and rested his cigarette on the edge of the desk. He looked wistful. 'It'll scorch this lovely old wood but then everything here will go the same way soon enough. Well, let's see. You tried to see Turner, didn't you? Of course, you did but, unfortunately for you, I saw him first. Oh, don't look at me like that. The man was a cockroach.'

I must keep him talking. My head was splitting and the light shining in my eyes was very distracting. I sought desperately for another question to ask. 'How did you persuade Carina to become involved?' I asked.

James smiled conspiratorially. 'She was up to her own tricks before all of this. I thought you would have worked that out by now.' He was enjoying himself, holding court, showing how clever he'd been. He eased back into a more relaxed position, perched comfortably on the edge of the desk. 'When Turner heard you'd arrived on the scene at Race, he demanded more money to guarantee his silence. We couldn't have that. When he saw me at his door, he realised things had gone up a notch.' James picked up the whisky glass and breathed in the aroma. 'Hmm smoky,' he said, grinning at me. 'Carina called me earlier, after she'd spoken to you. Very clever, taking your policeman with you to see the so-called lawyer. I take it Wilberforce pointed you here?'

I nodded. 'But I still don't understand why you would sell your company to Legerdemain and give up your stake? And how does Carina fit into all this?'

James laughed. 'We really have kept you in the dark, haven't we? Shall I share a secret? Carina owns Legerdemain.'

I forced my aching brain to focus. 'Carina took over Berrington and put up the cash to complete Artemis? But I don't understand, James. If you two became partners, why would you give up your stake? It doesn't make any sense.'

James was amused by my lack of insight. 'Patience, dear boy. Listen and learn. I need to take you back to the day in question, the Fifteenth of February. Roderick rang me in the morning, from France. He told me I must stop all work on Artemis immediately. I didn't bother arguing with him. He was coming back that afternoon, so I decided to go round to the house that same evening and have it out with him. When I got there, Helen practically tore the front door off its hinges. She looked wild. She had finally discovered the truth about Roderick's long-term affair, poor woman.' He took another sip of his whisky. 'I followed her into the sitting room. She sat and I put a stiff drink in her hands. The vitriol poured out of her. It was clear to me I would take the brunt of her anger in Roderick's absence.' James looked thoughtful as he re-lived the experience. 'She castigated Roderick for his affair, all the times he hadn't been there. The important events he'd missed in his children's lives and for all the sacrifices she'd made in support of his career. But then her monologue took an interesting turn. Having dealt with Roderick she began talking to me. How grateful she had always been to have me by her side.'

I nodded. 'She'd always appreciated your support.'

'Well, I have to tell you, I couldn't believe my luck. I started thinking, if she were to divorce Roderick and pick up half of his shares in the company, she'd be quite a prize. Added to my pathetic ten per cent, we'd be in control, which would change everything.'

The maths was beyond my woolly brain.

'You look puzzled, dear boy. Let me explain. When the company was set up, I had ten percent and Roderick had ninety. So, in a divorce settlement, Helen's half would have been forty-five per cent. Of course, when he died, he left his shareholding to Carina, the pension fund, Helen and Allen, in that order.' He laughed and shook his head ruefully. 'So, as a divorcee, Helen would have been quite a catch. And frankly, I wouldn't have been too proud to pick her up on the rebound. I confess that, having seen the opportunity, I was in too much of a hurry. Helen was having none of it. I misjudged the situation completely. And withdrew as gracefully as I could.'

'It must have been quite a blow to be rejected out of hand in that way.'

James shrugged, 'Oh, don't me get me wrong. I professed amorous inclinations in an attempt to deceive; it was, I confess, an unseemly attempt to get my hands on her shares. As you know, I'm usually quite convincing but on this occasion I failed utterly.'

'You went straight to the circuit to meet Rod?' I asked, quietly.

He nodded. 'If he wasn't at home, he was bound to be at the track fiddling with something.' James lifted his glass to his lips again, but looked at me and relented. He put the glass to my mouth. The whisky was cool and peaty to the taste. He put the glass down and straightened my shirt, before sitting once again.

'Did anyone ever tell you you're a good listener, Jake? But then I suppose we could call you a captive audience, couldn't we?' He smiled.

I continued to test my bonds discreetly, wriggling my wrists carefully, in an attempt to loosen the tape.

'Roderick was in the workshops. He was in a real mood. He kept interrupting me, flatly refusing to listen to any of my arguments. I knew at once, Race Engineering was over, it was just a question of time. We traded insults. He congratulated himself on how clever he had been, drawing me so far into the business. I said I'd go if I could take Artemis with me. He laughed in my face, took the loose change out of his pocket and threw it across the workshop. Not a chance, he said. And that's what you're worth without me.' James grinned at the memory. 'I wanted to shake him out of his cocksure complacency. I told him Helen knew about his mistress and was going to take him to the cleaners. She and I would control Race Engineering together and he wouldn't get a look in. He roared with laughter. He said there was no way Helen would settle for a loser like me.'

I saw the bitterness in James' face, however much he tried to hide it, Rod's insults had wounded him deeply. Good. Keep him distracted. Behind my back I kept stretching my arms, pulling at my wrists, working the tape whilst doing my best to maintain an equable, interested expression.

James continued. 'I was in a blind rage when I left. Roderick came out after me and stood in front of the car with a big grin on his face. I started the engine and drove at him. I thought he'd get out of the way but he didn't move. There was a sickening thud and he slid to the ground. He was clearly beyond any help, so I drove off.'

'You didn't try to avoid him,' I said.

James showed no remorse, holding his empty whisky glass up to the light and turning it gently from side to side, watching the patterns projected onto the wall. 'At that moment, I honestly didn't care if he lived or died,' he said. He topped up his glass again.

'You didn't think of calling an ambulance?'

'There was no point and besides, the longer I hung around, the more likely it was I'd be spotted. I drove back home, to Henley-in-Arden, to think.'

'What about fingerprints?' I asked.

James smiled cynically,' Not a problem, dear boy. I shouldn't think there was a surface or spanner in the place I hadn't touched in the last month.'

'What happened then?'

'I realised this was my big, once-in-a-lifetime opportunity. Roderick and I were the only ones that knew of Artemis. I hadn't told anyone that I was going to the circuit that night. If I could gather up all the parts and papers before news of his death got out, it would be as if it had never existed.'

'But there was the toolmaker you had working on it?'

'Fortunately for me, he was close to retirement age and ill. So, once I had the cash from Legerdemain, I topped up his pay-off from Race Engineering and he bought himself a charabanc and went touring.'

'You went back to Race that morning?'

'Yes, but when I left the house, I saw the damage to the Bristol. So, I drove to Berrington where I had the prototype Siren and swapped cars, just as it was getting light. Then, at Race, I went to the toolroom, to my office, anywhere I thought there might be Artemis parts or papers.'

'You missed Rod's copies of your original sketches.'

'The crafty bugger. I didn't realise he'd kept those.'

'There were rumours on the shop floor but nothing concrete until we found those drawings.'

James shook his head, grinning. 'And there was I thinking I'd covered it all. I was just loading the car up when Carina arrived. She'd come in early to prepare for a meeting. She saw me putting everything into the Siren and asked me what the hell I was doing. I calmed her down and persuaded her to follow me home for a chat.'

'How on earth could you convince her to side with you against her own family?'

James nodded, like a politician answering a difficult question. 'I asked myself the same thing. Then, during that drive, I had a brainwave. It seemed daft at first but the more I thought about it, the more I realised it could work. It relied on two facts I'd observed.'

'What were those?'

'She felt exploited by Roderick in the way he had manoeuvred her into the role of managing director but kept all the power. She wanted to be in charge, absolutely, but found in reality she was little more than an errand girl'

'And the second?'

'She constantly spent more money than the company could pay her. How do you fund a Kir Royale lifestyle on a sparkling Cava salary? You cheat, of course. I knew she would be interested in my proposal.'

'Even so, you'd just killed her father.'

James smirked. 'But she didn't know that until I told her. And that was the brainwave. I managed to convince her that Roderick wasn't her father and that I was.'

'What? Is that true?' I asked.

'It doesn't really matter, does it? Once she'd agreed to join me it was an irrelevance.'

He saw my confusion and laughed. 'I was always staying over when Roderick was away. Carina couldn't possibly have known whether or not Helen and I had been intimate, at any stage. But of course, the real trick, the clincher, was that it was in her interests to give me the benefit of the doubt. At first, she was dismissive but as she listened, she became more interested. I knew I had her hooked when she asked me the same question you did; how much it would take to finish the job.' He paused. 'I told her a million should do it but the payback would be at least ten times as much. Then it was her turn to surprise me. She explained how she'd caught Turner embezzling the racing business, how she'd blackmailed him, improved his scheme and set up Legerdemain to take in all that lovely money. And then we came to a deal. She would put up the cash, take over my company, I would complete Artemis and present it to the Germans and we would share the proceeds 50/50.'

'You were prepared to give up half of everything you'd lied, cheated and killed for?'

'What choice did I have? If I hadn't agreed, not only would I have lost out completely but I would be heading to prison. And besides, until Carina came along, I was wondering how on earth I was going to raise the money to finish Artemis.'

'How did you know you could trust her?'

'Easy. Only I knew how to make Artemis work. She needed me. We planned everything together, down to the last detail. We quickly realised how much neater things would be if the money disappeared through Legerdemain before Race Engineering went bust. By the time the creditors sorted out the mess we'd left behind, we would be long gone.'

James was coming to the end of his story, which meant he would soon be reaching for the petrol can. How long had we been talking? I was scraping the bottom of my question barrel. 'Having me around must have dropped a spanner in the works then. Is that why there were all of those tip-offs?' I asked.

'Oh, I can't take the credit for everything, Jake. But annoyingly, you kept finding ways to frustrate us, so we had to scatter obstacles in your path. And of course, some were just convenient distractions, nothing to do with us.' He sighed deeply, 'You know, all of our lives, including yours, would have been so much simpler if you had just accepted fate was not on your side with this one.' He drained his glass. 'So, now it's your turn. I need to know how much you've told the others and whether there is any threat to our plans I haven't allowed for.'

I really wanted to unsettle him, to tell him we were on to him and at any minute he would hear police sirens outside but I wanted to slow him down, not make him rush away. 'David and Allen know you sold Berrington to Legerdemain but that's about all, for certain.'

James reached out and tapped me on the knee. 'Excellent news! Thank you.'

Another question sprang into my head, 'I'm guessing it was you, then, who took the photographs of the crash at the circuit. How could you possibly know when the parts would fail?' I asked.

James positively preened. 'Mean time between failure. By choosing a particular quality of material I could predict almost exactly how long the parts would last. I knew how the cars would be run and could estimate when the failure would occur. I just had to wait at the circuit and let it happen.'

'Shame the pictures worked against you then?'

James grinned ruefully. 'True, but everything has worked out in the end.'

I reached desperately for anything else I could think of. 'I don't understand how you got to Turner when you did. He was already dead before I even knew I was going there.'

James looked at his watch and then folded his arms. 'Ok, last answer and then I really must make a move. You saw Carina and me in Stratford on Wednesday night celebrating our good fortune. I'd just received the offer letter. We'd already decided Turner was a liability and sooner or later you would track him down and he might well trade what he knew with you. I'd walked out of Race that morning and I was, shall we say, at something of a loose end. After I left The Vintner, I went home and had a few hours' sleep. I then drove to Liverpool and caught the early ferry to Douglas. I went to see Turner in his awful hovel.' He smiled callously, remembering the scene before him. 'We got into quite an intense conversation and then the most ridiculous thing happened. He slipped on some milk he'd spilt and banged his head; problem solved. I was back at the port in time for the afternoon sailing and drove back home.' James smirked, 'And before I forget, I've now fitted the Artemis device to the engine from a Vixen and popped it where it belongs, into the Siren. The car is a flier and the lighter engine makes for perfect handling. I'm sure your prissy Dr Phillips would approve.'

'You've already done it?'

'I'd always planned to use that combination in the Siren. It was Carina who came up with the absolutely brilliant idea of using a different engine to throw everyone off the scent. That old Australian lump I bought in proved to be just the job. Now, if there is nothing more, it's time for me to deliver Artemis to its new owners.'

I racked my brains but I'd run out of ideas. I could beg for my life but I wasn't going to give him the satisfaction.

'Our little chat has been highly amusing but as you know, I have a drive and a ferry to catch before I can enrich my bank balance and retire in indescribable wealth to somewhere tropical and decadent.' James stood and picked up the reel of duct tape, pulling off a section. 'We can't have you attracting the attention of any passers-by, can we?' he said as he smoothed the tape carefully over my mouth. 'I'm going to leave the desk light on for you but I shall move it so you have a good view of what's happening in the factory below. I want you to be able to enjoy every moment.' James repositioned the lamp so it once again formed a pool of light on the desk.

I watched, helplessly, as he collected up the papers from the desk and put them back into the box-file. Putting the box under his arm, he picked up his petrol can and placed the still-smouldering cigarette back in the corner of his mouth. He opened the office door. 'I'll say toodle-ooh, then. Don't get up.'

I heard him walk down the steel staircase. I imagined him removing the lid from the petrol can and sprinkling the contents liberally around the factory floor. There were plenty of cardboard boxes, other combustible materials and flammable lubricants stored down there.

14: The Last Lap

As soon as I was sure he wasn't coming back I really started to test my bonds. Whatever I did though, the tape would not give. I looked around desperately. Was there anything I could use to help get me out of this?

My eyes settled on the whisky glass. Maybe. I gathered up my strength, pulled up on the back of the chair with my bound wrists and thrust down with my legs. The chair hopped and moved a few inches. If I could back up to the desk, maybe I could reach the glass and smash it against the side of the desk. I could then use the shards to free my wrists. I couldn't think of anything else, so it had to be worth a try.

I heard a loud whooshing and the sound of crackling below, somewhere on the factory floor. The view through the office windows took on an orange hue. Looking towards the front of the factory, I could see the reflection of flames in the windows backing onto the ground floor offices. I didn't have much time. The combined smell of burning wood, paper and petrol vapour reached me.

I braced myself and jumped again. The chair rotated a few more inches. I repeated my manoeuvre until I was facing the side windows of the office. The seat of the blaze was in the corner of the factory where the Bristol had been parked. There was a loud "crump" - a dull explosion as the contents of the Bristol's petrol tank literally added fuel to the fire and a sheet of flame leapt through the storage area and began to lick at the underside of the roof.

James would be on his way now. I had cramp in my left leg and my thigh muscles felt like they were going to burst. He'd be driving fast to catch his ferry. I could feel the sweat running down between my shoulder blades. Was it starting to get hot in here or was it just the exertion? He'd stay within the speed limit, not wanting to be caught – three hours? Something like that. How long had we been talking? Maybe an hour? His ferry was at five and he was pretty relaxed about leaving.

Must work faster.

I shuffled the chair around, again. Three more squat thrusts and my hands were against the desk. I looked towards the side window where I could see a reflected view of the desk top, which was now behind me. The whisky glass was there on the desk. Was it to my left or to the right?

I strained to reach up to the desk but with my wrists secured to the back of the chair I was short of the surface. I braced my arms and pulled as hard as I could against the tape binding them to the chair. Beads of sweat ran down my face as I strained to free myself. Nothing gave. I remembered the steel ruler I'd left in the middle drawer to my right – just about the same height as my wrists! I shuffled my feet, propelling the chair along the floor.

Wafts of smoke drifted up behind the blackness of the side window, reminding me of the swirling, misted surface of an old mirror. I could taste the sharp, acidic tang of burning in the back of my throat. It felt warmer in here. How long would the office's steel and glass construction resist the flames? I felt the first waves of blind panic at the thought of being trapped in this frying pan over the fire.

Stop. Focus.

I took a couple of deep breaths then reached back and felt the edge of the middle drawer against my fingers. Crouching forwards, I pulled it towards me. Using my index finger and thumb, I groped around inside the drawer. I touched the cold, hard steel of the ruler and got my thumb nail under its edge, flicking it up. I lifted it carefully, making sure it wouldn't catch and get jerked from my hands. I inserted the end between my wrists and the tape binding them. I pushed gently on the ruler, moving it further and further down between my wrists, aiming to lodge the end against the back of the chair and then to use it as a lever to force the tape apart.

All was going well, until I felt the ruler stop. Try as I might, I couldn't budge it. I carefully felt around and realised it had snagged against the buttons on the sleeve of my jacket. I wriggled my wrists and pushed harder. I felt something tear.

No wetness, so it wasn't me. It had to be the suit. I stopped pushing as the ruler jammed against something solid. I stretched my fingers to feel along the ruler's edge to find the end had wedged solidly against the centre stem of the back of my chair. Now for it! I wrapped both hands around the end of the ruler, pushed myself back in the chair and lowered my wrists as far as they would go. I heard a ripping sound as some of the tape parted. The ruler slid out of my grip and I heard it clang onto the floor. But I had more movement now, maybe thirty centimetres from the back of the chair. Was it enough?

Only one way to find out.

I pictured in my mind's eye where James had last placed the glass on the desk. It was about two thirds of the way along, towards the other end. Using the side window as a mirror, I could see it was close to my side of the desk. I shuffled my chair painfully back along. It was exhausting but I had to try, it was all I could do. I looked around me, gauging the distance to each end of the desk. Smoke was starting to drift in under the door.

I lifted my hands towards the surface of the desk. Straining with my fingertips I still could not quite reach it. I looked to the window at my side. I was just short. There was only one thing for it. With an almighty squat thrust, I should be able to get enough height to reach back and grab the glass, then I could bash it against the desk and be in business.

I took some deep breaths through my nose. The smoke was sweeping across the floor of the office and billowing up towards me. I had to concentrate hard not to cough. I summoned all my strength. Right. Here we go. I tensed and then uncoiled my muscles in a single leap. I steadied my hand on the top of the desk and reached back. My fingers touched the glass but it eluded my grip. I heard it fall onto its side and start to roll towards the far end. My chair crashed back down and I sat uselessly listening to the sound of my only possible means of escape as it moved further away from me. It fell, crashing into fragments when it hit the floor.

Now what? I was exhausted. I could try to shuffle back along the desk and reach the glass but when I got there, what would I do? There wasn't enough slack in the tape to reach down to the glass. Could I throw myself onto the floor to reach it? I desperately racked my brains but I couldn't think of anything else. I started the slow, painful job of lifting the back of the chair with both hands and thrusting with my tired legs to move the chair a few centimetres at a time. My thigh muscles burned and my calves throbbed. The tension in my shoulders and upper arms was like a vice. It was getting hotter and the smoke was becoming more irritating. The desk seemed a mile long.

I could see flames now on the factory floor. The whole of the stores area next to where the Bristol was parked was alight. In places, the underside of the roof had caught fire and jagged lumps of insulation material were floating to the factory floor, with comet trails of flame chasing them down. How long would it be until they found something flammable on this side of the factory?

I modified my technique, simultaneously thrusting with my legs whilst seeking a purchase on the desk with my hands. I reached the corner and looking down, saw the circle of broken glass lying on the floor. The gap between the end of the desk and the wall was too narrow to fit the chair through. This was hopeless. I racked my brains. What else was there?

The noise from the factory floor was getting louder. The continuous roar of the fire was punctuated by a timpani of crashes and bangs as it increased its hold. Surely, someone had to see and report it? How long would it take for the engines to get here? When would the flames reach me?

Now there was a new noise, a crash somewhere from the side yard. Exhausted now, I swung my chair around painfully. Facing forward across the desk once more, I could witness this latest development. Another crash, this one louder and more distinct, like a stack of giant saucepans being knocked over.

The roller-shutter door trembled from the blow it had just received. I could hear a car engine revving hard, followed by the screech of tyres as yet another blow fell on the door. This time it gave. The wrecked door came crashing down and the white bonnet of Carina's Vixen burst into the loading bay over the tangle of steel. The car's polished chrome wheels reflected the light of the surrounding flames with dazzling energy.

The Vixen skidded sideways, it's ruined nose colliding with the forklift truck and a stack of palletised cardboard boxes collapsing, spilling steel components across it and smashing the windscreen. For a heart-lurching moment, there was no movement inside the car and I feared the driver had been knocked unconscious.

The in-rush of air through the shattered door fanned the flames which now leapt hungrily around the building.

From my vantage point, I could see bright orange peaks beyond the stores, taking hold in the toolroom. A dozen small fires dotted the factory floor, as if an absent-minded chef had set up multiple places to cook in a deserted campsite. Waves of grey and black smoke drifted across the scene, alternately obscuring and revealing the progress of the blaze.

I struggled uselessly against my bonds, glued to the spectacle unfolding below me.

There was movement in the car. The driver's door flew open, the flames illuminating a lone figure as she stepped out. She stood for a moment, transfixed by what confronted her. I saw her head turn this way and that, her pale, anxious face and short blonde hair picked out by the flickering amber light. She looked vulnerable, younger without the make-up and black wig. I saw her face tilt up towards me and I noticed a bloody graze on her forehead. I made to move, tried to make a noise through my taped lips. I slammed my chair up and down against the steel floor. I saw her tense. Now she was running across the factory floor in her high heels, her legs, clad in skintight jeans, pumping as she moved. She dodged around the pockets of flame. I heard the clatter of her shoes on the treads of the steel staircase and then saw her serious, beautiful face staring at me through the glass as she sprinted across the front of the office. The door burst open and she was inside. The tight white sweater she wore over her lithe figure was smudged with soot and she'd torn her jeans. As I watched she reached down to flick a piece of smouldering insulation material from her leg.

'Jake, Are you alright?' She looked into my face, anxious. She grabbed at the end of the strip of tape running across my mouth and yanked on it quickly. I felt the adhesive resist as it tugged at my skin.

'Yeeow!' I couldn't help it.

'Sorry. But quick is better. Are you hurt?'

I found my voice. 'I'm fine. We'd better get out of here. You'll need a knife or something.'

She grinned, 'I've had much practice.' She knelt down behind me. I felt her hot breath on my hands as she attacked the tape that bound my wrists, with her teeth. I heard a ripping noise as the tape came free and I was able to move my hands independently from each other. I reached around in front of me and pulled at the tape around my ankles. 'No,' she said, diving between my legs and brushing my hands away, her head bobbing as she pulled at the tape with her teeth and fingers.

As soon as I could stand, I took a vital second, in a fiery world, to offer a fleeting, grateful hug of thanks, smelling the smoke in her hair as we clung together momentarily. I stood back, sensing the awkwardness between us. There were things we needed to say. But not now.

'Let's move,' I said.

Her blue/grey eyes, full of trust, met mine. I took her hand and we left the office, surveying the factory from the walkway as we ran. I half fell down the steps in my hurry to get out, kicking lumps of burning roofing material out of our way as I went. Kat stayed close behind me. We reached the factory floor. Our eyes streamed with the smoke and the intense heat made my throat and nose feel like they were on fire.

'We have to get across to the roller-shutter.' My voice, hoarse from smoke inhalation, rasped close to her ear, fighting to be heard above the noise of the factory coming apart around us. I pulled at her hand and we ran, dodging and weaving our way through the chaos.

We reached the broken remains of Carina's Vixen and sprinted past, making it into the yard. Coughing like habitual smokers in the early morning, we took deep breaths of fresh air, clearing our irritated lungs.

'We need to get right away from here in case there's an explosion. There are all sorts of chemicals in this place,' I said, unable to keep the relief from my voice. We ran between the shattered yard gates, the tattered remains of which hung from their hinges like a set of ruined dentures. As we passed, I admired the lines of white paint scored into the surface where Carina's Vixen had forced its way through.

Kat grinned when she saw my expression. 'Don't mess with me, I'm dangerous.'

'I don't doubt it.'

We kept running until we reached the other side of the street. Now, at what I judged to be a safe distance, we stood, watching, as the fire increased its grip on the building. With a heaving groan, the roof collapsed in several places and clouds of sparks were released into the night sky. The front of the building was half blind now, with many panes of glass cracked or missing. Smoke billowed through the empty sockets. Kat and I stood together, watching the flames.

I turned to face her, looking deeply into her eyes. 'Thank you, Kat. You've just saved my life.'

'I couldn't leave you in there, after what I heard.'

'We need to talk,' I said.

She smiled. 'We do.'

There was a wail of approaching sirens.

Time flashed by as street theatre unfolded before us. The fire crews arrived first, followed closely by an ambulance. The two engines pulled up, the disciplined and well-ordered crew springing into carefully coordinated activity. An officer checked with us, was there anyone left in the building? Did we know what was stored in there? We watched from the back of the ambulance as the paramedics checked us over. A local night watchman, the one who'd made the call, brought steaming mugs of tea for everyone. A lone policeman arrived in a patrol car and listened carefully as I explained the protagonists were fleeing the country. I told him to contact DS Cooper. He took his mug back to the patrol car to get on the radio.

Kat and I sat next to each other in the ambulance, sipping tea. As the adrenalin wore off, the awkward feeling between us increased. We watched the flames and sparks roar up into the night sky. The building seemed to shudder and groan as parts of the structure surrendered to gravity and the tormenting heat.

'It's like fireworks,' said Kat brightly.

'Agreed. Just a bit more expensive,' I said. The fire brigade battled on, working to contain the blaze and prevent it from spreading to any neighbouring buildings. I reached into my jacket pocket, took out my mobile phone and turned it on, checking the message service. Three from David, increasingly anxious. I rang him. Though it was the middle of the night, he picked up in two rings.

'Jake, thank God.' Despite the hour, he sounded sharp and alert. I brought him up to date. His voice became brisk and commanding. 'Right. Stay by your phone and I'll make some calls.'

Kat was hunched over, holding her mug of tea in both hands, the steam rising in front of her face. The ambulance crew had cleaned the cut on her face and given her something for her headache.

'What will you do now?' I asked.

She shrugged, looked at me and smiled. 'A bath would be good.'

My phone rang. It was David. 'I've spoken to the Chief Constable. He's speaking to his opposite number in Paris and the gendarmes will be waiting for Bishop when his ferry docks in Calais. I'm sending a car to bring you and the girl back to Stratford where I've booked rooms for you. DS Cooper has been in touch and he'll join us tomorrow for a debrief. Get some sleep and we'll all meet over a late breakfast for a council of war.'

I heard the police car's engine start and saw the headlights illuminate. The driver waved a salute to us as he swung the car around and drove off.

The harsh glare of the fire trucks' floodlights revealed the devastation wrought by the fire. Most of the roof had collapsed and the remaining walls were stained in a monochrome mural of sodden soot. High pressure water jets were playing over the building's carcass. The flames were gone now, replaced by lingering tendrils of smoke and an acrid smell in the air. The fire crews were starting to pack up some of their equipment. One engine was being stood down, the crew hosing down their boots, stripping off their overalls and buttoning on smart tunics.

An officer peeled away from the group still working on the factory and came over to the back of the ambulance. His breathing mask hung around his neck and the chin strap of his grimy yellow helmet was undone. His deeply lined face was soot stained and grubby except for the area around his eyes where his goggles had been. He took off his gauntlets and accepted a mug of tea from the ever-present supply provided to us.

'Sorry I've not been over before but I'm sure you understand. Tackling the fire is the most important thing. I'm Bill Johnson, the officer in charge.'

The night watchman took his tray over to the remaining fire crew.

Bill swigged tea from his mug. 'That's better', he said. 'This job can dry your throat a bit. Surprising, eh?' He grinned.

'I'm amazed at how quickly you've brought it under control,' I said.

'It looked worse than it was. Fortunately, we managed to keep the blaze away from the lubricant store. Do you want to tell me what happened?'

I explained about James.

'Sounds like he's got a lot to answer for.'

A dark Jaguar saloon arrived discreetly, pulling up some metres from the ambulance. A uniformed driver climbed out and approached us.

Bill finished his tea. 'I'd better get back to my boys. We shouldn't be here too much longer. I've got your details from the policeman that was here. We'll be in touch.' We shook hands and he went back to the rear of the engine to join in with the clearing up operation.

'Mr Elderfield? I'm here to take you both to the Alveston Manor in Stratford.' Our driver opened the rear doors for us and we gratefully took our seats. The car's engine started and we took off. It purred over the sparsely occupied tarmac under dark grey sky, overtaking slow-moving delivery trucks and the odd car.

Two such grubby people really didn't belong in this immaculate interior. I looked at my filthy suit and blood-stained face in the driver's mirror and down at the singed and torn remains of my jacket and trousers. Kat looked no better. A white dressing now covered the cut on her forehead and a darkening bruise had appeared through the gash in the right thigh of her scorched, grubby jeans.

'Does that hurt?' I asked.

'It's nothing. I got it earlier. Tell me, do you usually travel in such style or are you just trying to impress me?'

We were still too revved up to properly relax. Time to clear the air.

'When I washed up this morning and put everything back in your bag, I found two things,' I said.

Kat smiled apologetically. 'A little bottle and a lot of money.'

'Talk to me.'

She sighed. 'Carina was angry after your meeting on Monday. She was determined to get back at you. The dinner invitation was a set up so we could act out our little scene for you.'

'This much you've already told me.'

'Ah – but you don't know why. It was her plan to get you into bed for a kinky threesome, then blackmail you.'

'Wow. That would have been some dessert.'

'The thing is, the way she described you, I thought you'd be a loud-mouthed bully; not someone who cared about people's feelings.'

'I meant every word.'

'I realised. That's why I treated you to my shoe dance at the end of the evening.' She put on her accent again. 'I think you liked it Mr Jake?' She said, laughing.

'You could have told me all this last night.'

'I had to be sure of you.'

'So, what was your trip over to me really about?'

'Carina wanted to stop you reaching the Isle of Man.'

'How was it supposed to work?'

'She had me change whilst she put up the bag. Then she showed me the envelope and the bottle and explained what to do.'

'Which was?'

'To add the liquid to your drink and once you were asleep, to hide the money somewhere in your house.' She grinned, 'I was then to stay with you and if you woke early, I should use my imagination and find some way to distract you.'

'I liked your imagination.'

'But you weren't distracted,' she smiled.

'What was the idea behind the money?'

'Once I was back with Carina, she would arrange an anonymous tip-off to the police to say that you had taken a bribe in exchange for failing to save Race Engineering.'

That hit me like a bullet. At our meeting on Wednesday, Carina had learned that the police still had a question mark hanging over me concerning bribery and the Marlowe case. She'd have thought this would have me locked up again. But there was no way she could have known that it was now Keating's name in the frame for that one.

'Why didn't you follow through on it?'

She ran her hand through her hair. 'Carina has become impossible these last months. The slightest thing would see her fly into a rage,' she sighed. 'I'd begun to question whether I should stay with her.' She looked up from under her long eyelashes. 'And I wanted to find out if you were for real.' She shrugged. 'If not, I could easily have carried out Carina's plan.'

'When she rang me yesterday afternoon, she thought I was at home with a hangover.'

'I'd never seen her so angry.'

'What did you do?'

'I turned on the tears and said I was sorry. I thought, it would calm her down.' Her eyes glittered as she spoke.

We both looked at the bruise on her thigh.

'I'm so sorry.' An apology seemed so inadequate but I didn't know what else to say.

'Have you ever read Nietzsche, Jake?

'I can't say I have.'

'That which does not kill us makes us stronger.' Her look was intense, passionate.

'Very insightful,' I said.

She half turned to face me and took my hands, looking deep into my eyes. 'It's true, isn't it? With all that we've been through, you and I, we have learned so much about ourselves.' She paused, her hand gripping mine to emphasise her words, 'It's time for us to choose how we want to live.'

Despite her dishevelled appearance, I'd never felt more attracted to her. Should I take her in my arms? Her warm smile was a shared intimacy between us. I hesitated a moment too long. She sat back, relaxing against the car seat, the moment lost. 'I'm glad,' I said. 'You're worth a thousand Carinas.'

'Thank you.' She smiled. 'I should finish my tale. Carina grabbed my wrist and dragged me down to the basement. At first, I wasn't concerned. This was how our games usually started.' She saw my expression and smiled defiantly. 'We often role-played. It was a big turn-on. I would have been naughty in some way and she would tell me off and threaten to punish me. But this time she really hurt me.'

'What did you do?'

'I cried and begged her to stop. That made her worse. I passed out and when I came to, she was gentle and loving. She half carried me and helped me upstairs and into the shower. Even washed my hair and when it was done, wrapped me in a big fluffy towel. The phone rang and she went through to the bedroom to take the call.'

'James from the factory.'

'Yes,' she said. 'I was in the dressing room with the door slightly open between us. Everywhere was a mess. The safe door was open and our passports had been taken out. I was curious, so I put the hair dryer on, so she wouldn't realise I could hear her. I stood behind the door to listen. Our suitcases were open on the bed. I heard her speak with you and with James. I was shocked when I heard Carina ask James if he was going to kill you. I closed the bedroom door very gently, pulled on some clothes and picked up my shoes. I tiptoed downstairs and took Carina's car key from the hall table. I walked carefully across the gravel so I did not make a noise and only put on my shoes when I reached the car.

'How did you find the way?'

'I'd been with her to the factory a few times. It was not difficult to find.' She smiled.

We lapsed into silence as the car slowed for the exit from the M40 and glided around the junction towards Stratford.

Kat looked out of the window, avoiding my eye. When she spoke, it was hesitant, careful. 'As soon as I saw your face last night, I knew that I wouldn't go through with Carina's plan. I couldn't do that to you and besides, without you, the company would fail and everyone would lose their jobs.'

The Jaguar pulled up in front of the Alveston Manor Hotel and the driver jumped out to open the door for us. He handed me his card and said he was at my disposal, to just ring if he was needed. Despite the early hour, the duty manager came rushing out to greet us as if we were VIPs. The car pulled away and we were shown into reception. The normal check-in process was waived with the manager saying "it had all been taken care of". He handed me an envelope with my name written across it in David's handwriting. I tore it open and read quickly.

Dear Jake,

> *You have done an amazing job and through your hard work we now have clarity about all that has happened at Race Engineering. We'll get together in the morning but in the meantime, get a good sleep. We'll see you both at 11am.*

Well done,
David.

I felt numb and exhausted after the events of this last week. The manager showed us personally to our rooms. He put the large old-fashioned key in the lock of the first door and opened it with a flourish.

'These are the best rooms in the house,' he said, smiling. He handed the key to Kat and followed her inside.

I leaned against the door frame, watching them. It was a beautiful room, traditionally furnished with a large four-poster bed. Having shown Kat where everything was, he steered me from her doorway and along the corridor to the next room.

'The layout is exactly the same as the young lady's,' he said, handing me the key. 'If you need anything, please call.' He bid me good night and closed the door behind him.

I sat on the edge of the sumptuous four-poster, too tired to move. I looked at my ripped sleeve and blackened hands. The pungent smell of smoke was on my skin, hair and clothes. Fibres clung to my stained suit where the ambulance crew had wrapped a blanket around me. A discreet knock at my bedroom door made my heart jump. I leapt off the bed to open the door.

It was the night porter. Disappointing. He was holding a tray with a bottle and a glass on it. 'Manager's compliments, Sir. He thought you could use a night cap and if you would like to put on the dressing gown from your bathroom, I will take your clothes and shoes and arrange to have them cleaned for the morning. We will, of course, be doing the same for the young lady.'

He placed the tray on a side table and whilst he waited, I slipped into the bathroom and changed, handing over my battered garments. I placed the contents of my pockets on the bedside cabinet – including the keys to the Vixen I'd left parked in Birmingham. I turned off my mobile phone to preserve what little charge was left and poured myself a healthy measure of the single malt Islay whisky from the tray. "Lagavulin." I read from the label that it "takes out the fire but leaves in the warmth". Could have been made for the job. The whisky was smooth and powerful and I felt its heat infuse me, reaching down my throat into the pit of my stomach and spreading out through my limbs. I put down the glass and lay back on the bed.

15: Saturday: The Chequered Flag

I awoke suddenly, several hours later, my heart racing and my body clammy with sweat. The smell of bonfires lingered around me still. The curtains were open and I'd left the lights on. Outside, it was getting light and the birds were singing. In my nightmare, I'd been back in that office, bound to the chair, alone, with smoke swirling around and the orange light of flames writhing sinuously around the walls. I sat up and reached for the whisky glass I'd left on the bedside table, draining the last drop. Despite the nightmare, I felt better for the sleep, wide awake, with all synapses firing. Half-formed ideas were trying to connect in my head. I closed the curtains and sat naked at the desk, pulling a sheet of hotel notepaper and a pencil towards me, listing my thoughts. I remembered George Doubleday's wise words. All the elements were there. I just needed to check a couple of points before ringing the States. I figured Randy would forgive me for disturbing him. I looked at the bed-side clock. It was still early but I knew my trusty solicitor, Dean Channing, would be up, preparing for his morning run. Ten minutes on the phone with Dean added to my level of confidence. I dialled the CEO of Nalco's home number, mentally apologising to David for the cost I was about to add to this hotel bill. Calls made, I could relax and return to bed.

The alarm sounded at ten and I slipped out from under the covers to take a hot, refreshing shower, scrubbing my body clean. Hot jets of water pummelled my skin and massaged my scalp. My head was tender on the back where James had hit me. I towelled myself dry and put a robe on. I returned to the bedroom and threw the covers over the now soot-stained sheets.

The phone rang. It was reception. 'Good morning, Mr Elderfield. I'm afraid the garments we took from you last night for cleaning were very badly damaged. Mr Lansdowne authorised us to arrange replacements for you. May we bring them up?'

Some moments later there was a knock on the door and two members of staff trailed in carrying a series of bags and boxes. They put everything on the bed and left me to it. I ripped off lids and opened bags. Underpants, socks, shirt, a pair of smart grey chinos and a dark blue unstructured jacket. Expensive labels, nice. Accessories to match, a dark brown leather belt and a matching pair of slip-on shoes in my size. I dressed. There was another, more hesitant, knock at the door. Kat stepped into the room.

'Do I look alright?' she asked, performing a slow twirl. 'They said my clothes were ruined and Mr Lansdowne has replaced them.'

Kat's new jeans were a pale, designer-label pair, as body-hugging as the previous ones. Her blue/grey cashmere sweater matched the colour of her eyes perfectly and the replacement heels conformed to her usual criteria – high, black and with wine-red soles. Very expensive.

She blushed, 'I have underwear, too. How did he know size?' She looked at herself in the mirror.

'You look great. You know, the store staff probably worked out your size from your clothes,' I said. She looked so different from the Kat I'd first met at Carina's on Tuesday evening. More natural, less knowing, almost innocent. But those quick, intelligent eyes betrayed her vivid imagination and a whole wealth of experience that was a closed book to me.

She gave me a shy glance. 'You look nice,' she said. 'This is only the second time I've seen you out of a suit. How did you sleep?'

'Really well,' I lied, thinking of the strange and restless dreams I'd endured. 'And you?'

She looked thoughtful. 'Not so good. Once the lights were out, all that has happened to me kept going through my mind. It was horrible. But I will start again; build a new life.'

'Good for you,' I said. There was an awkward silence between us whilst we both tried to think of something to say. I won.

I looked at my watch, 'We're about to be late. Let's make a move'

I turned my mobile phone on and it instantly started ringing. I looked at the number – USA.

'You go on ahead. I'll catch you up.' I finished my call and came out of the room.

Kat was waiting for me, looking out of the window towards Clopton Bridge. She turned to me. 'It's nice here, isn't it? I shall miss it.'

'Well, we can't live in hotels all our lives.'

'Silly. I mean Stratford.'

'You can't leave now. I've only just met you.'

She frowned and smiled gently. 'You are very kind, Jake, but I need to work out who I am and what I want.'

'That's understandable,' I said.

We went down to reception and were directed to a private room, where we found Helen, Allen, David and DS Cooper waiting for us. I wasn't surprised to also see Trevor Woods, Race's bank manager, there.

I introduced Kat to everyone and she promptly thanked David for her new clothes and her room.

'Think nothing of it,' he said. 'We are very grateful for all you have done.'

Everyone was pensive and serious. Allen thanked us for attending, particularly DS Cooper who had left Ronaldsway airport at eight that morning. It felt like we were guests at an Edwardian country house party. The dining table bristled with highly polished cutlery and a side table against the wall held an array of covered, stainless steel warming dishes. Small labels described the contents of each dish. David looked amused as Allen took charge. DS Cooper, wearing jeans, white T-shirt and his leather biker's jacket today, was first to stack his plate with their fragrant offerings. Woods followed him along the buffet and similarly did justice to the hotel's collation.

David was next, helping himself to a more modest plateful. I offered Kat a plate but she shook her head and took a seat at the table. I poured coffee for us both and collected a couple of croissants for her. I took scrambled eggs and toast for myself. She smiled her thanks as I sat next to her. Helen and Allen made do with tea and toast.

Once appetites had been sated, the hotel staff discreetly cleared the breakfast things, replenished our coffee and tea and left us to talk. I noticed Allen take his Palm Pilot from his pocket and lay it reverently on the table in front of him.

He rapped a spoon on a glass. 'David has called us together this morning so we can share what we all know and decide what to do with the company. Jake, can I suggest you and Miss Dominova start us off?'

I ran through all that had happened since my conversation with David and Allen yesterday afternoon. DS Cooper shook his head in disbelief at my escape from Man, but agreed if he'd known my plans in advance it would have given us both a problem. Then I came to my raid on Berrington Pressings, my incarceration and the conversation with James.

Allen interrupted me. 'I didn't realise how damaged Dad's relationship with James was.' He shook his head. 'But the idea that James is Carina's father? That's just outrageous. It is nonsense, isn't it mother?'

'Absolute poppycock,' she said. She sank into her own reverie, her hands in her lap and her head down. 'If only Rod had treated James fairly. None of this needed to have happened.'

'I'm truly sorry for you both,' I said. 'All this must have come as a huge shock. But desperate people do and say desperate things. James was desperate; he'd just killed the man who'd exploited and belittled him and now he had another hurdle to jump through. Carina just happened to be in the wrong place at the right time.'

'And she'd been ripping us off all this time,' said Allen.

'That's true. She already had the money parked in the Isle of Man and here was James offering her a way to make a lot more. It seems she could resist anything except temptation.'

'We can't change any of that,' said Allen. 'Jake, please continue with your story.'

There was silence as I told of watching the fire take hold and my attempts to escape. I gestured to Kat and she took up the tale, describing Carina's actions and her role in them. Everyone listened with rapt attention as she told how she stole Carina's car and embarked on her bold rescue mission.

Helen was deeply shocked to hear of Carina's cruelty towards Kat. Allen pursed his lips and shook his head. Kat came to the end of her tale. I looked at David inquiringly. He deferred to Allen.

'All of us here owe you a huge debt of gratitude, Miss Dominova. Perhaps now, we should hear from Detective Sergeant Cooper?'

'Certainly, Mr Race. We alerted the police in Rio of Carina Race's anticipated arrival there. Unhappily, although the airline was able to confirm she travelled on the expected flight, she managed to evade detection on arrival and has gone to ground. The authorities there are confident of apprehending her and have put a watch on all points of exit from the country, in case she tries to move on from there. From our point of view, Miss Race faces a number of serious charges.' He glanced at Kat, 'Of course, after what we have heard, Miss Dominova may wish to consider adding a charge of assault.'

Helen shook her head slowly in despair. 'How did we ever come to this?'

'Turning to James Bishop, the Chief Constable's office made a direct request to Paris and he has been detained. He's currently on his way to Paris for interview but he and his car will be returned to us over the weekend.' He smiled. 'He should be safely back in Stratford nick by Monday night.'

'James must face the consequences of his actions,' said Helen, shaking her head.

Cooper continued, 'We'll be interviewing Mr Bishop at the earliest opportunity. I want him to repeat what he told Jake, on the record. We are also hopeful of lifting forensic evidence from his Bristol, despite the fire damage.'

'Appalling, truly appalling,' muttered Helen.

Allen put his arm around his mother. He spoke gently, 'You mustn't distress yourself. What's important now is that we find a way through this.'

David moved things along. 'Perhaps, Allen, we should hear from Trevor as to the bank's position?'

'Thank you, David. Yes, quite right.' He looked expectantly at Woods.

Trevor Woods cleared his throat. 'I must say we have been delighted at the way Allen and Jake have set about rescuing Race Engineering. We feel considerable progress has been made in a very short time, despite everything. But I have to confess things have not been straightforward at the bank.' He met David's eye across the table. 'I raised my concerns when Adrian Keating was appointed but my reservations were dismissed. The truth is whilst there were rumours, there was no hard evidence of his wrongdoing. For some weeks, David and I had been speaking, off the record, about the developing situation at Race and when the crisis occurred, David shared his plan with me to put Jake into the company to help turn it around. We agreed that putting Keating up against Jake once more might well precipitate a situation where Keating stepped out of line.'

'Thank you for that,' I said bitterly. 'You might have told me I was your fall guy.'

David was contrite, 'I'm sorry, Jake but there was no way to warn you. We needed your reaction to be completely natural. All I can say is, it's worked to your advantage.'

DS Cooper took up the story again. 'After Mr Lansdowne's call to the Chief Constable's office, regarding Mr Keating's demands for a bribe, the Marlowe case was reopened and between the two events we had more than enough to bring him in for questioning.'

Which meant I was finally off the hook for that one. 'A red line crossed off, you might say,' I said.

David smiled.

Cooper deferred back to Woods. 'Late last night, I received a call from my Area Director to inform me Keating had been arrested and the Credit Committee were handing the Race account back to me.'

'Keating and James are under lock and key and Carina has gone AWOL. So far, so good,' I said.

'Which doesn't get us any closer as to what we are going to do with the company,' said Helen.

DS Cooper stood. 'There's a pile of paperwork waiting for me at the station and I need to get everything ready for the boss on Monday.' He nodded to us all. 'You know where I am if you need me. I'll be in touch once we have Bishop in custody. Thanks for breakfast.' He grinned. 'I really should take a dim view of you breaking into the factory last night. But, well done.'

He and I shook hands and he left.

'So, Allen, Jake, what do you propose for Race Engineering?' said David.

Allen was the first to respond to David's question. 'We've made real progress in trading over the last week but if Nalco press their claim for immediate repayment, we simply can't meet it.'

'How much of the stolen money is still in Berrington's account?' asked David.

'Not much. Judging by James' ledgers, less than a hundred thousand,' I responded.

'I have spoken to Legerdemain's bankers, Royal Argent, this morning and there is very little left in that account.' said Woods.

'The most we could pull together in a hurry would be around half a million and only then with the bank's support,' added Allen.

David watched me discreetly. He knew I was up to something. Woods too, was watchful, sensing more to come. Kat sat quietly, next to me, waiting, as she had so often in the recent past.

'I put an idea to the CEO of Nalco this morning,' I said.

Now I had everyone's attention.

'What did he say?' Allen asked.

'If you all agree to the proposal I discussed with him, he'll jump on a plane tomorrow and be with us for a meeting on Monday.' I waited for ten seconds before I added, 'And he'll bring his chequebook.'

David prompted me, 'Well? Are you going to give us the details?'

I held up my hands in surrender and gave them a big grin. 'Ok, here goes. I couldn't sleep last night – no idea why. I did some thinking and made a couple of phone calls. We have Race Engineering under control. James' invention, the Artemis Supercharger/Turbo is a game changer. Berrington Pressings has a lucrative offer on the table to buy out the rights. We can prove Artemis rightfully belongs to Race Engineering and Berrington has spent Nalco's money to complete the project. But if we wait for the courts to sort things out, we'll all be old and grey before it happens.'

'Out with it, Jake,' said David.

'We do a deal with James.'

David frowned and shook his head. Helen looked up, surprised.

'How do you see this working?' asked Allen quietly.

'I said we should do a deal with him, not forgive him.'

'What kind of deal?' asked David.

'Everything is in a tangle at the moment. Artemis has been presented for sale as if it belongs to Berrington Pressings. The Nalco money went to Beckmann Turner, who transferred it to Legerdemain, who then bought Berrington with it. The simplest way out of this is for James to gift Berrington to Race Engineering.'

'But that won't work, Jake – Berrington belongs to Legerdemain,' said Allen.

'I checked with my lawyer, before I spoke to Parks. Unless we take the initiative, the courts are likely to freeze James' assets. But Legerdemain's acquisition of Berrington was made with stolen money. It was a fraudulent transaction. Making over Berrington to Race Engineering would restore Artemis to its rightful owner'

'What good is a fire-damaged plant to us?' said Allen.

'It can be repaired. We're going to need to increase production at Race Engineering and we'll need the extra component capacity Berrington can give us.'

'How so?' said Allen.

'Nalco have agreed, in principle, to become shareholders in the expanded business and to treat the outstanding monies as a down payment. I'm also confident we can take over the deal James negotiated with the Germans and license the manufacture and use of the Supercharger/Turbo to them. Crucially, we would retain the right to install it in a relaunched version of the Siren, which we can call the Siren ST. Nalco believe, as I do, that with their help, we can sell the car in the States as well as into our other established markets.'

There was silence as everyone considered what I'd said.

'My bank would be very happy to endorse such a plan, subject to seeing a formal proposal. In the meantime, I'd be happy to extend the existing line of credit, to give you time to complete a deal,' said Woods. 'Well done, Jake. I can see why David was so keen to hire you.'

'I only see one problem with this proposal,' said David. 'Why would James agree to it?'

'That was another part of my conversation with Dean. Although James is associated with two deaths, he will argue the first death was not premeditated and the second was an unfortunate accident. If we drop the fraud charges in exchange for this deal and if Bishop cooperates fully with the police, it will work in his favour when it comes to sentencing.'

'I don't understand how can you be so reasonable about this,' exhorted Helen. 'He left you for dead in a burning factory. If it hadn't been for Miss Dominova, you would have perished there. And what about the lives he risked at the circuit with his stupid attempt to sabotage the Siren. Don't you think he should pay for that?'

'I'm not out for revenge. He's ruined financially and all his plans have come to nothing. He will certainly serve a sentence for what happened to Rod and I'm sure the other matters will lead to charges which will extend his time in jail. He's a broken man.'

Helen's response was quiet and introspective, 'Yes, I see,'

'You've thought this through, Jake,' said Allen. 'I would like to add my own proposals to these. Our board is sadly depleted with the loss of two of our directors. If we are going to take on these challenges, we need to beef up the team. I would propose that we ask David to become our chairman and Dr Phillips to take over as engineering director.' Allen turned to me. 'And what about you, Jake, will you take over as MD?'

I smiled. 'No,' I said. 'That's your role now, Allen.'

'Then be our operations director, please,' he said.

I nodded my agreement.

David took over. 'As chairman designate, I think, if everyone agrees, I should run this part of the meeting. First of all, I would like Miss Dominova and Trevor to leave us for the moment whilst we convene a shareholder's meeting to appoint a new board. We can then vote on Jake's proposal as directors. I would like to add one proposal to Allen's and Jake's, that we ask Helen to take over from Allen as company secretary.'

Helen nodded, looking pleased.

It was the work of a moment for those shareholders present to approve the new board.

The Nalco/Berrington proposal was then unanimously approved. David stood, signalling the end of the meeting. He came around the table to me, holding out his hand. 'I knew you could do it, Jake. Very well done.'

I shook his hand. 'You really did set me up, didn't you?'

David smiled. 'I'm not going to apologise. With so many issues in the air and so little time to fix them I needed you to bring things to a head.'

I felt the bump on the top of my crown from James' torch. 'I certainly did that,' I said.

Helen and Allen joined us. Allen slapped me on the back.

'How can we possibly thank you, Jake?' said Helen.

'Amazing, Jake,' said Allen. 'I've learned so much from you in the last week. I'm really excited to see what we can do with the business. I'm so glad you're staying on to help.'

I smiled. 'For a while, anyway. Then we'll see.'

We said our goodbyes. David and Allen made arrangements to go and look at the Berrington factory and survey the damage. I passed across the keys for the Vixen I'd left parked up there. They went off together to say goodbye to Trevor.

Kat was sitting in a corner of the bar. She was watching a couple at another table, listlessly. They were holding hands, talking and laughing together.

I sat next to her.

'Look at them,' she said. 'So happy on their romantic weekend.'

'Are you jealous?' I asked.

She laughed, 'No. I'm done with romance for a while.' She looked at my face.

'That wasn't aimed at you. You're nice but I'm not ready to jump into another relationship with anyone.' She smiled, 'And you're not my usual type.'

'But we can be friends, you and I?'

'That's very generous of you, thank you.'

We looked up. Helen was standing in front of us. She spoke to Kat. 'I didn't want to leave without having the chance to apologise properly to you. I never dreamed my daughter would treat you so badly. If there is anything we can ever do for you then you only have to ask. I am so sorry, for everything.'

Kat accepted the apology with good grace and Helen was met by Allen at the door. He and David offered to drive her home before going on to Birmingham.

'They are nice people. It's a shame I never got to know them.'

'It's not just the family who are indebted to you. I still owe you my life.'

Kat smiled. 'Oh, those nice firemen would have got you out.'

'I'm not so sure. After all, you were the only one who knew for certain I was there. It was a brave and selfless act. Thank you.'

She shrugged, looking down at her lap but no words came.

'Ok, here's what we do. Come home with me whilst you work out your plans. You'll be free to come and go as you please.'

'So not like when I was with Carina, then?'

'I can even offer you your own room as long as you allow me the time to tidy it up first.'

We laughed. I phoned last night's chauffeur and summoned him to take us to Carina's so Kat could gather up her things.

The Jaguar pulled up at the kerbside outside the familiar house. Kat came to life and jumped out of the car.

'Come,' she said. 'I want to show you.' She took my hand and led me to the house.

'Do you have a key?' I asked.

'Carina was always losing them. She kept a spare outside.'

We walked up to the front door and she reached up to a ledge above the porch. She felt around and took down a key.

She grinned. 'Good. It's still here. I thought we might need to throw a rock.'

We went along the hall to a door which I would have assumed was the entrance to a cupboard under the stairs. She opened it and turned on a light switch. A flight of black-painted concrete steps led downwards, illuminated by a row of bulkhead lights fixed high on the plain grey walls. I followed Kat down. At the bottom, we were confronted by a steel door with large bolts at the top and bottom. Her fingers flicked against a bank of switches on the right-hand wall and she slid back the bolts and turned the door handle. She beckoned me to follow her.

There was a vaulted ceiling of old brick, its barrel shape too high for me to touch in the centre. The plain brick walls were stark and barren. The floor was bare concrete. Ceiling-mounted spotlights conjured funnels of bright white light, highlighting selected places, leaving the rest of the space murky and mysterious. A steel chain hung from the centre of the ceiling. It ran through a wall-mounted pulley to a crank, allowing its length to be adjusted. At the end of the chain was a pair of professional-looking, steel handcuffs. I looked across the room to where a cupboard stood in another circle of light. I went to it and opened the doors. Kat watched my face as I looked through the contents. The smell of leather and latex was almost overpowering. Clothing, shoes, boots, gags and an assortment of implements designed to inflict pain.

She picked up a well-used riding crop and whacked it firmly into the palm of her other hand. 'This was her favourite thing.' Kat laughed when she saw my face, 'Don't be such a baby,' she said. 'The idea of it was so powerful, so erotic.'

'Until the last time.'

'Yes,' she said, 'But the thrill stays with you long after the pain fades.' She put the crop back in the cupboard, closed the doors and walked back to the cellar entrance.

I followed her, trying to imagine what she must have been through down here. Horrifying. How could one person do this to another?

'I'll stick to a bed. Far more comfortable.'

She grinned and shook her head. 'I wanted you to see it so you could really understand Carina.'

'You think I was in any doubt about her?'

'Just making sure. In case she should ever come back. It's what friends do. Look out for each other.' She smiled.

We left the cellar. She closed the bolts on the door and turned off the lights.

'I'll get my things,' she smiled.

I waited in the hall whilst she went upstairs. I heard her moving around as I studied the décor and thought about what I'd just seen.

I hadn't recognised the deep intimacy binding them together. Kat had trusted Carina with her most valuable possession; herself, body and soul. She'd chosen a life on the edge with no control, never knowing where it would lead her. More red lines.

Kat came back down the stairs clutching an expensive-looking leather holdall. She smiled, tapping the bag. 'I've borrowed one or two extras.'

'No more than you deserve. Let's go.'

We closed the front door behind us and replaced the key, walking back to the waiting Jaguar. The chauffeur got out and opened the door for us.

'Where to?' He asked.

I gave him my address in Old Town.

16: Spray the Champagne

I stuck by my promise and Kat got her own room. She stayed with me whilst I helped the team at Race to wrap things up and get the company on the right path. Randy Parks, Nalco's CEO, came over and followed through on our agreement. DS Cooper and Dean Channing helped us negotiate with James. Berrington and Artemis were transferred to Race's ownership and we sorted out the shareholdings so the right people would get rewarded for their efforts. The endurance race was delayed for us to manufacture and test the Supercharger/Turbo with our new German partners and when it took place it was a huge success. Dr Phillips accepted a permanent place on Race's board of directors and the Siren ST was successfully launched across Europe and North America with Nalco again sponsoring the racing programme. After his baptism by fire, Allen did a great job as managing director with David mentoring him. Carina couldn't be traced. Helen started to visit James regularly in prison.

Allen gave the ten thousand pounds I'd taken from Kat's bag to her as some small compensation for all of her trials at the hands of his sister.

Having Kat around was great. We both had issues that it was good to talk through with someone who understood. She stayed just long enough for me to start to believe we might become more than friends. We looked after each other, in a way I could have got used to.

But one night I returned to an empty house. There was a casserole keeping hot in the oven and a brief note of thanks and love on the table, with a small bunch of flowers she'd picked from the little garden she'd restored in the back yard.

I got paid handsomely for my contribution to Race Engineering's rebirth. It was a great delight to go and see my parents and repay money that I'd borrowed, adding generous interest. My debts were cleared and the pressure was off me, for a while, at least. And my stock in the business community had never been higher. It looked like Keating would be away for some time. I went to see him, just to gloat, not that I bear a grudge, you understand.

With the exciting bit over it was time for me to give Allen the space to do his job. He would be fine now, with a properly financed company, professional business partners and David advising him. I could focus on my own future.

One last piece of hot news before I go. It happened this morning. I was sitting at the dining table pondering my next move. A break, maybe, somewhere warm? I heard the letterbox rattle. It couldn't be the postman, too early. There was an envelope on the mat, no writing on it. I ripped it open. Inside were a set of car keys. I opened the door. Outside was a metallic silver Siren ST, registration number, J4KE.E

Jake and Kat will return soon in DANGEROUS ART.

A Free Gift for My Readers!

I really hope you enjoyed reading REDLINE as much as I loved writing it. If so, would you mind penning a review on Amazon? It can really help other potential readers to decide whether REDLINE is for them.

If you'd like to be kept up to date on Jake and Kat's future exploits, please go to my website [www.terry-green.co.uk.](www.terry-green.co.uk) In exchange for your email address and your consent to join my mailing list I'll keep you informed as to my progress in charting their adventures. And to say thank you, for a limited time, I'll send you a free e-copy of Kat's back story - THE VELVET REVOLUTIONARY.

Thank you.

Afterword

It's fair to say I've taken a number of liberties in writing this story and I am entirely guilty of making the facts fit the plot where it suited me. As with any work of fiction, I hope that you've have been able to suspend your disbelief and enjoy the journey.

Place

To the best of my knowledge, Race Engineering, its founder and the Prospero Road Industrial Estate in Stratford Upon Avon have never existed. Stratford was a great place to live and I have a huge affection for the town. I last lived in Narrow Lane, Old Town and was warmly welcomed by my friends and neighbours there. As far as I know, what I have written about Old Town and Narrow Lane is correct. With the exception of the entirely fictitious Glovemaker's Arms, my other location notes for Stratford, including the fabulous restaurant that is The Vintner, are as correct as I can remember.

The Long Marston (ex) Airfield does exist and was in the hands of the RAF from 1941 to 1954. I don't believe it has ever been used as a test track but it has played host to a range of events and activities, including the Shakespeare County Raceway dragstrip, various forms of aviation and gliding as well as a host of summertime music festivals including the Godskitchen Global

Gathering, the Bulldog Bash and the Phoenix Festival. Hobbs Yard in Bristol is pure invention.

Jake's brief visit to the Isle of Man relies on my memories of visiting Douglas in the period when the story is set, plus a certain amount of desk research which has hopefully provided a reasonably realistic representation of this beautiful island. Needless to say, Tony Peters' home, Stelladimes, Wilberforce's' office and Turner's cottage have all been conjured from my imagination.

I'm indebted to my great friend, Peter Soddy, for helping to invest some realism into my sketchy idea for Jake's boat trip back to Liverpool. Jake's journey through Liverpool airport and the helicopter ride back to Birmingham are pure invention.

The Hay Mills Industrial Estate certainly existed and a number of manufacturing businesses that operated within the motor industry were based there. Berrington Pressings was never one of them. Memories of visiting my grandparents there as a child brings back a vivid recollection of the unique industrial smells that emanated from long-forgotten factories with names like Wilmott Breedon and Lucas Industries, (affectionately known as Lucas, Prince of Darkness).

People

All of my characters are pure invention but I couldn't resist slipping a couple of famous motor racing names into the story.

In real life, John Cooper, (not my policeman, Guy), was an innovative engineer, the son of Charles Cooper, who founded the Cooper Car Company in 1947. Through the 1950s and early 60s their rear engine, single-seat cars were a great influence in Formula One and the Indianapolis 500. Through his friendship with Alec Issigonis, John Cooper became involved with the creation of performance versions of the Mini and the Cooper name has become synonymous with today's Mini, as owned and marketed by BMW.

My ironmonger's name, Gordon Bennett, is one which is often taken in vain. In 1900 he sponsored the first ever international motor racing competition – The Gordon Bennett Cup Race, which was the forerunner of modern Grand Prix Racing.

Period

I've chosen to set this story in the late nineties. I thought it would be fun for a number of reasons, D: Ream's "Things can only get better" has a resonance with the story's theme and flow and its use by the Blair team in that year's election campaign made it a big noise. The ability to slip in one of the most influential devices in the development of the mobile phone, The Motorola Startac, along with the Palm Pilot electronic organiser, before such concepts converged into the digital smartphones most of us carry around today, was irresistible. But the untold story of the period was the behind-doors focus on developing the efficiency of the internal combustion engine. There was a quiet revolution in progress that few were aware of. Vehicle manufacturers and their suppliers were spending millions of dollars looking for ways to eke extra mileage and performance out of the cars we were driving. Electric cars were a future fantasy which would need to see significant progress in the development of the battery before the dream could edge towards reality.

Product

James' Artemis device would probably be called a twin-charger today. As Dr Phillips describes to Allen and Jake, such a device strives to deliver the benefits of both a supercharger and turbocharger but to eliminate the weaknesses of both. The concept predates Redline by over ten years but the devices of that period were very much a work in progress.

The earliest application of a twin-charger I'm aware of was, as Allen says, by Lancia in 1985 but since that time many manufacturers have applied their research and development resources to creating solutions which edged forward in performance and reliability.

I have complicated James' Artemis device by reference to a US Patent No US 6,269,642, B1, dated Aug 7 2001. This paper describes a design for a variable geometry turbocharger. It seems to me if James had the technical prowess and experience that I describe in this story and was operating at this time, in the late nineties, he might well have been looking at ways to combine all of this thinking into one device. So, I would just like to pay tribute to all of the great and worthy engineers around the globe who spent their waking hours making our cars work more efficiently and to hope you, the reader, enjoyed the ride.

Finally, the tyre bath.
If you have read this far, you may have forgotten James' first encounter with Jake where, in response to being put on the spot by him, James says, 'It's my turn in the tyre bath, is it?' Back in 1988, I had the excellent fortune to be working for Peter Soddy, then Marketing Director of SP Tyres UK Ltd, makers of Dunlop Tyres. We were at the Le Mans circuit in France for the legendary "24-heures du Mans" motor race. The Dunlop presence behind the pits was significant as quite a number of the entrants were running on our tyres that year. One such team were Jaguar, who had the distinction of winning the race for the first time since 1957. It was also the Centenary of John Boyd Dunlop's invention of the pneumatic tyre, so with that and Jaguar winning on our tyres everyone was in a very good mood. When I was asked to attend the race, I was unaware of the tradition that "race virgins" should be "baptised" in the tyre bath – literally a tub of water large enough to submerge a race tyre in, in order to locate a puncture. To this day, I don't know how I avoided being dipped.

Acknowledgements:

I would like to express my grateful thanks to my extended family, friends and volunteer readers who have been more than patient as I wrestled with Redline. They have given me the confidence to complete it and to plan future works. I also need to thank my friends and members of "Chasing Our Tales" - our very own writers' group for their generous re-reading of this manuscript as it developed. And the practical advice of the team at Jericho Writers.

And finally, Sharon, whose tireless preparedness to re-read and re-apply her journalistic experience with unstinting generosity has proved invaluable.

About the Author

Many of you may already know me as "Cashier Number Three!"

And over the last twenty years around 25 million shoppers every month heard me summoning them from the queue in banks, shops and post offices everywhere.

My career has taken some interesting twists and turns – from cars to queues – cellular phones to celebrity chefs.

But I needed something more which is why <u>I turned to a life of crime.</u>

A reader commented that my first business book, You're Next, read like a thriller. That got me thinking. Could I come up with a twist on the classic detective story? Could I write an entertaining, compelling series of novels set against the background of my career? Oh sure, there would have to be lies, fraud and murder, along with some delicious scandal and just a touch of romantic intrigue – in short, all the elements you'd expect in a compelling, page-turning thriller. And how about serving those up on a bed of gritty business challenges for our hero?

Thanks for reading REDLINE – I hope you enjoyed the race?

Best wishes,

Terry

www.terry-green.co.uk

https://www.linkedin.com/in/thevoiceofcustomerexperience/

Printed in Great Britain
by Amazon

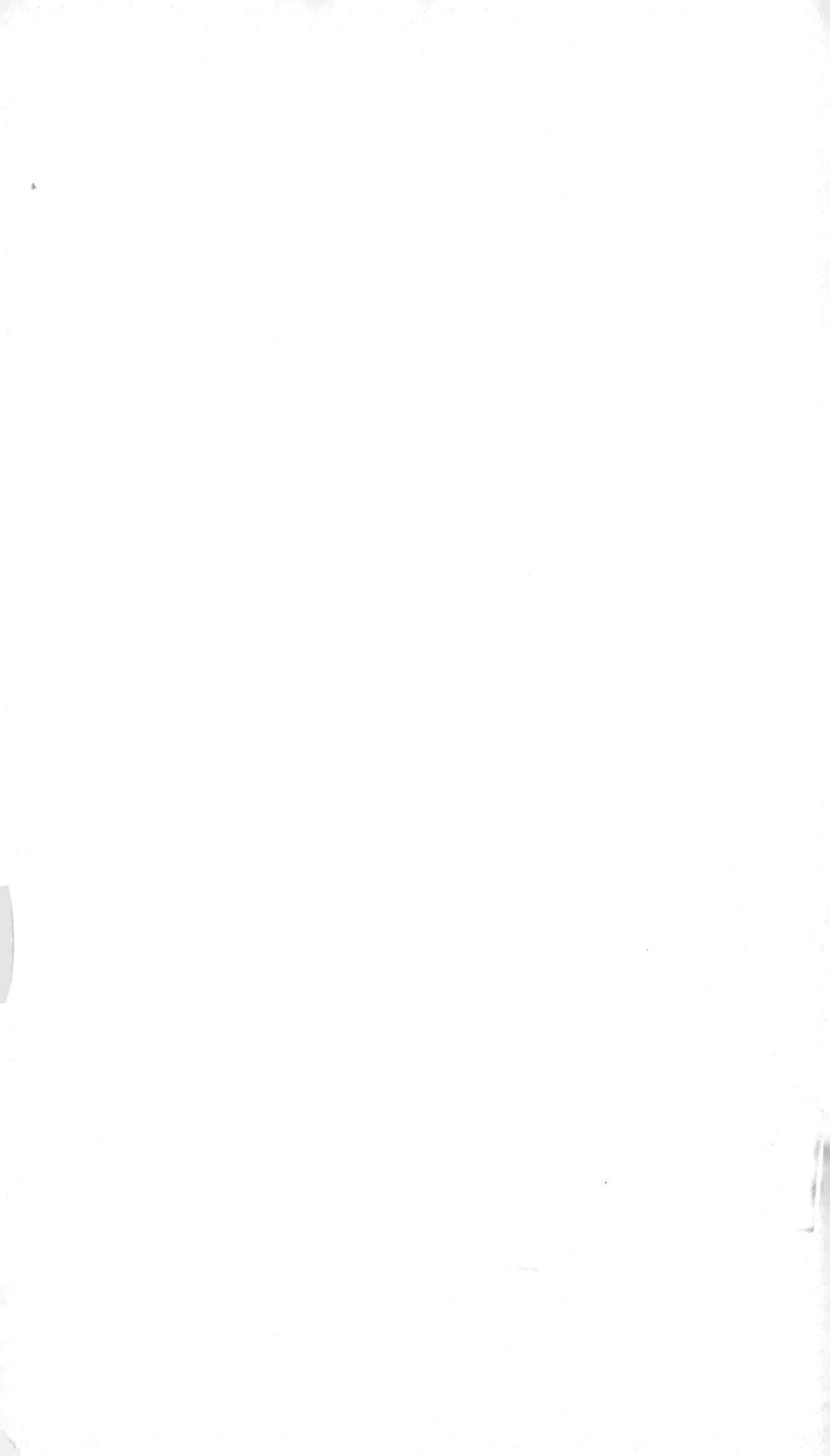